ART IN THE BLOOD

Art in the Blood

A SHERLOCK HOLMES ADVENTURE

BONNIE MacBIRD

COLLINS
CRIME
CLUB

COLLINS CRIME CLUB

An imprint of HarperCollinsPublishers
1 London Bridge Street
London SE1 9GF
www.harpercollins.co.uk

Published by HarperCollinsPublishers 2015
1

A catalogue record for this book
is available from the British Library

Hardcover 9780008130831
Paperback 9780008129675

Set in Sabon by Palimpsest Book Production Ltd, Falkirk, Stirlingshire.

Printed and bound in the USA by RR Donnelley

For Alan

Contents

Preface

During the Olympic summer of 2012, while researching some Victorian medical information at the Wellcome Library, I chanced upon a discovery so astounding that it completely altered my course. After requesting several old volumes, I was brought a small, dusty selection, some so fragile that they were held together by delicate linen ribbons.

Untying the largest, a treatise on the usage of cocaine, I discovered a thick sheaf of folded and yellowed papers had been tied to the back.

I opened the pages carefully and spread them before me. The handwriting was strangely familiar. Was I seeing clearly? I turned back the cover of the book; on the title page, in faded ink, was inscribed the original owner's name: Dr John H. Watson.

And there, on these crumbling sheets of paper, was an unpublished, full-length adventure written by this same Dr Watson – featuring his friend, Sherlock Holmes.

But why had this case not been published with the others

so long ago? I can only surmise that it is because the story, longer and perhaps more detailed than most, reveals a certain vulnerability in his friend's character which might have endangered Holmes by its publication during their active years. Or perhaps Holmes, upon reading it, simply forbade its publication.

A third possibility, of course, is that Dr Watson absent-mindedly folded up his manuscript and, for unknown reasons, tied it to the back of this book. He then either lost or forgot about it. And so I share this tale with you, but with the following caveat.

Over time, perhaps from moisture and fading, a number of passages have become unreadable, and I have endeavoured to reconstruct what seemed to be missing from them. If there are any mistakes of style or historical inaccuracies, please ascribe these to my inability to fill in places where the writing had become indecipherable.

I hope you share my enthusiasm. As Nicholas Meyer, discoverer of *The Seven-Per-Cent Solution*, *The West End Horror*, and *The Canary Trainer* said recently for himself, and all fellow lovers of Conan Doyle – 'We can never get enough!'

Perhaps there are more stories yet to be found. Let's keep looking. Meanwhile, sit down by the fire now, and draw near for just one more.

PART ONE

OUT OF THE DARKNESS

'I've got a great ambition to die of exhaustion
rather than boredom.'

Thomas Carlyle

.

CHAPTER 1

Ignition

y dear friend Sherlock Holmes once said, 'Art in the blood is liable to take the strangest forms.' And so it was for him. In my numerous accounts of the adventures we shared, I have mentioned his violin playing, his acting – but his artistry went much deeper than that. I believe it was at the very root of his remarkable success as the world's first consulting detective.

I have been loath to write in detail about Holmes's artistic nature, lest it reveal a vulnerability in him that could place him in danger. It is well known that in exchange for visionary powers, artists often suffer with extreme sensitivity and violent changeability of temperament. A philosophical crisis, or simply the boredom of inactivity, could send Holmes spinning into a paralysed gloom from which I could not retrieve him.

It was in such a state that I discovered my friend in late November of 1888.

London was blanketed with snow, the city still reeling from the extended horror of the Ripper murders. But at that moment, violent crime was not my concern. Married earlier that year to Mary Morstan, I was ensconced in a nest of comfortable domesticity, living at some distance from the rooms I had formerly shared with Holmes in Baker Street.

One late afternoon found me reading contentedly by the fire when a note arrived by breathless messenger. Opening it, I read: 'Dr Watson – he has set 221B on fire! Come at once! – Mrs Hudson.'

In seconds I was hurtling through the streets in a cab towards Baker Street. As we tore around a corner, I could feel the wheels slipping in the mounding snow, and the cab lurched dangerously. I rapped on the roof. 'Faster, man!' I shouted.

We skidded into Baker Street and I saw the fire wagon and several men leaving our building. I leaped from the cab and ran to the door. 'The fire,' I cried. 'Is everyone all right?'

A young fireman stared up at me, eyes shining from a smoke-blackened face.

'It's put out. The landlady is fine. The gentleman, I ain't so sure.'

The fire captain pushed him aside and took his place. 'Do you know the man who lives here?' he asked.

'Yes, quite well. I am his friend.' The captain eyed me curiously. 'And his doctor.'

'Then get in there and see to the fellow. Something is not right. But t'weren't the fire.'

Thank God Holmes was at least alive. I pushed past

them and into the hall. Mrs Hudson was there, wringing her hands. I have never seen the dear woman in such a state. 'Doctor! Oh, Doctor!' she cried. 'Thank heavens you've come. It's been terrible these last days, and now this!' Her bright blue eyes brimmed with tears.

'Is he all right?'

'From the fire, yes. But something, something awful . . . ever since he was in gaol! He has bruises. He won't talk, he won't eat.'

'Gaol! How is it that—? No, tell me later.'

I raced up the seventeen steps to our door and paused. I rapped loudly. There was no reply.

'Go on in!' called Mrs Hudson. 'Go!'

I flung open the door.

A blast of cold, smoky air assailed me. Inside the familiar room the sounds of carriages and footsteps were muffled to near silence by the new snow. In one corner, a wastepaper basket lay upended, blackened and wet, with charred paper nearby on the floor and a small area of drapery burnt away, now sodden.

And then I saw him.

His hair awry, his face ashen with lack of sleep and sustenance, he looked, quite frankly, at death's door. He lay shivering on the couch, clothed in a shabby purple dressing gown. An old red blanket tangled around his feet and with a quick movement he yanked it up to cover his face.

The fire, along with stale tobacco smoke, had filled the study with a sharp acrid odour. A blast of freezing air blew in from an opened window.

5

I crossed to it and shut it, at once coughing at the foetid air. Holmes had not moved.

I knew immediately from his posture and ragged breath that he had taken something, some intoxicant or stimulant. A wave of anger swept over me, followed by guilt. In my newly wedded bliss, it had been weeks since I had seen or spoken to my friend. Holmes had, in fact, suggested we attend a concert together not long ago, but along with married social life, I had been busy with a critically ill patient and had forgotten to reply.

'So, Holmes,' I began. 'This fire. Tell me about this.'

No response.

'I understand that you were imprisoned briefly. What for? Why did you not send word?'

Nothing.

'Holmes, I insist you tell me what is going on! Even though I am married now, you know that you can call on me when something like . . . when . . . if you . . .' My voice trailed off. Silence. A sick feeling crept over me.

I removed my greatcoat and hung it in the old familiar place, next to his. I returned to stand next to him. 'I need to understand about this fire,' I said quietly.

A thin arm emerged from the ragged blanket and waved vaguely. 'Accident.'

In a flash, I grabbed his arm and yanked it into the light. It was, as Mrs Hudson said, covered with bruises and one substantial cut. On the transverse side was something more alarming: the clear evidence of needle marks. Cocaine.

'Damn it, Holmes. Let me examine you. What the devil happened in gaol? And why were you there?'

With surprising strength he wrenched his arm away and curled into the blanket. Silence. Then finally, 'Please, Watson. I am fine. Go away.'

I paused. This went far beyond the occasional dark mood I'd witnessed in the past. He had me worried.

Sitting down in the armchair facing the couch, I vowed to wait this out. As the mantelpiece clock ticked and the minutes turned into an hour, my concern deepened.

Some time later Mrs Hudson entered with sandwiches, which he refused to acknowledge. As she puttered around mopping up the water left by the firemen he shouted at her to leave.

I stepped with her on to the landing and closed the door behind us. 'Why was he in gaol?' I asked.

'I don't know, Doctor,' said she. 'Something to do with the Ripper case. He was accused of tampering with the evidence.'

'Why did you not call upon me? Or upon his brother?' I asked. At that time, I knew little of the considerable influence in government affairs that Holmes's older brother Mycroft commanded, and yet my sense was that some help might have been offered.

'Mr Holmes told no one, he simply vanished! I am not sure that his brother knew for a week. Of course he was released right after, but the damage was done.'

I learned much later the details of this horrific case and the ill-directed trials it put my friend through. However, I have been sworn to secrecy on this account, and it must remain a matter for the history books. Suffice it to say that my friend threw considerable light on the case, something that proved most unwelcome among certain individuals at the highest levels of government.

But that is another tale entirely. I returned to my vigil. Hours passed, and I could neither rouse him, engage him in conversation, nor get him to eat. He remained unmoving and in what I knew to be a dangerous depression.

The morning drew into afternoon. While placing a cup of tea near him, I happened to notice what appeared to be a crumpled personal letter lying on the side table. Unfolding the bottom half silently, I read the signature: 'Mycroft Holmes'.

I opened it and read. 'Come at once,' it said, 'the affair of E/P requires your immediate attention.' I folded the note and put it into my pocket.

'Holmes,' I said, 'I took the liberty of—'

'Burn that note,' came a shrill voice from beneath his cover.

'Too wet in here,' I said. 'Who is this "E slash P"? Your brother writes—'

'Burn it, I say!'

He would say nothing further but remained buried and unmoving. As the evening wore on, I decided to wait him out and remain there through the night. He would eat – or collapse – and I would be there, as his friend and his doctor, to pick up the pieces. Valiant thoughts indeed, but shortly after, I fell asleep.

Early the next morning, I awoke to find myself covered with that same red blanket I now recognized from my old rooms. Mrs Hudson stood over me with a tea tray and a new letter – oblong and rose-tinted – resting on the edge of the tray.

'From Paris, Mr Holmes!' said she, waving the letter at him. No response.

Glancing at Holmes, and the unfinished food from yesterday, she shook her head and threw me a worried look. 'Four days now, Doctor,' she whispered. 'Do something!' She placed the tray next to me.

From the rumpled figure on the couch the thin arm waved her away. 'Leave us, Mrs Hudson!' he cried. 'Give me the letter, Watson.'

Mrs Hudson departed, throwing me an encouraging look.

I snatched the letter from the tray and held it away. 'Eat first,' I demanded.

With a murderous look, he emerged from his cocoon and slammed a biscuit into his mouth, glaring at me like an angry child.

I held the letter away and sniffed it. I was rewarded by an unusual and delicious perfume, vanilla, perhaps, and something else. 'Ahh,' I said in pleasure, but Holmes succeeded in snatching the letter from my hand, immediately spitting out the biscuit. He examined the envelope thoroughly, and then tore it open, extracting the letter and scanning it quickly.

'Ha! What do you make of it, Watson?' His keen grey eyes were shaded by exhaustion, but lit by curiosity. A good sign.

I took it from him. As I unfolded the letter I noticed that he was eyeing the teapot uncertainly. I poured him a cup, added a splash of brandy and handed it to him. 'Drink,' said I.

The letter bore a Paris postmark with yesterday's date. It was written in bright pink ink and on fine stationery. I glanced at the delicate handwriting.

'It's in French,' I stated, handing it back. 'And hard to read even if not. Here.'

Impatient, he snatched the letter and announced, 'Writing – most definitely female. Scent, ahh . . . floral, amber, a touch of vanilla. I believe this is a new scent of Guerlain, "Jicky", in development but not yet released. The singer – for this is how she describes herself – must be successful or at least very much admired to have obtained a bottle in advance.'

Holmes moved to better light near the fire and began to read with the theatricality I have come to enjoy at times, and tolerate at others. His fluent French made translation simple for him.

'"My dear Mr Holmes," she says, "your reputation and recent recognition by my government has led me to make this unusual request. I seek your help in a highly personal matter. Although I am a concert singer in Paris, and as such may perhaps be considered by you to be of lower "caste" – caste, an odd choice of word for a chanteuse – "I beg you to consider helping me." Ah, I cannot read this; the ink is so pale!'

Holmes held the letter to the gaslight over our fireplace.

I noticed that his hand was shaking and he looked unsteady. I moved behind him to read over his shoulder.

'She continues, "I write on a matter of the greatest urgency concerning an important man of your country, and the father of my son—" here the lady has crossed out the name – but I perceive it is— What the devil?'

Holding the letter up closer to the light, he frowned in puzzlement. As he did so, a curious thing began to happen. The ink on the letter began to fade so quickly that even I noticed it standing behind him.

Holmes cried out and immediately pushed the letter under the cushion on the couch. We waited a few seconds, then pulled it out to look at it again. It was completely blank.

'Ah!' said he.

'It's some kind of disappearing ink!' I cried, silenced immediately by Holmes's sidelong glance. 'The father of her son?' I asked. 'Did you catch the name of this important personage?'

'I did,' said Holmes, standing quite still. 'The Earl of Pellingham.'

I returned to the couch wondering. Pellingham was one of the wealthiest peers in all of England, a man whose generosity and immense power in the House of Lords – not to mention his virtuous reputation as a humanitarian and collector of fine art – made him nearly a household name.

And yet here was a French cabaret singer claiming ties to this well-known figure.

'What are the chances, Holmes, of this lady's claim being valid?'

11

'It seems preposterous. But perhaps . . .' He moved to a cluttered table and spread the letter out, under a bright light.

'But why the disappearing ink?'

'She did not want a letter with the gentleman's name to fall into the wrong hands. The Earl is said to have a long reach. And yet she has not told us all, I think—'

He now aimed his magnifying glass at the letter. 'How curious, these scratches!' He sniffed the page. 'This blasted perfume! Yet I detect the slightest odour of— wait!' He began rummaging through a collection of glass bottles. With small dabs, he applied droplets to the page, muttering as he did so. 'There must be more.'

I knew better than to disturb him at such work and turned back to the newspaper I was reading. Not long after, I was startled from my dozing reverie by a cry of triumph.

'Ha! Just as I thought, Watson. The letter that disappeared was not the entire message. I have revealed a second letter underneath, in invisible ink. Clever indeed—a double use of steganography!'

'But how—?'

'There were small scratches on the page that did not match the writing we saw. And the faintest odour of potato. The lady has employed a second ink that only appears upon the application of a reagent, in this case iodine.'

'Holmes, you amaze me. What does it say?'

'It reads: "My dear Mr Holmes, it is with the utmost panic and terror that I write this to you. I did not wish a letter naming the boy's father to remain extant; hence my precaution. If you are as astute as reputed, you will discover this second note. Then I will know you are the man to help me.

'"I write to you because my young son, Emil, aged ten, has disappeared from the unnamed's estate, and I fear he has been kidnapped or worse. Emil has until recently lived with this man and his wife under complicated conditions which I would like to make known to you in person.

'"I am allowed to see him only once a year at Christmas time, when I travel to London and must follow explicit instructions for a most secretive assignation.

'"A week ago, I received a letter telling me that our meeting, to have taken place three weeks hence, is now cancelled and I will not see my boy this Christmas, nor ever again. I was enjoined to accept this on pain of death. I cabled at once, and a day later I was accosted in the street by a vicious ruffian, knocked to the ground and warned to stay away.

'"There is more, Mr Holmes, but I fear a strange net is closing in on me. May I call on you in London next week? I implore you in the name of humanity and justice to take my case. Please cable your reply to me signed as Mr Hugh Barrington, London Variety Producer. Very sincerely yours, Emmeline 'Cherie' La Victoire."'

Holmes paused, thinking. He picked up a cold pipe, grasping it with his teeth. His tired features took on a hint of animation. 'What do you make of this "strange net," Watson?'

'I have no idea. She is an artist. Perhaps a touch of the dramatic?' I said.

'I think not. This letter displays intelligence and careful planning.'

He tapped his cold pipe on the page in a sudden decisive gesture, glanced at the clock and stood, his eyes afire. 'Ah, there is just time to make the last ferry from Dover. Pack your bags, Watson; we leave for the Continent in less than ninety minutes.' He moved to the door, shouting downstairs, 'Mrs Hudson!'

'But the lady is coming here next week, she said.'

'Next week she could be dead. Concerned as she is, this young woman may not fully appreciate the danger she faces. I will explain all en route.'

And with that he was at the front door, again shouting into the hallway, 'Mrs Hudson! Our bags!'

'Holmes,' I cried. 'You are forgetting! My bags are elsewhere. In my own home!'

But he had left the room and entered his bedchamber. I wondered if his brain was even functioning to forget such a thing. Was he healthy enough to—?

I leaped from my chair and tore back the cover from the couch. There, tucked under one of the cushions, lay Holmes's cocaine and hypodermic. My heart sank.

Holmes appeared in the doorway. 'Please convey my apologies to Mrs Watson and collect your things at . . .' Here he paused, seeing the bottle and syringe in my hand.

'Holmes! You told me this was finished.'

A flicker of shame crossed his proud countenance. 'I'm . . . I'm afraid I need you, Watson.' There was a slight pause. 'On this trip, that is. If perhaps you would be free?'

The words hung in the air. His thin frame stood silhouetted in the door, poised, nearly quivering with excitement, or perhaps the drug. I looked down at the needle in my hands. I could not let him go alone in this state.

'You must promise me, Holmes—'

'No more cocaine.'

'No, I mean it this time. I cannot help you if you will not help yourself.'

He nodded, once.

I replaced the syringe in its case and pocketed it and the cocaine. 'You are in luck, then. Mary leaves for the country tomorrow to visit her mother.'

Holmes clapped his hands together like a child. 'Very good, Watson!' he cried. 'The Chatham departs for Dover from Victoria Station in three-quarters of an hour. Bring your revolver!' With that he vanished up the stairs. I paused.

'And the sandwiches,' he shouted down from above. I smiled. Holmes was back. And so, for better or worse, was I.

CHAPTER 2

En Route

I returned home for my things and managed to make it to Victoria Station barely in time to leap aboard the train to Dover.

The man facing me across our private compartment was no longer the man who had been languishing at 221B only hours before. Clean-shaven and even elegant in his travelling costume of black and grey, Holmes was every inch the imposing figure he could be when so inspired.

Certain that his rapid transformation was due entirely to the stimulation of this new case, and nothing to do with my ministrations, I admit to feeling a bit resentful. Nevertheless, I put these thoughts from my mind and decided to be satisfied that my friend was once again returning to himself, whatever the cause.

He began an unusually voluble explanation of our situation, his eyes burning with an excitement I hoped would not turn manic.

'The double encoding of the letter was not without interest, don't you think Watson? She evidently needed to mention the real name of the gentleman, yet to take that kind of precaution must mean she fears him as well. But it is the secondary message which intrigues.'

'Yes. How did she know that you would find it?'

'My reputation of course.'

'And so my recounting of *A Study in Scarlet* has done you some good, then, Holmes?'

'You forget I am known in France. Given her interest in chemistry, I would consider her choice to hide the second message a kind of litmus test.'

I sat back in puzzlement while peeling an orange with a small knife. 'I'll admit the double-ink trick is a clever touch. But what about the case itself? The lady wishes to travel to you. Why, then, this haste and our trip to Paris?'

Holmes smiled mischievously. 'Don't you fancy a trip to Paris, Watson? Leave the gloom of London for the City of Lights? Surely you cannot object to a brief holiday. You have not yet seen the curious ongoing construction of a rather grandiose edifice called La Tour Eiffel.'

'I have heard it is an abomination. And you do not travel for recreation, Holmes. Why do you think the danger to the lady is imminent?'

'I believe the attack in the street, Watson, is only the tip of the iceberg. I am concerned by her connection to the Earl. My brother believes there is a well-hidden but dark cloud of violence surrounding this man.'

I felt a sudden dawning. 'Ah, the "E/P" of Mycroft's note

18

to you! But I have always heard that Pellingham is a respected philanthropist, and a paragon of *noblesse oblige*, is he not?'

'So goes the story. You have heard of his art collection?'

'Yes, started by his father, as I recall.'

'It is legendary, but currently kept private. Are you aware that no one has seen it in years?'

'I'm afraid I do not follow these matters, Holmes.'

'Mycroft suspects the Earl of a less than scrupulous method of obtaining his treasures. There is a recent case in particular.'

'Why would a man of his standing risk being branded a thief over some stolen paintings?'

'The Earl is in a position difficult to imagine. His connections render him almost untouchable. He sheds suspicion like water off a well vulcanized mackintosh, Watson; surely you know that. And the artwork in question is a sculpture, not a painting. Not merely any sculpture, but the Marseilles Nike. You have heard of it?'

'Ah . . . that Greek statue discovered earlier this year! I believe there was a murder connected to—'

'Four murders, to be exact. The Nike is considered the grandest find since the Elgin Marbles, and she is said to surpass the Winged Victory in beauty. An enormous work in excellent condition. Priceless.'

I offered Holmes a section of orange; he waved it away, continuing with enthusiasm: 'No less than three foreign powers lay claim to her discovery and possession. She was being transferred somewhat controversially to the Louvre when she disappeared in Marseilles some months ago. Four men were killed during the theft in a particularly brutal manner. The Greek, French and British governments have been exhausting resources to trace her and solve the murders, to no avail.'

'All three countries? Why would so many lay claim to this Nike?'

'The discoverer – one of the four murdered men – was a titled Englishman, working on a French-funded dig in Greece.'

'Ah, I see. And so *you* were asked—'

'Mycroft did request that I look into it, and the French government as well, but I have hitherto declined.'

'Why?'

Holmes sighed. 'An acquisitive nobleman and a bungled art theft are not of sufficient interest to me, until the moment I received Mlle La Victoire's note. It seems that Pellingham may have wider interests. Mycroft has been investigating rumours of business and personal transgressions in and around his estate that bear a closer look. And while Mycroft has been keeping an eye on the Earl, even he must tread carefully because of Pellingham's immense power. He needs more data to go on.'

'More?'

'The mackintosh, Watson, the mackintosh. Mycroft needs to justify an investigation, and Mademoiselle Emmeline La Victoire may very well provide us with an *entrée* into the Earl's world.'

We paused briefly and I stared out the window at the

passing countryside growing dim in the fading light. Above were darkening, clouded skies. In the distance, lightning flashed. It did not bode well for our crossing. I turned back to Holmes.

'And there is the matter of the child. And the attack upon the lady herself.'

'Precisely.'

'Well, she is certainly frightened, judging from her letter.'

'Indeed. Her request to disguise my response indicates she is being watched. It is my opinion that we cannot reach her too quickly.'

'But exactly who is this Emmeline La Victoire?'

'You have not heard of the singer "Cherie Cerise", Watson?'

'I confess that I have not. My taste for recreation runs to bridge, and a quiet book by the fire, as you well know, Holmes.'

'Ha! A polite fiction! You are a crack shot, with a gambling habit, a passion for the yellow-backed novel, and a penchant—'

'Holmes!'

But my friend knew me only too well. 'Cherie Cerise is currently the toast of Paris. She is a *chanteuse extraordinaire*, if one is to believe her publicity, and alternates between the Chat Noir and the Moulin de la Galette, packing that large establishment to near riot every evening she appears.'

'The Chat Noir? The Black Chair?'

'Cat, Watson, the Black Cat, an intimate venue of great cachet. I visited it twice last year during my work for the

French. It is remarkable for the music, the clientele, and even the artwork which adorns the walls.'

'But I still do not understand the connection.'

'Peace, my good doctor, all will be made clear. And now rest, for there is work ahead of us. We will be hearing the lady sing, possibly this very night.'

I sighed. 'Is she at least beautiful?' I wondered.

Holmes smiled. 'Ah, and this from a married man! You are not likely to be disappointed, Watson. When a Frenchwoman is not a beauty, she is yet a work of art. And when she is beautiful, there are none of her sex to surpass her.' With that he pulled his hat low over his eyes, leaned back and was promptly asleep.

PART TWO

THE CITY OF LIGHT

'Art is born of the observation and investigation
of nature.'

Cicero

CHAPTER 3

We Meet Our Client

s it turned out, we were forced to spend the night in Dover, sharing a cramped room in a hotel crammed with stranded travellers, all delayed by the rising storms. Holmes had briefly slipped out into the sleet and had sent several telegrams, including one to Mlle La Victoire. Our client was now expecting us at eleven that morning at her apartment.

Leaving the Gare du Nord, we made our way through snow-fogged streets, past rows of trees garlanded with crystal icicles, gradually moving towards the hills of Montmartre. There Holmes had a favourite bistro, the Franc Buveur, where we could pass the hour before we were to meet our client. It was still early, and I longed for a coffee and perhaps a roll, but Holmes ordered us both a *bouillabaisse provençal*. This proved to be a hearty and flavourful fish stew from Marseilles, apparently available all hours at this establishment. It was perhaps somewhat extreme for my taste, but I was relieved to note he consumed his with gusto.

I made a mental note to return with my friend to Paris any time I noticed his thin frame becoming dangerously gaunt. I have never been plagued with this problem, but at thirty-five I knew that, for myself, precautions in the other direction might be wise.

We made our way through curving, tree-lined streets to Mlle La Victoire's address. This part of Montmartre had an almost rural tranquillity that belied its proximity to the area's renowned nightlife. The occasional empty plot and cottage garden, now blanketed by snow, stood tucked in between the old houses. Windmills poked through from behind, just beyond the nearby streets.

Approaching an elegant three-storey building with delicate grillwork at the windows, we rang and were shortly standing on the third floor, facing a door painted an unusual shade of dark green. An ornate brass knocker invited use. We knocked.

The door was opened by one of the most beautiful women I have seen. Cherie Cerise, *née* Emmeline La Victoire, stood before us in a velvet dressing gown of the same deep green, perfectly accentuating her startling green eyes and auburn hair. It was not merely her physical beauty that struck me, but a rare quality which emanated from the lady – a sparkle of intelligence coupled with a womanly allure that nearly took my breath away.

However, deep shadows under her bright eyes and a distinct pallor spoke of grief and worry. Her glance swept us both, taking in every detail in an instant.

'Ah, Monsieur Holmes,' she said with a smile to my companion. 'I am so relieved.' She turned to face me with radiant warmth. I flushed for no reason at all. 'And you must be Mr Holmes's most wonderful of friends, Dr Watson, I believe?' I held out my hand to shake hers, but instead she leaned in to kiss me, and then Holmes, on both cheeks in the French manner.

She smelled of the same delicious scent as her letter – Jicky perfume, Holmes had called it – and it took considerable self-control not to grin from ear to ear. But we were there on serious business. 'Mademoiselle, we are at your service,' I offered.

'Madame,' she corrected. '*Merci*. Thank you for coming, and so quickly.' Her charming French accent only added to her allure.

Soon we were seated in front of a small, cheery fireplace in the *salon* of her sumptuous apartment, decorated in the French style in shades of tan and cream, with high ceilings, a light-coloured oriental carpet and silk-upholstered furniture in subtle stripes. Bright against this neutral background were several bouquets of fresh flowers, expensive at this time of year, and a rainbow array of silk scarves strewn about. Our client was a woman of sophisticated tastes.

With apologies for the absence of servants, the lady herself brought us hot cups of coffee.

'My husband will return soon,' she said. 'And the maid, with groceries.'

Holmes sighed.

Mademoiselle La Victoire studied him. 'It is true; I did not mention a husband.'

'You are not married,' stated Holmes.

'Ah, but I am,' began the lady.

Holmes grunted and stood up abruptly. 'Watson, come. I fear our journey has been a waste of time.'

The lady leaped to her feet. 'Monsieur Holmes, *non!* I beg of you!'

'Mademoiselle, you are not married. If you desire my assistance, I require nothing less than complete frankness. Do not waste my time.'

She paused, considering. I reluctantly rose to my feet. Holmes reached for his hat.

'Sit, please,' she said finally, doing so herself. 'I will agree. The matter is urgent. But how did you know?'

I sat, but Holmes remained standing.

'You have claimed to have a husband and his name is mentioned in several articles about you. And yet he is never seen, nor described. My inquiries have revealed no one has seen him. And now, in your apartment, I note many female, but no male, touches; your scarves left over the back of the one easy chair which would be his if he existed, the choice of books on your mantelpiece, the lack of smoking paraphernalia except for your own cigarette case here.' He indicated a small delicately worked silver case on a side table.

'Yes, it is mine. Would you care to smoke, Mr Holmes? It will not bother me.'

'Ha! No, thank you. The details I mention are small

indications, but the proof is the ring on your left hand. False, I perceive, and not only of poor design, but slightly too large for you. Given the careful attention to the colour and fit of your attire, and the decoration of this room, this oversight indicates that your marriage is a fiction which I must assume is to keep male admirers off balance as you require. It is helpful that you seem quite out of bounds.'

It all seemed so obvious, and yet I had noticed none of these facts.

Mlle La Victoire remained silent, but a slight smile played upon her face. 'Well, all that is clear enough,' she said. 'But it merely shows you to be more observant than most.'

Holmes snorted. 'I am not finished . . .'

'Holmes—' I warned.

'My theory, and this is unproven, but I judge it likely from my first impressions upon meeting you, is that you trust no man.'

'I am merely assessing your capabilities,' said she.

'No. You have already done so. The letter.'

'Then how do you arrive at this intimate pronouncement, from five minutes of contact and a view of my *salon*?'

'Holmes,' I entreated again. We were headed into dangerous territory.

He ignored me, leaning forward, his grey eyes boring into hers. 'You are an artist, a great one from your reputation, and therefore are tempestuous, changeable . . . and vulnerable to flights of fancy as well as fits of despair. Your talent in music, when added to the exquisite sense of colour and refined taste, shown both in your décor here and your personal attire, attest to the acutely sensitive nature of the fully developed artist. You mask your strongly emotional nature with a crisp and intelligent manner. But it is not simply a mask; your critical thinking has enabled you to create a successful career on your own, in spite of these personal weaknesses. Nonetheless, you deceive yourself; you are at heart and quite essentially – a creature driven by emotion.'

'I am an artist; we are emotional. There is nothing new here,' she said sharply.

'Ah, but I have not got to my point,' said Holmes.

I placed my cup back into its saucer with a clatter. 'Coffee. This is quite delicious. Would it be possible to have another cup?' I asked.

They both ignored me.

'And what is your point?' asked the lady.

'You have an illegitimate son by the Earl. While I do not yet know the particulars, you must have been quite young. Most probably this was your first love. You were how old?'

Mlle La Victoire sat very still. I could not read her, but the temperature had dropped in the room. 'Eighteen.'

'Ah, I see that I am right.'

'*Peut-être.* Go on.'

'His betrayal, obvious as you are not married to the Earl, must have wounded a young person of your sensitivity quite deeply. It is my belief that since this time you have trusted no man and yet you long to with every part of your romantic soul.'

A small gasp came from our client.

Holmes's words hung in the room like tiny icicles. He was occasionally unaware of how they might wound. However, Mlle La Victoire recovered immediately.

'Bravo, Mr Holmes,' she said with a smile. 'It is as though you have personal knowledge of the subject.'

'I had no prior information—'

'Ah, *non*! I perceive that you speak from personal experience.'

A flicker of surprise crossed his face. 'Hardly. But now, let us turn to the matter at hand and examine the facts of your case.'

'Yes, indeed,' said the lady.

Both of them sat back, composing themselves and taking in the other with something akin to the guarded admiration of champion boxers before a match. I became aware that I was sitting nervously on the very edge of my chair. I cleared my throat and shifted, attempting to relax.

'Cigarette, anyone?' I ventured.

'No,' they said simultaneously.

Holmes began. 'Your son. What, nine? Ten?

'Ten.'

'How did you discover he was missing? *En français . . . plus facile pour vous?*' said Holmes, adopting a more gentle tone.

'Ah, *non*. I prefer in English.'

'As you wish.'

Mlle La Victoire drew a deep breath and pulled her green dressing gown around her. 'It is every Christmas that I see *mon petit* Emil in London, at Brown's Hotel. There is a man who brings him to meet me, a "go-between". We have a luncheon together in their beautiful tea room, Emil and I, and I give him gifts. I ask him about his year, and try to know him. It is precious, but too little. This year, the meeting was cancelled. I wrote, and sent a telegram. No reply. Finally I heard from this go-between that Emil is with his uncle at the seaside and would not be available for some time.'

'But you doubt this story.'

'He does not have an uncle.'

'These yearly visits, have they been every year since his birth?

'Yes. It is the arrangement I have made with his father, the Earl.'

'That would be Harold Beauchamp-Kay, the present Earl of Pellingham?' asked Holmes.

'Yes.'

'Begin at the beginning, please. Describe the boy.'

'Emil is ten. Small for his age. Slender.'

'How small?'

'About this tall,' Mlle La Victoire held her hand some four feet from the ground. 'Blond hair like his father, with my green eyes. A sweet-faced child, quiet. He enjoys music and reading.'

'And who does the boy think *you* are?'

'He believes me a friend of the family, no relation.'

'Does the Earl accompany the boy to London?'

'Emil,' I prompted. 'His name is Emil.'

'*Non!* I have not seen Harold – er – the Earl since . . .'

Here her voice faltered. She looked stricken. I felt Holmes suppress a sigh of impatience.

'Then who brings Emil to Brown's?'

'The Earl's valet, Pomeroy. He is of French descent, and very kind. He understands a mother's love.' Abruptly her façade cracked and she gasped to cover a sob. I offered my handkerchief. She took it graciously and touched it to her eyes. Holmes remained unmoved. But her feelings were genuine, of that I was sure. She struggled to compose herself.

'I must explain. Ten years ago I was a poor singer here, in Paris. It was three days of love; we spoke of marriage. I did not know he was an Earl or that he was already married. But then—'

'Yes, yes, of course. Moving forward in time. So, this valet Pomeroy is complicit? What happened this year?' he barked.

'Holmes!' I admonished, once again. The lady was evidently in a state of great agitation.

'Pray continue,' he pressed on, only slightly altering his tone. 'What did you do upon hearing your Christmas visit was cancelled?'

'I wrote, demanding an explanation.'

Holmes waved his hands in impatience, 'And . . . ?'

'A reply warned me to cease contact, or I would never see Emil again.'

'A letter from the Earl?'

'*Non*. I have had no contact with the Earl – either in person or by letter – once our agreement had been made. The letter was from his man, Pomeroy.'

'No further explanation or contact?'

'I wrote and sent a third telegram but with no response.'

'What kept you from travelling to the Earl's estate to investigate?' asked Holmes abruptly. 'I will take that cigarette now.'

The lady offered him one from her case. He patted his pockets for matches. I retrieved one and lit it for him.

'This is all very recent, Monsieur Holmes,' she replied. 'The original arrangement was that I make no other attempt to reach Emil except the Christmas visits. Those were the terms.'

'And yet this arrangement has been breached by the other party,' snapped Holmes. 'Have you entertained the notion that your son may be dead?'

'He is not dead!' Mlle La Victoire stood up, eyes blazing. 'I do not know how I know this, Monsieur Holmes, and you may analyse or sneer if you wish. But somehow, as a mother, I know that my son is alive. You must help me! I need you to act.'

'Mademoiselle! We are not finished.'

'Holmes,' I said gently, 'you are distressing this lady with your harsh questions. It seems we do not yet know the half of this story.'

'Which is precisely the point. I cannot assist you, unless I know not only the half but the whole of it,' said Holmes. 'Sit down please, and let us continue.'

She sat, composing herself.

'Who else at the Earl's estate knows that Emil is your son?'

'Lady Pellingham knows.'

Holmes leaned back, surprised. 'The Earl's wife, the American heiress! Does she know the full story? That the child is the Earl's?'

'Yes.'

'And she has accepted her husband's illegitimate offspring in her home?'

'More than that. She is a mother to Emil. She loves him dearly and he returns the feelings. In fact, Emil thinks that she *is* his mother!' Here she broke off, her voice catching in a sob.

'That must be very difficult for you,' I said.

'Go on,' said Holmes.

'At first it did pain me,' she admitted to me. 'Greatly. But later I realized it is for the best. Lady Pellingham is a kind woman and lost a child at birth, close to the time Emil was born. My little Emil was substituted in secret for their dead child, and the rest of the world believes him to be theirs. Emil will inherit the estate and will be the next Earl of Pellingham. And so you see—'

'I see,' said Holmes, once again abrupt. 'It is a fortunate arrangement in many ways.'

The lady stiffened. 'You think me mercenary,' she said.

'No, no, he does not.' I jumped in, but Holmes overrode me.

'I think you practical.'

'Practical, yes. At the time of the adoption I was but a poor artist, with no way to offer Emil an education or any advantages. And life with a performing artist would place a small child into a world full of dangers, bad influences. Imagine a baby backstage—'

'Yes, yes of course. You wrote that you were attacked, Mademoiselle La Victoire,' said Holmes, 'which is the reason we are here. Elaborate, please.'

'It was exactly one day after my last telegram to the Earl. A ruffian approached me in the street. He pushed me rudely and brandished a weapon, a strange kind of knife.'

'Describe this knife.'

'It was very odd. It resembled a ladle, but the end was very sharp, a kind of blade,' said our client. 'I pulled away and slipped in the ice, falling to the ground.'

'Were you hurt?'

'I was more frightened than hurt. I received only a small bruise from the fall. But there was something else—'

'What? Be precise.'

'After I fell, the man helped me up.'

Holmes's leaned forward in excitement. 'Ah! Did he speak to you? His exact words?'

'After helping me up, he held this strange blade to my throat and said I had better watch out.'

'His exact words? No mention of the Earl?'

'No, nothing specific. He said, "Leave it alone. Or someone might die."'

'His accent. English? American? Greek?'

'French,' she said. 'But hard to understand. A low voice.'

'Did anything about this man, his clothing, his voice, the knife, seem familiar to you?'

'Not at all. The man's face was in shadow from a large hat. It was dusk and snowing heavily. I could not see him clearly.'

'Do you know anyone who works as a tanner?'

'A tanner? You mean he prepares leather? Er . . . *non.* No one. Why?'

'The knife,' said Holmes. 'You described a tanner's dry scraper. A tool particular to that trade.'

'In any case, I do not take kindly to threats, Mr Holmes.'

'No, you would not. However I believe this was not a threat, but a friendly warning.'

'*Non!*' she exclaimed.

'*Attendez.* I do believe there is danger. The danger may be to your son, rather than to yourself. However, it is possible that your very efforts to find him could put you both in peril.'

Mlle La Victoire sat frozen, listening.

'In the interests of safety, I ask that you not venture out alone. Do nothing, but allow Dr Watson and myself to search for your son unimpeded. Now, one more question. Did you sense anything wrong before this? In previous visits to your son perhaps?'

'You must understand me, Monsieur Holmes,' said the singer. 'I love my boy. I have observed over the years a healthy and happy child, well adjusted and thriving. I would never have let things proceed if not. It is my feeling that he has been treated kindly and generously by the Earl and his wife.'

Holmes remained impassive. From the doorway leading

into the rest of the apartment came the sharp sound of a chair scraping. Holmes stood, immediately on the alert. I joined him.

'Who is in the apartment with us?' said he.

Mlle La Victoire rose. 'No one. It is the maid with the groceries. Now if you will excuse me, please.'

'Her name?'

'Bernice. Why?' But Holmes did not reply. Mlle La Victoire moved to the door, which she opened in a clear gesture of dismissal. 'Now, gentlemen, I must rest and prepare for my performance tonight. Please join me at Le Chat Noir. I sing at eleven. We can meet afterwards and continue this interview.'

'We will be happy to be there,' I said. 'Thank you for the coffee, and your kind hospitality.' I approached and kissed her hand. Turning, I saw my companion already had his overcoat on and was reaching for his scarf.

Moments later we found ourselves in the street. It had begun to snow. 'Come Watson. What do you make of our client?'

'She is exceedingly beautiful.'

'Guarded.'

'Charming!'

'Complex. Masking something.'

'I was glad to hear the boy was treated well at the Earl's.' I said. 'Don't you trust her on that account?'

Holmes snorted and walked faster. 'We cannot yet be sure of Emil's treatment at home. Children often learn stoicism early.'

'But surely Mademoiselle La Victoire would have noticed,' I said.

'Not necessarily. Even a mother can miss the signs.'

I was taken aback by this comment. As I had often in the past, I wondered again briefly about Holmes's own story. Of his childhood, I knew nothing. Had his own mother missed signs? And of what?

A sturdy woman approached carrying an armful of groceries. Holmes called out to her in a cheery voice and perfect accent, '*Bonsoir*, Bernice!'

'*Bonsoir, monsieur*,' she sang back, and then, seeing we were strangers, hurried on.

Holmes looked at me. *Who had been in the apartment with us?*

CHAPTER 4

Le Louvre

he sleet had turned into a light snow during our visit to Mlle La Victoire. We had several hours to pass before the evening's performance and, hailing a cab, we proceeded to a small hotel near the Madeleine. To my surprise, Holmes next suggested a visit to the Louvre. I entreated him to rest, but his nervous energy had returned, and he pointed out to me that a short and leisurely perusal of some of the world's great art treasures would be more restorative than a nap. It seemed a reasonable idea at the time.

I should have known that he had a second, unspoken reason; it was a hallmark of my travels with Holmes. We stowed our luggage, and hailed another cab.

Holmes directed the driver slightly out of our way, taking a scenic route through Paris, heading first east to the Place de l'Étoile. Circling the magnificent Arc de Triomphe, we proceeded next to the Champs Élysées, moving past the impressive Palais de L'Industrie. Arriving at the Place de la

Concorde, Holmes pointed out the Luxor obelisk, before directing our driver south to the river. From there the unfinished apparition of La Tour Eiffel loomed vaporously off to our right through the snowy air. It looked ridiculously like something Jules Verne might construct as a ladder to the moon.

'A monstrosity!' I commented. Holmes smiled. I wondered how long Parisians would put up with the blasted thing.

Upon entering the Louvre, we began with a tour of the galleries in the southern wing. There Holmes surprised me with his vast knowledge of the collection, and the pleasure he took in introducing me to its finer points. I was happy to see him refresh both mind and spirit, as there were few things other than work and his violin which could relieve his churning, restless mind.

Perhaps I had been wrong, and this trip to Paris would be the exactly the tonic he needed for his recovery.

Moving quickly through several great halls, we came to rest in front of an unusual portrait. The subject was a somewhat eccentric-looking gentleman, dressed in a Bohemian style of eighty years or so ago, with a broad fur collar, a bright red scarf, his white hair in disarray, and a look of devilish, amused intensity on his vivid features. Holmes paused in front of this portrait, apparently taken by it.

I wondered aloud, 'Who is this strange-looking fellow, Holmes, a friend of yours?'

'Hardly, the man is long gone. But this painting is a

recent acquisition and I have read of it. The subject is the painter Isabey, renowned for his miniatures.'

The slightly odd expression and clothing of the gentleman in the painting struck me. 'He looks a bit mad!' I remarked. 'Or perhaps ready to embark on some shady diversion.'

Holmes turned to me in amusement. 'Possibly. One never knows with an artist.'

I read the name below the portrait. It had been painted by Horace Vernet – the brother of Holmes's grandmother! While he spoke little of his upbringing, he had once mentioned this.

'Ah, your great-uncle is the artist!' I exclaimed. 'This is unusual for him, is it not? Wasn't he more known for historical, and later military and oriental subjects?' I wondered aloud, proud to demonstrate knowledge in at least one very small corner of the visual arts.

Holmes looked at me in some surprise, and then smiled, returning to his study of the painting.

I had made it a point to familiarize myself with the Vernet family in an effort to understand my friend. Horace Vernet was an odd chap, born in the Louvre itself in June of 1789, while his artist father (Holmes's great-grandfather), Carle Vernet, hid out there during the violence of the French Revolution.

Carle's sister, arrested for associating with the nobility, had been dragged screaming to the guillotine. Carle never painted again, but his son Horace went on to become a renowned artist, discarding the trappings of classicism and forging his own path as a renegade painter of a much more natural style whose topics were chiefly soldiers and orientalism.

While the other side of Holmes's family were English country squires, and therefore probably more conventional (though I could not be sure), I have always felt, after learning of Holmes's French ancestry, that it explained something of his 'art in the blood' theory.

Holmes, the cold reasoning machine, did have a deeply emotional side to him. And some of the leaps of thought which came to him – after amassing the facts, of course – displayed an imagination that could only be termed artistic.

As we strolled out of this gallery and into the next, Holmes leaned in close and whispered, 'Have you noticed the man who is following us?'

I started and began to turn.

'Don't give it away! Continue to walk.'

'Oh, give me more credit than that, Holmes!'

We drew presently into a room containing some drawings of Ingres. These pen-and-ink studies of women and children might have been pleasing but I could not focus. I glanced behind me. Was there someone who withdrew immediately behind the door to the next gallery? Or was Holmes, in his precarious state, imagining things?

Who would know we were there, or have the slightest reason to follow us? It must be merely another tourist. What was I thinking?

'The gentleman with the large umbrella is quite skilled at concealment.' Holmes nodded discreetly in the direction of the gallery from which we had just come.

'I see nothing, Holmes,' said I. 'Most people leave their umbrellas in the cloakroom.'

'Precisely.'

I glanced around again. I saw no man with an umbrella. A small trickle of worry began to take hold of me, coupled with impatience. 'May I suggest a coffee?'

'Follow me, Watson,' he said, 'and we shall lose the fellow.' He took off at a brisk walk.

'Ridiculous,' I muttered, hurrying to follow. What could be the point of this mysterious game?

Ten minutes later, and after a breathless trot through a maze of galleries and rooms large and small on a route which seemed to be well known to my companion, Holmes decided we had succeeded in losing our shadow.

'Good,' I remarked. 'Perhaps our follower has joined one of the tour groups of American ladies and will find himself a suitable wife, enabling him to give up a life of crime.'

Holmes ignored me and presently we came to a large, public staircase in front of a remarkable statue. It was the headless form of a woman, striding intemperately forth, wings spread behind her.

'Behold the Winged Victory of Samothrace, or Nike,' Holmes announced. 'One of the finest examples of Hellenistic art in the world, if not *the* finest.'

But our fictional follower had grabbed hold of my imagination. 'They are probably charming him now with their astute comments on the art,' I said. 'One of them will capture his fancy. Together, they will move to Philadelphia, opening a small umbrella shop where—'

'I told you, we've lost him,' snapped my companion.

'He was never there, Holmes!' I said, exasperated. But he ignored me, lost in contemplation of the statue.

'Just look, Watson. Isn't she magnificent? Notice the vivid stance, the spiral structure, the rendering of wet cloth – perhaps as if at the bow of a ship. The style is from the island of Rhodes, and the sculpture probably commemorates an ancient victory at sea. It is said that the Marseilles Nike I mentioned to you in the train bears a resemblance to her – which would make that statue most coveted indeed!'

He stared at it, rapt, entranced by which feature or idea, I could not say. It was lovely, I suppose. It was certainly dramatic, bordering on the histrionic. She was missing her head. Where was the head? I sighed, suddenly tired.

Holmes shot me a withering glance.

'Is the tea room nearby? Perhaps a French pastry would revive me,' I said.

'Watson, don't be such a Philistine. You are in the presence of one of the finest pieces of art in the Western pantheon—' He stopped in mid-sentence and pulled out his pocket watch. 'Ah, it is time! I have an appointment with the Curator of Sculpture to discuss the stolen Nike statue. It appears that a rare photograph is in their possession. Come, we must not be late.'

'What? I thought you were not interested in this stolen statue.'

'A favour to my brother; nothing more. And simple curiosity.'

I doubted this. Holmes was purposeful at all times. I

46

tried to control my annoyance. 'But when did you have time to make this appointment?'

'I telegraphed from Dover,' he snapped. 'Obviously.'

It was typical of Holmes to disguise his agenda, even from me.

'Holmes, there is only so much art I can imbibe at a time,' I said, somewhat testily. 'I am going for a cup of tea. Now.'

Thus I found myself alone in the galleries, scheduled to meet up with Holmes at the Rue de Rivoli entrance in three-quarters of an hour. He admonished me to take care and remain in sight of others.

I thought the warning pointless. No one could be following us in the Louvre. Who would know we were there, other than the art expert he was now seeing? I wondered if the residual effect of the cocaine, aggravated by too much artistic stimulation, had my friend's imagination working overtime.

I attempted to find my way to the tea room but became lost and wandered for a good fifteen minutes, growing ever more fatigued and annoyed. Finally a sympathetic guard pointed out a short cut to the restaurant through a doorway and down some stairs normally reserved for employees of the museum.

I entered the dark spiral stairwell and began my descent. In retrospect, it was a foolhardy move. But I was yet to understand the extreme danger of our investigation.

As I passed the next landing, the door on the floor above opened behind me with a soft click. Having discounted our mysterious pursuer's existence, I ignored this for perhaps a second or two. I became aware of the lack of footsteps behind me.

Had someone entered the stairwell and remained standing, in the doorway above? Strange, I thought, and was turning to look when I was struck a sudden hard blow to the legs by a large figure shrouded in grey and wearing a low hat – and wielding an umbrella! I tumbled down the marble staircase like a child's toy thrown in a fit of pique.

With a thud I slammed into the rails at the next landing, and lay there, my breath knocked out of me. A sharp pain in the ribs stabbed into my consciousness and I groaned. I heard the door on the landing above click shut. And then I blacked out.

When I regained consciousness I was lying on some sort of couch. The face of my friend, Sherlock Holmes, floated hazily above mine with an expression of fearful concern.

'Watson! Watson!' he entreated. His hand patted mine, as he tried to rouse me.

My eyes focused and I took in the scene. Behind Holmes were two security guards. We were in someone's office. I blinked a few times.

'I am fine, Holmes,' I managed to say. 'It was a small tumble.'

'You were pushed down a steep flight of stairs,' he said.

'Well, yes.'

'But you did not see your attacker?'

'It happened too quickly,' I replied, attempting to sit up. 'I only glimpsed a hat. And an umbrella.'

Holmes snorted.

'I suppose I did not believe you,' I admitted sheepishly.

Holmes brusquely dropped my hand and whirled on the guards.

'I shall ask you again! Who entered the stairwell?' demanded Holmes of one of them, whom I now recognized as the guard who had shown me the stairwell.

'Not a person,' said the guard, in a defensive whine. 'I go. I see nothing.'

'No one?' Holmes stared at him. 'Idiot!' he muttered under his breath, and then turned back to me. 'Are you well enough to walk, Watson? We must get you to the hotel, and perhaps to a doctor.'

I sat up with a lurch, feeling a wave of nausea and some sharp pains in my legs, rib, and the back of my head. But taking stock, I realized that nothing was broken, and that I was probably no more than badly bruised.

'I won't need a doctor,' I said, 'but I could use that cup of tea. And perhaps a bit of rest before tonight.'

Holmes smiled with relief. 'Good man, Watson,' he said.

CHAPTER 5

Les Oeufs

fter a brief rest at our hotel, my headache abated and I was left with nothing more than sore ribs. We changed into our evening clothes, stopped briefly for something called *oeufs mayonnaise* and proceeded in a cab towards Montmartre. A light dusting of new snow lit by golden gaslights gave Paris a sparkling mystique.

'You begin to realize, of course, that this case is more complex than it initially appeared.'

I could read from my friend's expression that this did not altogether displease him.

'Who do you suppose pushed me down the stairs?'

'Ha! Our "imaginary" follower no doubt,' he said with a smile.

'Yes, but other than our client, and this expert at the Louvre, who knew we would be in Paris?'

'From those two, and Mycroft additionally, stretch many possibilities,' said Holmes impatiently. 'But most probably it was the person at Mlle La Victoire's apartment who was "not Bernice".'

'Do you have any theories?'

'Four. No, five. But I believe my primary suspect will reveal himself tonight.'

I was not unaware of the keen pleasure my companion took in the increased danger of our situation. His eyes burned with the excitement of the chase.

I fingered the revolver, cold and reassuring, in my pocket. Against my better instincts, I found the thrill of adventure rising inside in me like an unwanted fever.

CHAPTER 6

Le Chat Noir

ur cab gradually left the Grands Boulevards as we made our way once again through the increasingly narrow and hilly streets towards Montmartre, home of colourful Bohemians and the centre of the art world in Paris. The ramshackle houses, crowded with trees and vines, gave the area an air of a country village gone mad.

Until relatively recently, this area had been on the very outskirts of Paris. I wondered if the windmills were still in the service of grinding grain.

One surely was not. Le Moulin de la Galette was now a beacon for one of the most famous nightclubs in the world, a scene of wild evenings – where Parisians and visitors from many lands gathered to hear beautiful women in arresting attire sing of love, despair and, through thinly veiled references, more intimate matters.

There, too, strange clowns cavorted in wild acts calculated to disarm and shock, and rows of shapely dancers performed the famous cancan, revealing glimpses of more than propriety would bear. Not that I had ever seen such things.

But I held out hope.

We passed the Moulin de la Galette and I was drawn to the colourful posters, glistening in the cold evening light, harbingers of this rich entertainment. They depicted swirling skirts, bright colours, strings of electric lights.

We were certainly far from London in every respect. I smiled at the thought of Mary at home and what she might think of this colourful locale. It would fall into her 'I will just enjoy the postcard' category.

Our cab pulled up outside 68 Boulevard de Clichy. A bold sign announced that we had reached our destination. The building itself looked like a country home, crowded in between two larger buildings, which leaned in like overly solicitous relatives. It was the famous cabaret Le Chat Noir, or 'the Black Cat'.

I took a deep breath and willed myself to be on the alert. As we stepped down from our cab, I glanced up and down the street, but no one stood out in the milling masses.

Inside, after depositing our capes, hats and sticks with a blonde coquette who flashed me a wink and a smile, I reluctantly felt myself swept forward by the arriving crowd down a narrow hallway and up a steep stairway lined with French political cartoons. While the French sense of humour, I'll admit, is not my own, I was struck by the bitter under-tones, the funereal slant of the subject matter, the scorn and the anger beneath the humorous caricatures.

The contrast between the hostess's inviting smile and the sarcastic political commentary was as unsettling as the tendency of the remarkably varied crowds to, well, *push*.

And then I got a glimpse of the main room.

My first impression was of utter chaos – the noise, the smoke, a hodgepodge crowd of Parisians of all classes, jammed in like sardines; the walls covered with paintings, posters, ornate cornices, lanterns, bizarre sculptures. An enormous stuffed aquatic creature hung from the ceiling. A porpoise? A giant catfish? I could not be sure.

The crowd was a milling, laughing mass. The noise was oppressive. In one corner were several Swiss Guards. I later learned Le Chat Noir was a social mecca for these odd mercenaries in their startling blue-and-yellow striped Renaissance clothing and white ruffs. A rowdy burst of laughter came from a cluster of them at a far table.

I'd heard of Le Chat Noir of course, but never imagined it would be a place that I would visit. It seemed a madhouse.

Holmes and I pushed our way through the dense crowd towards a couple of empty seats. A bearded ruffian in corduroy abruptly rammed into me, splashing his glass of wine on my waistcoat.

'I beg your pardon!' I said. The man stopped in his tracks and turned penetrating dark eyes to my face.

'*Anglais!*' he literally spat, the viscous wad narrowly missing my polished boots. '*Va te faire foutre, espèce de salaud! On ne veut pas de toi ici!*' He turned and disappeared into the crowd.

I shot Holmes a questioning look, and he took my arm,

guiding me to our seats. I blotted at the wine with my handkerchief, feeling my face turning red from the insult.

'Sit,' said Holmes, as we squeezed into two empty seats at the end of a long banquette against a back wall. 'I see this is your first encounter with the virulent form of anti-English sentiment which has grown over the past years here.'

'Still angry over Agincourt, I suppose,' I replied, my dignity ruffled.

'You do not understand the French,' he said.

'No one understands the French!' I replied. Holmes grinned.

But it was true that there was a flavour to the crowd and the place itself that was impenetrable to my sensibilities. Looking around me, I sensed we were at the epicentre of some cultural movement, but I could not grasp its significance . . . or its meaning. I felt a bit like the stuffed creature hanging above us – an observer – separate, and quite out of place.

My attention was next drawn to a decorative circular frame enclosing a large translucent screen of some sort on the wall behind the stage. Noticing my puzzlement, Holmes explained. 'That is the screen of the famous *Théâtre d'Ombres*, the Shadow Theatre,' he said. 'Shadow puppets, figures cut out of zinc, are projected there nightly. The writing is quite amusing. Very popular now.'

'You've seen it, then?' I wondered.

'Several times. But, aha! There is the man of the hour.' He indicated with a nod a tall, handsome fellow in a well-cut suit of European style, sporting a jaunty moustache and gliding effortlessly through the crowd. He was French, from his elegant dress and dark good looks. 'Exactly whom I expected,' said Holmes.

The gentleman looked our way, and Holmes nodded in greeting. I thought I detected a flash of annoyance from the man but his face then broke into a charming smile. He bowed mockingly in our direction before taking his seat.

'Old friend?' I asked.

'In a manner of speaking,' replied Holmes. 'Is he familiar to you, by chance?'

I studied the man, recognizing nothing. 'Who is he?'

Before Holmes could answer, a server placed before us two carafes of water, and two curved glasses with a strange green liquid nestled in the lower part of each. A perforated kind of knife balanced across each, with a lump of sugar on top. Holmes paid her and turned to me with a smile, indicating I should pour the water over the sugar. 'We'll discuss it later. Now, do give this a taste; it is quite unique. But no more than a single sip, Watson; I need you sharp tonight.'

Absinthe! Was he mad? I watched Holmes add water, and with a stir, the liquid took on an eerie glow. It looked like something one might imagine oozing from under the sea in a Jules Verne novel. Of course I had read of the stuff. The famed concoction was an extreme depressant renowned for its hallucinogenic effects.

'No thank you, Holmes.' I pushed my glass away.

He took one sip and did the same. 'Wise choice,' he said.

'I once spent an afternoon at a nearby establishment, working off an absinthe-induced reverie.' He shrugged. 'It is worth trying once – in the name of science, of course.'

My attention returned to Holmes's 'old friend'. He was seated near the door, engrossed in conversation with a young couple, the girl staring at him in frank admiration. I could see from his gestures and her enraptured expression that he possessed that very particular Gallic charm which was easy to spot and impossible to emulate. What was Holmes's interest in this man?

I noticed another small group, off to the side, also regarding the Frenchman. There were four men, three very tall and muscular, and a smaller, almost delicate man. There was something quite odd about them. In addition to being clad entirely in black, almost like a group of clerics, they somehow conveyed an air of menace. While the crowds around them laughed and gestured, they remained preternaturally still, their drinks untouched. The smallest man, whose manner subtly commanded the others, made me think of a cat, coiled and waiting at a mouse hole.

I started to point them out to Holmes, but he'd risen and, taking our drinks, crossed the room towards the bar. I observed that the Frenchman kept a careful eye on Holmes while remaining in conversation. His regard caused the group of four to follow his gaze to Holmes. I did not like the look that passed over the small man's face. It seemed to be recognition, and something more. A chill came over me in the crowded, warm room.

Holmes returned with a carafe of red wine and two fresh glasses.

'Holmes,' I began. 'There are four men over there who seemed very interested to find you here.'

'The Americans. Yes, I noticed.'

This should not have startled me, but it did.

'You are referring to the oddly dressed gentlemen in black?' he smiled. 'Not exactly your Grand Tour types. They are more interested in our French friend, not me.'

'And yet they seemed to recognize you,' I pointed out. 'Or the small one did.'

'That is unfortunate,' said Holmes. 'It may change our plans slightly.' He thought for a moment. 'If there is any trouble, or if I so signal you, escort our client safely away from here and to some place other than her home. Do you understand me?'

'Of course I understand you,' I replied peevishly. 'What is it that you expect to happen?'

But before he could answer, we were drowned out by a loud musical flourish from the small band.

There was an audible murmur of anticipation as our client took the stage.

PART THREE

THE LINES ARE DRAWN

'Art, like morality, consists of drawing the
line somewhere.'

G. K. Chesterton

CHAPTER 7

Attack!

f she was beautiful this afternoon, she was now transformed into a goddess! Dressed entirely in red, Mademoiselle La Victoire as Cherie Cerise positively glowed, her tumbling curls of flaming red hair tied up loosely in the topknot so stylish here, her exquisite pale bosom promising a passionate heart just below. She moved across the stage as if floating on air, her mischievous smile tempting the imagination. All traces of her dire situation were concealed by the consummate performer that she was.

'You are gaping, Watson,' Holmes whispered. Perhaps I was. But save for Holmes, so was everyone else.

A unanimous shout, 'Cherie!' rose up from the room. Our client, Mlle Emmeline La Victoire, was unquestionably a star.

In retrospect, I realized that what I had anticipated was a bawdy, music-hall-style performance with half-shouted melody and swishing skirts. But as the music started up and she began to sing, what came from the lovely creature was the voice of an angel, soaring and clear. She conveyed a sweet melancholy that ripped at one's heart.

For nearly an hour I sat transported.

As she finished a song about a rare tropical bird which flew many leagues to be with its lover (or perhaps it was a dog, I cannot be sure), I turned to my friend – only to discover that the space where Holmes had been sitting a moment ago was now filled by a rude-looking peasant, red nose aglow with drink.

Where the devil had he gone? Scanning the room, I observed that the Frenchman he had pointed out earlier was missing and the black-clad men as well. I grew uneasy and stood up. Holmes was nowhere to be seen. Damn his secrecy!

Just then, a series of shouts burst from backstage, followed by a loud crash. Our client froze, and the music ground to a halt. What happened next was so fast I can barely recount it.

There, against the backlit, glowing screen of the *Théâtre d'Ombres*, the small puppets were overshadowed by the distorted silhouettes of two men locked in mortal combat. The struggling figures bashed against the oiled canvas.

A spray of some dark liquid spattered in a wide arc across it. The crowd gasped.

A rending tear sounded as a knife split the fabric. The torn screen peeled forward revealing the splatter as bright red blood!

I was up and pushing through the crowd towards Mlle

La Victoire when a man hurtled through the tear, landing on the stage at her feet. An arterial wound in his chest shot a fountain of crimson several feet into the air. Mademoiselle screamed.

The crowd leapt as one and clambered to get away from the stage. I lost sight of our client through the churning mass of bodies. Using every ounce of strength, I shoved my way towards the stage against the tide of the mob.

I reached the stagehand on the floor and saw instantly that the wound was fatal. I looked up and Mlle La Victoire was gone. Leaving the dying man in the arms of a colleague, I ran backstage.

Chaos! In a dark room lit by a piercing ray of white light aimed at the back of the screen, struggling figures bashed into large wooden frames on wheels.

The spotlight was blinding. I tried to shield my eyes. 'Mademoiselle!' I cried.

I heard nothing but the shouts of men. I dodged as the highly flammable light crashed to the floor next to me. There was a small explosion. The room went black and flame erupted near my feet. There was more shouting as several stagehands rushed towards it to put it out.

Mlle La Victoire's voice rang out. 'Jean!'

Two large stage doors swung open to a nearby courtyard dimly lit by a single street lamp. The fight spilled into it. The cobblestones gleamed with black ice and the struggling men slid and tumbled on its slick surface, falling with sharp cries of pain.

I recognized the mysterious Frenchman of Holmes's

acquaintance, and two of the black-clad men I'd observed earlier. I drew my revolver and followed.

Mlle La Victoire dashed out from backstage into a circle of light. Brandishing a large vase, she brought it down on one of the black-clad men. The vase glanced off his shoulder. He grunted, whirling to grab her wrist. She screamed.

The thug, his bald head gleaming in the lamplight, pointed a knife under her ribs and backed her towards the wall of the adjacent building, as the tall Frenchman continued to battle one of the others.

'Bitch!' snarled the bald villain, raising the knife to her face. 'I'll cut you good for that.'

American? I aimed but had no clear shot. Pocketing my gun, I dashed forward at the exact moment the Frenchman downed his red-haired attacker and did the same. Both of us leapt towards the man with the knife, and as if we were choreographed, the Frenchman knocked the weapon from the man's hand, as I threw a punch straight at the kidneys. The bald man in black dropped to the ground, his knife flying into the darkness.

Two were down. But there had been four at the table.

'Jean!' cried Mlle La Victoire, flinging herself into the Frenchman's arms.

'*Allez-y!*' he said, pushing her away. *Run!*

She hesitated. In that instant, her bald assailant rose from the ground like Lazarus, and in a flash knocked me into the wall. We struggled as the second attacked the Frenchman with renewed vigour.

The four of us slid and tumbled on the ice like drunks.

My revolver fell from my pocket. It skittered away into the darkness.

As I struggled with my attacker, a third man grabbed Mlle La Victoire and slapped her, hard.

Furious, I tried to wrench free, but at my momentary distraction, my attacker took his chance. I felt myself choked from behind, and gasping for air.

It was then that the fourth man in black, the small man whom I had spotted as the leader, moved into the light. The odds had worsened. He ran towards me, butting me hard in the stomach. My knees buckled.

He pulled out a long stiletto which glittered like a deadly icicle in the pale light. The man choking me altered his grip and grabbed me by the hair, forcing my head back. The small man now slowly raised the stiletto to my throat, and began caressing it with the flat of the knife.

It was a strange gesture, like a surgeon cleansing the skin with carbolic before his incision. Time slowed.

His pale face and beady eyes were strangely rat-like. 'The dangerous one dies first,' he said. The sharp side of the blade pricked my skin. I felt a warm trickle of blood down my neck and it seemed the end. I closed my eyes.

But the Frenchman had prevailed and suddenly the Rat was knocked aside!

Seizing the moment, I yanked the man who was choking me off balance. Dimly I was aware of the Frenchman struggling in the corner of my vision but I could not dislodge my assailant and his chokehold tightened. I dropped to my knees, growing faint.

We were outmatched.

The Rat regained his footing, and charged. But a sharp crack of something hard on bone caused the small man to tumble before me with a high-pitched cry of rage. Somersaulting skilfully out of his fall like a circus acrobat, he leaped to his feet and turned to face a new attacker.

Backlit by the streetlamp was a tall, cloaked figure brandishing a stick. It was Sherlock Holmes!

The odds were looking up.

I slammed an elbow into the gut of my assailant. He loosened his grip and staggered back. I turned and we grappled, slipping in the ice and landing on the ground.

Holmes's voice pierced through the sounds of the mêlée. 'Your pistol, Watson!'

'Gone!' I cried. 'Where the hell have you been?'

In a single glimpse I saw the Rat now facing the Frenchman, as two others advanced on Mlle La Victoire.

'Busy!' shouted Holmes, as he ran to her aid.

Out of the corner of my eye I glimpsed him battling two assailants, walking stick held out before him in both hands, like the trained singlestick fighter he was. He whirled it above his head and then rained it down in a series of quick blows on the men facing him.

My own assailant leaped on top of me, and as we struggled, I heard Holmes's stick connect and the cries of his attackers.

I landed a sharp uppercut to the thug charging me and he fell. I turned to see if Holmes needed help. But he had one man down, and as Mlle La Victoire cowered behind him he neatly felled the second of her attackers with a blow to the legs.

Then he took the lady's hand, and pulled her away from the light and off into the darkness.

Where? I wondered.

The Rat, across the small courtyard and advancing on the Frenchman, saw it, too. But he did not follow. Instead, he uttered a curse, and turned, slashing at my tall ally. The Frenchman fell with a cry and the Rat leaped on him.

Without thinking, I plunged towards the two and for a moment the Frenchman, the Rat and I rolled like marbles on the icy cobblestones. I managed to land a sharp blow on the Rat's collarbone and he screamed but rolled free and up on to his feet.

The Frenchman lay unmoving. I was on my own!

The Rat gave a quick glance to my mysterious ally. Dead? He barked a short command and his three cohorts – two downed by Holmes and the third trying to help them up – froze and looked up. Then all four vanished into the darkness.

I paused, waiting for a further attack. Silence.

From the ground came a sigh. 'Ah,' said the Frenchman. '*Enfin, c'est fini!*' He stood up with barely a wince, brushing off his elegant suit.

I was panting, exhausted. What in the hell had just happened?

I felt my neck; it was still bleeding. I took out my handkerchief and pressed it to the cut. I looked over at the Frenchman. His face was now a mask of pain, and he had a hand to one shoulder.

'Are you all right?' I asked. 'I am a doctor.'

He flashed me a look I did not understand. Guilt? Embarrassment? Then it was immediately replaced by an impudent grin.

'I have never been better,' he said, straightening up and shaking off his pain like a man would fling a bead of sweat on a summer's day. For the first time I noticed his size. He had at least two inches and fifty pounds on Holmes, hardly typical for a Frenchman. Could he really be French? He glanced around and casually retrieved his top hat, lost in the struggle, replacing it at a jaunty angle.

My doubts were at rest; he was most definitely French.

'Jean Vidocq,' he said. 'And you must be Dr Watson.'

'How do you know my name?'

'You fought well, Doctor,' he said, still smiling. 'Not injured too badly?' While his words were friendly, there was an undercurrent of mockery.

'No,' I replied stiffly. 'Thank you.'

I looked about me. Mlle La Victoire and Holmes were nowhere to be seen.

The Frenchman noticed this as well. '*Merde!*' he said. 'Where did Holmes take her?'

'How do you know us?'

At that moment, Holmes strode into the light, alone, and carrying my cape and hat. 'Good work, Watson,' he said, handing me my things. Then – 'Watson, your neck!'

'I'm fine.' I removed the handkerchief. The wound still bled but only a little. I pressed harder on it.

"Will it . . . ?" he asked, concerned.

"It will be fine. It is just a scratch. I will keep pressure on it."

He was relieved. 'You are lucky, '

As my breathing slowed, the chill hit me. I was exhausted and confused. Holmes and the Frenchman knew each other, but beyond that I had no idea. I took my cape and hat from Holmes and put them on, pulling my gloves from the pockets.

'What have you done with Cherie?' the Frenchman demanded.

'It is not so easy to secure a cab at this hour,' Holmes replied with a smile. 'Mademoiselle La Victoire is now en route to a safe location.'

'You left to call a cab?' I said.

'*What* safe location?' demanded Vidocq.

'A trusted friend's,' said Holmes, studying our fellow combatant. 'Ah, your shoulder, I see, Vidocq. You were not expecting the skill of the little man with the stiletto, were you? Obviously a professional.'

'Brilliant deduction,' sneered the Frenchman.

'It is fortunate we were here, then,' said Holmes, unruffled. He took my arm. '*We* will look to the lady now.' He smiled at Vidocq. 'You can attend to your more pressing matters. Do have someone look at that shoulder.'

I heard a snort of disgust as we turned to leave. 'I know all her friends!' called out the man named Jean Vidocq.

'That is too bad,' muttered Holmes as we moved away.

CHAPTER 8

A Slippery Slope

olmes pulled me along through the icy streets. The hilly terrain and the frost-slicked cobblestones made for rough travel, and the cumulative blows of the day took their toll. It was all I could do to keep up with my long-legged companion. Where exactly were we headed?

He paused at the intersection with Rue Lepic. I seized the moment. 'I am out of breath. Explain to me what is going on.'

'Not now, Watson, we must arrive before Vidocq.'

'Arrive where? Who is this man, and how do you know him?'

'He's a detective, claiming to be the great-grandson of the famous Eugène Vidocq, the man who founded the Sûreté a hundred years ago. Let's go.'

'Ah, I remember now! Jean Valjean of *Les Misérables* was based on the man.'

'Yes, a literature lesson is just what we need,' snapped Holmes. He took off up the hill.

'But there was something odd about him, wasn't there?' I gasped, following with difficulty.

'The Vidocq of yore was a criminal as well as a lawman. He was a forger and a murderer, and it caught up with him. Hurry! Marriage has turned you soft.'

'But this "Jean Vidocq" tonight, is he a relation?'

'No. There are no descendants on record. Can you not speed up, or must I leave you behind on the ice floe like a dying Esquimau?'

We laboured up the hill. Around us rickety buildings of all sizes leaned in ramshackle angles, like drunks holding each other up for the journey home from the pub. Fruit trees and small vegetable gardens were jammed between the houses, and to our right, the eerie shadows of a cemetery. The streets grew steeper and more treacherous, and our breaths came out in white puffs.

'How do you know this man?' I gasped, pressing on.

'We worked on a case last year in Nice. He is reasonably intelligent, but not to be trusted.'

'He does have a certain style,' I pointed out.

'Brilliant, Watson. He is also extremely jealous of me. Please hurry.'

He turned on Rue Lepic and started up another hill. I grabbed his sleeve to slow him down and we both slid on the icy street and nearly tumbled to the ground. It must have been exhaustion, but I suddenly laughed.

'Damn it, Watson!' cried Holmes.

'I can't keep up!' I said, coming to a stop. 'Wait! I remember now . . . This Vidocq . . . I read . . . wasn't he the one assigned to recover that stolen statue, the Nike in Marseilles? The one you told me about?'

'Yes, yes. It is in all the papers.'

'But what is his relation to our client?'

'That is the question of the hour. How is the neck?'

I removed my handkerchief. 'It has stopped bleeding.'

'Come on!'

We pressed on up the hill, the air so cold it burned my lungs. The picture became clearer. 'Four men were killed in Marseilles,' I said. 'Stabbed, I believe, with a stiletto. Tonight, that rat-faced little man—'

'Watson, you scintillate. Yes, yes, of course it is the same man.'

'But you were called, as you said, on that Nike case—'

'Yes, and I refused.'

Holmes turned to leave.

'But, *are* you on that case? Because it certainly seems to me—'

'I told you, no.'

Yet Holmes had arranged to consult the Nike expert at the Louvre. My frustration with his secrecy got the best of me, and I stopped in my tracks. 'If you want my cooperation you must tell me what is going on!' I shouted. The sound reverberated in the empty street.

A window above us opened and a slop pot of God knew what rained down several feet away. We both dodged instinctively. '*Fermez les gueules!*' someone shouted from above and slammed the window shut. It was Holmes's turn to laugh. He grabbed my arm and began to drag me up the hill. We picked up speed.

'All right. It is possible that the cases are connected,' he admitted.

'Fine,' I gasped. 'But you said Miss La Victoire is going to a safe place. Can't we resume this in the morning?'

'No.'

'Why not? Let go of my arm.'

'I must speak to Mademoiselle La Victoire tonight. Vidocq may be there soon and will interfere.'

'The man did save my life, Holmes. He can't be all bad.'

Holmes sighed. 'I know Vidocq well. He would like nothing better than for us to return to London. He thinks I may take over his case.'

'Perhaps you are worried he may take over yours,' I said, wrenching free. 'Go on ahead. What is the address?'

'Turn right at the corner, and two more blocks: 21 Rue Caulaincourt.'

'I shall meet you there.'

'Fine,' he said, with a smile. 'Oh, and Watson, my dear fellow, Vidocq is the man who pushed you down the stairs at the Louvre. Perhaps you may wish a word with him yourself.'

Holmes knew me too well. I took off at a run.

CHAPTER 9

L'Artiste en Danger

oments later, we arrived at the corner of the elegant Rues Tourlaque and Caulaincourt at a luxurious building with a gracefully curved portico and ornate grillwork. As a maid took our coats and hats in the entry hall of an apartment on the fourth floor, I noticed Mlle La Victoire's velvet cloak and Vidocq's top hat and cape hung on pegs nearby. Holmes's rival had arrived before us. I seethed with desire to settle my account with this Vidocq. But of course the case took precedence.

We were ushered into the main *salon* and left alone. Surrounding us in the brightly lit room were the strangest curiosities imaginable – a veritable circus of wonder – costumes, a trapeze, painted backdrops, a bathtub, Japanese prints, theatrical lights, a hookah, and more . . . with an artist's easel, canvases and paints crammed into one corner. Alice down the rabbit hole could not have felt more out of place than I did at that moment.

The room was empty and a fire roared in a large fireplace off to one side. We stood there, waiting for someone to appear. 'Mademoiselle?' called out Holmes in a shrill voice.

Instead a small, dwarf-like man, oddly attired in a Chinaman's silk pyjamas and hat, weaved uncertainly into the room. He was gloriously ugly and at the same time fascinating, with thick lips and large, dark eyes, a pair of pince-nez resting on his nose. He had a certain refined dignity, despite being deeply inebriated.

'Welcome friends! *Bienvenue!*' he said in heavily French-accented English. 'We are expecting you, Monsieur Holmes!'

'Monsieur Toulouse-Lautrec,' said Holmes, striding forward and bending down to shake the little man's hand. It was the world-famous artist himself! '*Bonsoir.* I need to speak to Mademoiselle.'

The little man reached up to shake Holmes's hand with enthusiasm. 'Soon. Soon. She is in the bath. I have read of your exploits, Monsieur Holmes, and Docteur Watson! Look, I am the great Anglophile!'

'Monsieur Lautrec, it is urgent,' said Holmes.

But Lautrec had turned to me, and now pumped my hand with vigour. He broke off, caressing my sleeve. 'Ah, the fine English tailoring,' he murmured. Then, with a wink, he added, 'As you see, the English of me is perfect! Or nearly.'

He dived in and embraced us in the French manner, kissing us on both cheeks. The scent of alcohol radiated from every pore.

'Monsieur, the lady?' Holmes enquired again.

'And,' I ventured, 'if Monsieur Vidocq might be available?'

'First you must refresh,' said Lautrec, snapping his fingers for the maid. She reappeared instantly. 'Marie! *Tremblements de terre pour tout le monde!*' He smiled at us. 'Earthquake, she is a recipe of me for the drink – cognac and absinthe. You will enjoy. The earth, she move.'

Then, to Holmes, he added with a wink, 'We must wait. The lady finish her bath. Always after a performance.'

Always, I wondered? How did this man know? As if in answer, he turned to me.

'Mademoiselle, she model for me. The bath. The cabaret.'

'And Vidocq?' I prompted.

Lautrec shrugged. 'The back, perhaps he help to wash?' He winked at me, and then turned to Holmes, who had been unable to mask his surprise. 'Ah, Monsieur is jealous,' he observed.

Holmes snorted. 'Of course not! She is my client. I need to speak to her, that is all.'

The little man stepped nearer, staring up at my friend with that artist's peculiar close regard, not unlike Holmes's own. He shrugged in sympathy and then smiled. 'Everyone love Mademoiselle Cherie.' He squinted at Holmes. 'But do sit down. She will come.'

Grateful for the chance to rest, I took a seat on a red velvet sofa strewn with silk pillows. I would see to my business with Vidocq when the time was right.

Holmes moved towards the fire, rubbing his hands briskly before it. He was disturbed, and attempting to hide it. It would be unusual for him to take a personal interest in a client, even one as beautiful as the lady. But for all his cold reasoning, Holmes could be a very emotional man. In the flickering firelight, I could see the pallor of exertion and fatigue colouring his countenance.

'Sit down, Holmes,' I entreated. He ignored me.

Lautrec continued to regard him.

'The cheekbones very strong, and the eyes, there is something there. You, Monsieur Holmes, must sit for a portrait,' he said.

Holmes said nothing but continued to regard the flames.

'You are a haunted man; I will capture this!' Lautrec said. He stared intensely at Holmes. 'Yes. Who are your ghosts?'

Holmes looked up, startled, from his reverie. 'I do not believe in ghosts!'

The maid entered with the drinks, followed by a tall, sombre man in conservative dress. He introduced himself to us as Dr Henri Bourges, friend of Lautrec. Holmes refused a drink, nodded almost rudely to Bourges, and returned to his contemplation. I, however, recognized the name. Henri Bourges was a rising young medical man, whose recent paper on diphtheria had impressed me profoundly. What was he doing in this madhouse?

It became immediately apparent.

The man turned to Lautrec, who had already consumed half his drink in two large gulps. '*Mon vieux,*' said Dr Bourges, gently removing the glass from the artist's hand, replacing it with a sketchbook and pencil, 'you must not miss the opportunity to sketch our honoured guests.' He led Lautrec to another sofa, settling him there. With a quick move, he surreptitiously dumped Lautrec's unfinished drink into a potted plant.

Holmes had grown more agitated, pacing in front of the fire. I crossed to him and taking his arm, I whispered, 'Holmes, pray take a seat!' Holmes shook his head violently and moved away to pace by the window.

'Dr Watson? It is a pleasure to find another medical man. May I have a word?' said Henri Bourges from across the room. I stepped away from Holmes and joined him.

We exchanged pleasantries, and I complimented him on his paper. At a lull in the conversation we looked over at Holmes and Lautrec. Holmes had finally sat down, jaw clenched, but was still in motion, his knee bouncing as though driven by St Vitus's Dance. I felt simultaneously concerned and embarrassed for him. I hoped Mlle La Victoire would arrive soon.

Dr Bourges, too, was staring at Holmes.

'Do you live here?' I asked him, intending to distract.

Bourges nodded. 'Some of the time. Henri and I are friends since childhood. He is a great artist. A talent which burns too brightly. I consider it a mission to keep him from his excesses.'

We smiled in mutual understanding. 'I recognize the temperament,' I said.

'I see that you do,' he replied, eyeing Holmes. 'Cocaine?'

I hesitated, but one cannot fool a medical man. I nodded. 'And the work.'

'Of course. It is agony for them without the work,' said Bourges. We stood a moment in silence.

Mlle La Victoire swept into the room. She was stunning and refreshed, in a forest-green Grecian dress embroidered with iridescent beading which set off her colouring and beautiful figure.

Vidocq followed her in. I felt my blood rise at the sight of him.

'Mademoiselle,' said Holmes stiffly, rising to greet her.

'Thank you for your help tonight, Mr Holmes,' she said, moving easily past his awkwardness, and kissing his cheeks. He blushed, self-consciously.

'You and Dr Watson both.' She blew me a kiss.

Vidocq grinned at this and I noticed that he too, was refreshed, debonair in his tailored evening attire, and hardly the worse for wear after our pitched battle. Yes, he'd saved my life, but I'd saved his as well. And he'd pushed me down a flight of stairs. I walked straight up to him.

'Sir,' I said, 'you have not been a gentleman. Is there anything you wish to say to me?'

He laughed and glanced at Holmes. 'Ah, I am discovered.' Then, to me, 'Your friend may tell you, I am rarely a gentleman,' he said with a grin. 'But sometimes I am an ally.'

'One last chance,' I said. There was no response. 'Please forgive me, Mademoiselle,' I said to our client. 'But he leaves me no choice.'

I hesitated no longer, but turned to Vidocq and struck him a hard right to the jaw. He dropped like a stone.

'*Mon Dieu!*' cried the lady.

Vidocq stared up at me from the floor, rubbing his chin. '*Alors*,' he said.

'That was for the Louvre,' I said, shaking out my hand.

'What happened at the Louvre?' Mlle La Victoire asked.

No one answered her. Holmes smiled down at Vidocq, who shrugged, grinning up at us with insouciant charm. 'A little disagreement,' he offered. Then, to me, 'I only hoped to frighten you off. But you are more, how shall we say, robust than I anticipated. We are even now. Help me up.' He held his hand up to mine.

My manners deserted me. I walked over to a sideboard where I poured myself a glass of water, or what I thought was water. I took a hearty gulp and choked. Gin! Bourges appeared and handed me a glass of water. 'I never liked him either,' he whispered with a wink. 'Lautrec thinks he is, how do you say, a bounder?'

Mlle La Victoire glided to where Holmes stood. 'Monsieur Holmes!' she said in her charmingly accented English. 'I am sorry to make you wait, and after your so kind rescue tonight. I will admit I am shaken.'

Holmes led her to a settee and seated her gently, but remained standing. Vidocq insinuated himself next to and quite close to the lady, raising a protective arm behind her. She shrank ever so slightly from his touch.

'Monsieur Vidocq,' said Holmes with considerable irritation. 'I would like a word with Mademoiselle alone.'

Vidocq did not move. 'Cherie and I have an understanding. I will remain to protect her interests.'

'Mademoiselle's interest, and my own, is to find and recover her son, Emil,' stated Holmes. 'You, however, are on the trail of the Marseilles Nike, are you not? A trail with a rather large reward at the end?'

Vidocq said nothing, but looked away. Holmes turned to Mlle La Victoire. 'Mademoiselle, what do you think has transpired this evening?'

The dear lady seemed surprised. '*Mais, évidemment . . .* those men, they came to Le Chat Noir to kill me . . .'

'Really? Is that what this gentleman has told you?'

She shrugged. Vidocq broke in. 'Of course. It is the truth.'

'Then why, pray tell, did our attackers not follow you, Mademoiselle, in your cab, but instead stayed to fight the three of us?'

Mlle La Victoire looked doubtful.

'Let me answer,' said Holmes. 'Because they were there to kill Vidocq, and you were merely in the way.'

She turned to her lover. 'Jean! But why would they want to kill you?'

He shrugged and said to Holmes, 'You cannot prove this.'

'They were hired professional killers, probably with a contract to kill and the same weapon used at Marseilles,' said Holmes. 'Vidocq, as *you* are the only one investigating the stolen statue, might they not have been after you?' He turned again to Mlle La Victoire. 'I am curious, Mademoiselle. Has Monsieur Vidocq questioned you closely on the habits of your acquaintance, the Earl of Pellingham?'

Vidocq interjected. 'Of course. He is the father of Emil.' He kissed our client on the cheek. 'Anything to find your dear son.'

'Convenient, then,' said Holmes, cheerfully, ignoring Vidocq's gesture. 'Were you aware, Mademoiselle, that the Earl is a primary suspect in the Nike theft?'

Mlle La Victoire hesitated. 'No, I was not.' She turned to Vidocq. 'You have been very curious, Jean.'

'*Cherie, ma petite!*' exclaimed Vidocq, 'My feelings are quite genuine for you!'

But the singer stood up, putting a little distance between them. 'What does this mean, Mr Holmes?'

Holmes turned to Vidocq. 'Your feelings did not prevent you from placing her in harm's way this evening,' he stated coolly.

Vidocq snorted. 'Ridiculous. I had no way to predict they would attack tonight.'

'You noticed them in the audience, as I did,' said Holmes. 'I saw you.'

'But then I have a question for you,' said Vidocq. 'If you are on Mademoiselle's case, and not the Marseilles Nike, why then your visit to the Louvre and the Greek curator earlier today?'

'I am a lover of great art,' said Holmes smoothly. 'That is all.'

Mlle La Victoire looked from one man to the other uncertainly. Vidocq stretched his arms towards his lover. 'Surely you do not believe this nonsense?' he said with the broadest of smiles. '*Ma petite*, where is your faith?'

She paused, and then, to my great surprise, rushed into his arms.

'I believe you, Jean,' she said with passion. He embraced her and the two turned to face us.

Holmes snorted. 'Mademoiselle, I ask only this. You summoned me here. Allow me the privilege of a private conversation before you choose sentiment over logic.'

'She will not listen,' said Vidocq.

Mlle la Victoire turned to Vidocq and silenced him with a look. 'Do not force me to choose, Jean. I believe you. But I will speak to Mr Holmes, alone. Please leave us.'

Vidocq paused. Something passed between the two men; then, with a shrug, Vidocq melted again into his relaxed, Gallic charm. 'But of course,' he said with a grin. Turning to the lady he added, 'I will be in the next room if you require me.' He sauntered out.

'Yes, take Monsieur Lautrec with you,' called Holmes.

I turned to see that the little man had seated himself on a nearby mound of cushions and had been sketching Holmes throughout the conversation, Bourges standing appreciatively by. Lautrec shrugged. 'Perhaps some more drinks,' he said, following Vidocq into the next room. Dr Bourges trailed after him with a nod to me.

Holmes's demeanour immediately changed. He sat down next to Mlle La Victoire, patting her hand in a surprisingly comforting gesture. 'Mademoiselle,' he began, his voice much kinder now but with a distinct urgency. 'Monsieur Vidocq's feelings may or may not be genuine. But you know his reputation. I can assure you that his feelings for you aside, his primary interest is in the Marseilles Nike and not your son. You know of this famous statue?'

'I know of it.'

'Ah! Pray let us continue so that I can help you find Emil. Those men who attacked tonight, did any of them look familiar to you? Perhaps one resembled the man who accosted you on the street.'

'*Non*. I am sure he was not among them.'

'As I thought. And Jean Vidocq? What are your feelings for him?'

Here the lady paused. It was my impression that a kind of veil slipped over her and came between her true intentions and us. 'I . . . we . . . I will admit that we have grown close,' she said.

'Clearly you are intimate,' Holmes stated flatly. 'And yet you have reservations.'

She started. 'How do you know this?'

'Really, mademoiselle, it is obvious.'

She shifted uncomfortably. 'Please do not think harshly of me. I am an artist, and many assume that I am promiscuous as a matter of course. But that is far from true.'

'Trust and intimacy are separate issues for you,' said Holmes. 'It strikes me that you may be using the gentleman, if I may refer to him thus, for your own purposes.' It was a statement rather than a question.

A glimmer of surprise passed over her features, but was quickly hidden.

'When exactly did this relationship with Monsieur Vidocq begin?' Holmes inquired without hesitation.

'A month or so ago. And I do love him.'

Holmes grunted. 'Not months then. But how long before the attack?'

'I do not remember. Perhaps three weeks. I had contacted him to help me find Emil,' she stated. 'Jean frightened off my attacker! As tonight! I owe him my life.'

'As I pointed out earlier, the man in the street was merely warning you,' snapped Holmes. 'Mademoiselle, why did you write to *me* asking for help . . . when you have a man you love close to hand?'

Tears sprang into her eyes. 'Honestly,' she said. 'I do not know. There is something about Jean . . . about Monsieur Vidocq . . . that I do not understand. He is very attractive and we . . . and yet . . .'

Holmes remained still, his keen grey eyes boring into the lady's. 'And yet you are not sure of his intentions. Your instincts are finely honed, Mademoiselle.' He paused and smiled. 'The reward for recovering the Marseilles Nike for France will probably be a Chevalier.'

'I do not see how this relates.'

'But you see very well, Mademoiselle. Of course you know that your former lover, the Earl, is one of the great art collectors in the world. Did it never cross your mind that he might be involved in the Nike case, which floods the headlines? Your information about him might be useful to a detective on his trail.'

The lady rose. '*Oui*, all right then, Mr Holmes. Yes, it is possible that Jean Vidocq wishes to use me in some way to get to the Earl. Although . . . I cannot help. I have had no contact with the Earl for years. I have asked Jean to help me find Emil and he is pursuing inquiries here in Paris. Perhaps, as you said, I am using Monsieur Vidocq just as you think he uses me.'

'But he has disappointed you. And I have been engaged . . . in reserve, I suppose,' said Holmes a little bitterly.

'I will do anything to find Emil,' said the poor lady. 'That is all I care about. I believe you are here for that reason alone, as you must have turned down the Nike case for your brother to have hired Monsieur Vidocq.'

This startled Holmes. 'How did you know that my brother hired Vidocq?' he asked. It seemed that even Holmes did not know this fact until now.

'I chanced to see a cable from a Mr Mycroft Holmes before Jean destroyed it.'

'So, I see. This makes me your second choice to find Emil, and Vidocq the British government's second choice to locate the statue.' Holmes barked a laugh. 'This is all quite amusing.'

In a fury the lady crossed to Holmes and slapped his face. He stepped back in surprise.

'You laugh, but my son is missing, Mr Holmes,' she said. 'Two of the most famous detectives in the world have offered help, and yet I believe neither of you cares about this fact, but only about an antique piece of carved stone. Emil is ten years old. Wherever he is, if he is alive, he is very frightened. Or worse. I care nothing of your rivalry with Jean Vidocq, or a Greek statue, no matter how valuable. Can't you work together? Will you, or will you not help me?'

Holmes approached and took her hands tenderly in his 'My apologies. I am at your service, Mademoiselle. And I will find Emil. It is why I am here.'

The lady considered his words.

'Mademoiselle. Mr Holmes is a man of his word,' I said, stepping forward. 'As am I. We will do everything in our power to find your son.'

'I believe you both,' she said. 'I do not know why, but I do. Please forgive my doubts.'

'Forgotten,' said Holmes. 'I have reason to believe Emil is still in England. Whoever has taken him is probably connected to the Earl, and would wish to keep a close eye. We will depart, the three of us, for London in the morning. It is now four o'clock. We must get some rest first.'

'There is an eleven o'clock train for Calais from Gare du Nord in the morning,' she said, gathering her shawl around her.

'We will be on it,' said Holmes.

'The *four* of us.'

'We shall see,' said Holmes sharply.

CHAPTER 10

Mlle La Victoire's Story

e slept a few hours on two of the various chaises longues in Lautrec's apartment. From his maid's practised and quick accommodation with cushions and blankets, it was clear we were not the first adventurers to take our repose in this *salon* of wonders. But exhaustion made short work of the novelty.

In the morning we were served coffee and croissants. Then, despite her professed trust in Holmes, our client again insisted on Vidocq coming to London with us. In contrast to the night before, Holmes acquiesced easily.

I bade a grateful farewell to Dr Bourges, collected our belongings from the hotel, and in the cab to the Gare Nord, asked him why.

'Keep one's friends close, and one's enemies closer,' said Holmes with a grin. 'He will follow us there anyway. This way we can keep an eye on him.'

Shortly after, we were London-bound on the Chatham in a private first-class carriage.

The frosty countryside flew past us. As Vidocq dozed against the window of our compartment, Holmes questioned our client more closely regarding the Earl.

'Tell me, Mademoiselle, the circumstances surrounding your brief relationship with the Earl. Any detail may be important; leave nothing out. You were eighteen, were you not? And working where?'

The lady hesitated, and drew up a soft wool travelling blanket around her shoulders. A dreamy look came over her face as she began to recount her start in Paris.

'I came up from Provence,' she said, 'the small village of Eze. I had a letter of introduction and began to model first at l'École des Beaux Arts, and soon for a number of private artists in the Latin Quarter, where I met Degas, Renoir, and later, Lautrec.

'My heart was in music, and I had hoped to make my way as a singer,' she said with a smile . . . 'Through a small group of writers called *Les Hydropathes* I received an invitation to sing at one of their *soirées*. From there, I soon began to sing in several cabarets, while still working as an artist's model.'

As she continued her story, we learned that Lord Pellingham had spotted Mlle La Victoire one evening at one of these small cabarets. The handsome Earl had been carousing across Europe incognito, apparently in an alcoholic ramble disguised as an art acquisition trip, and hidden from all, including his peers in the House of Lords and every member of his family.

I kept to myself the thought that the singer had been, perhaps, the most important of his 'acquisitions'.

After her performance, she and the Earl – whom she knew as 'Count Wilford' – had a brief liaison which lasted for three deliriously happy days and nights ensconced at the Grand Hôtel du Louvre. There he wined, dined, and courted the young girl in a way that seemed destined for a bright future.

The young singer was in heaven. She understood herself to be entertained by some minor royal personage, but on the third morning, as 'Count Wilford' slept off the previous night's champagne, a missive arrived on a silver tray which she received at their suite.

Her paramour slept on and, curious, she opened it. It was an urgent business communication regarding a crisis at one of the gentleman's largest holdings, a silk factory near the family seat in Lancashire. It detailed some worker unrest and dire financial challenges. But that was not all. It also revealed details of his life that froze her in his tracks. 'Count Wilford' was indeed a member of the peerage – but actually named 'Lord Pellingham' né Harold Beauchamp-Kay, an art collector, major figure in the House of Lords, and most shocking of all . . . married.

His American wife, Annabelle, had taken ill, and he was requested to return to his home in Lancashire immediately.

Upon reading this letter, and realizing she had been pinning false hopes on a married man and a famous one at that, the young girl replaced it carefully in its envelope, quietly gathered her things and disappeared into the predawn mist of Paris.

She wandered round Montmartre for four days, bereft

at the deception and furious at herself, for she had quit her cabaret singing post, nurturing the classic and sadly romantic hope of nearly every poor, beautiful young woman across the world – that she would be rescued by some form of royalty and whisked into another life altogether, her true destiny. She was but eighteen years old, and could be excused for this rather naive dream.

She heard nothing from Pellingham in the days following and tried to put him from her mind.

She was hired at another cabaret, and her talents and stunning beauty took her back into the limelight. Within a month, however, she realized she was pregnant, but disguised this fact by creating a fashion statement with a rainbow of flowing silk scarves which hid her burgeoning curves. It was at this time that she earned the sobriquet '*la Déesse des Mille Couleurs*' or 'the Goddess of a Thousand Colours'. The scarves had remained as her personal signature ever since.

After she discovered her pregnancy, Mlle La Victoire wrote to Lord Pellingham but received no reply. She wrote a second and third time with the same result.

Nine months later, at the home of a friend in Montmartre, she gave birth to a baby boy whom she named Emil. It was a difficult birth but the baby was healthy, handsome, and thriving.

Holmes had listened patiently to this story. But at this juncture he leaned forward with keen interest. 'How exactly were the arrangements made to give Emil to the Earl?' he asked.

'Two weeks after Emil was born,' said the lady, her eyes glazing over at the memory, 'a man named Pomeroy came to me.'

'Describe him.'

'Dark and how do you say, stocky. An Englishman of French descent, who spoke to me in French. He said he was a close associate of Lord Pellingham. He had an offer to make me. Ah, I regret—'

'Describe the offer exactly.'

'Lord Pellingham would adopt Emil, and raise him on the estate as his own, with his American wife Annabelle. Our son would have every advantage, and he would inherit the estate upon Lord Pellingham's death. But there were conditions.'

'Naturally; what were they?'

'I was to tell no one. It must seem my new baby had died. I had to sign a paper, a legal paper. I would receive no money. But Lord Pellingham would, through his connections in Paris, open doors for me to sing and perform throughout Europe.'

'And did he do so?'

'I like to think he did not need to do so.'

'Of course not; your talent is beyond question,' I remarked.

She smiled but the smile faded quickly, and she continued her tale. As she had mentioned before, she would be allowed to see Emil once per year, at Christmas time, in London, with very specific and immutable conditions.

Holmes pressed her for details.

Each year this Christmas meeting took place in the tea room of Brown's Hotel, and as I watched her describe her pitiably short hour with the child over the years, my heart broke for them. She had been introduced only as a friend of the family. Each year she brought the child a small present, usually some beautiful, valuable handmade plaything – once a toy theatre; later, a hand-carved horse which had enchanted the child and became his favourite toy.

Emil seemed to respond to his mother and her gifts with sensitive appreciation, and she swore that there was a bond between them, even though it remained unspoken. The boy, in accordance with the arrangement, was never to be told of their real relationship.

Holmes had listened to this description with eyes closed, leaning back in his seat. He opened them now, regarding Mlle La Victoire with curiosity.

'You seem intelligent. What inspired you to entrust your son to this man who so cruelly deceived you?' asked Holmes.

Mlle La Victoire paused. 'An instinct. I felt . . . I don't know why . . . that this was best for Emil. And at first, it surely seemed so. Emil was a happy child . . .'

'Why in the past tense?'

'I . . . No reason.'

'There was no hint of disturbance in the child's demeanour last Christmas? Any unease?' asked Holmes.

'No,' the lady said, puzzled.

'Think! Was the child withdrawn at all, sombre? Or was he changed in any way?'

'I did not notice anything wrong,' said Mlle La Victoire.

'Except . . . except that as he left, he looked back at me. I saw tears. Never before were there tears.'

Holmes exhaled sharply. 'And yet you did nothing?'

Her own eyes moistened. 'I thought perhaps he had missed me.'

Holmes said nothing but I could sense the wheels of his mind turning. He looked away, to stare out of the window. The southern English countryside hurtled past us, an icy blue-white blur. The snow had turned to sleet, and even in our heated compartment I could feel the chill seeping in from the windows.

Vidocq rose and removed himself briefly from our compartment. Immediately, Holmes seized the moment and leaned forward to speak in low, earnest tones. 'One last thing, purely as conjecture. Do you continue to believe your son to be alive?'

'I do,' she said without hesitation. 'I am as certain about it as I am of your word, Mr Holmes.'

She paused.

'Please. I have made a terrible mistake; I know you think it. But I cannot find Emil alone. I need your help, Mr Holmes.'

'And that is why we are at your service, Watson and I.'

'And now, I have a question for you,' she said. 'You have not fully explained. Why London?'

'I am not certain that he is in the city itself,' he replied. 'But I believe him to be in England. Whoever has Emil may wish to ensure his safekeeping. It would be too hard to arrange in another country. As for London, there are a great many tanners there. I believe there is a chance that Emil has been removed by friendly hands, but because he is in danger for some reason. That is why we must tread very carefully, so as not to lead the threat to him.'

'I see. But who or why?'

'We have much to learn. But I do think the danger is real. I must make a request of you.'

'Anything that will help,' she said.

Holmes regarded her with that peculiar piercing stare. 'You must not allow your feelings for Jean Vidocq to stand in our way,' he said, watching her carefully.

Mlle La Victoire's face became a perfect mask. As a performer, she had an uncanny ability to appear transparent at one moment, opaque at the next. 'Of course not,' she said finally.

And then she smiled. The compartment was immediately warmer.

PART FOUR

BEHIND THE SCENES

'The artist must be in his work as God is in creation, invisible and all-powerful; one must sense him everywhere but never see him.'

Gustave Flaubert

CHAPTER 11

Baker Street Irregularities

e returned to 221B to find that Mrs Hudson had arranged for repair of the sitting room from Holmes's recent fiery adventure. It was a comfort to return to the familiar rooms, where even the furniture had been restored to the state of my residence there.

All evidence of Holmes's drug-fuelled debacle had been eliminated, his papers and chemical equipment tidied, the room aired and scrubbed. A cheery fire had been laid and tea, brandy, and scones set out on the table awaiting our arrival.

There also was a note from Mary. Her mother's needs necessitated her staying longer, and so I was free, at least for the time being, to continue with Holmes. 'My only request, dear John,' she wrote, 'is that you promise to take care of yourself as well as you do me . . . and your friend. Please stay safe.'

It was with tremendous relief that I set down our valises,

hung up my coat, and poured a cup of tea. However, Holmes surprised me by offering Vidocq and Mlle La Victoire my old bedroom, where they were to be his guests during the London search for Emil.

Since my marriage, the room had been unused except as a kind of laboratory and dumping ground for Holmes's equipment, papers, and research projects. These were summarily removed to the basement by Mrs Hudson and a boy.

'Holmes, this is unlike you,' I ventured when Mlle La Victoire and Vidocq went upstairs for a rest. 'And more than a little improper.'

'Watson, you know I care little for propriety. This way I can better ensure Mademoiselle's safety.'

'It is all about her wellbeing, then, I suppose,' said I. 'You are not attracted to the lady? Perhaps even a little.'

Holmes snorted. 'Watson, really. If I were, would I lodge her so cosily with a lover right under my nose?' He paused and grinned impishly. 'Were you by chance wishing to return to your old room for the duration?'

In fact I had rather looked forward to it. 'No,' I replied, more sharply than intended.

Nevertheless I lingered to write up my notes, spending a companionable afternoon as Holmes busied himself with telegrams, a visit from the Irregulars, and some reading. However, as our French visitors came and went, the apartment grew redolent of soft, ripe cheeses, and filled with flowers as if France had annexed our old rooms. Holmes left on an errand later without explanation, and as I awaited his return, my irritation became intolerable. I gathered my things to leave.

At that moment Holmes sauntered through the door and flopped down on the couch with a sigh. Once again I noticed a distinct pallor of exhaustion. 'What have you been up to, Holmes?' I asked.

He rolled his eyes upwards, indicating the presence of his guests in my upstairs room. 'Later, Watson.'

'Get some rest,' I said. 'Doctor's orders. Now I must be off.'

'Do stay for supper.'

'I will see you in the morning,' said I, and departed.

After stopping at a pub for a sandwich, I returned to my residence to sleep. Both irritated and exhausted, I fell into bed, dropping immediately into a dreamless slumber. After what seemed only minutes, I was awakened by a loud ring of the doorbell. I glanced at the clock.

It was barely six in the morning and before our housekeeper was awake to answer it. I reluctantly dragged myself to the door, a dressing gown thrown over my nightclothes.

There before me was an ancient derelict with broken and stained teeth, cringing on the doorstep like a malevolent rat. A sailor of some sort, judging by his clothing. 'What is it, man?' I bellowed in none too friendly a fashion.

'Get dressed, Watson,' came Holmes's voice from this apparition. 'We are summoned to Mycroft's immediately.'

CHAPTER 12

Suspension Bridge

have always held that life with Holmes is a bit like walking across a suspension bridge that hangs from ropes over a jungle chasm. The adrenalin may be invigorating, but one never knows what lies beneath, and one is constantly in danger of losing one's footing.

Any equilibrium I might have recovered from a night's sleep in my own bed was quickly erased by a tumultuous dash across town in a hansom cab, heading to the Diogenes Club, that peculiar lair of his even more peculiar older brother Mycroft Holmes.

Why? Why the rush? Why the disguise? Why did Mycroft summon us both? As Holmes removed the false teeth and wig, peeled rubber from his face and began to scrub the mahogany colouring and grime from his cheeks, he explained in part.

'I visited the docks last night – well, early this morning – as an old sailor who cannot keep away from the action, bearing a small offering of friendship.' He raised a battered flask concealed in his ragged clothes.

'And what did you learn there?' I asked. 'You have missed a bit under your left ear.'

Holmes scrubbed further. 'Simply this. Three recent shipments arrived, any one of which could have been our missing statue. However, one in particular seemed to be more closely watched than the others, and I managed, with considerable trouble, to catch a glimpse of its contents. It is, I am quite sure, our Nike.'

'Ah,' I said, digesting this. I had not yet had my morning coffee. As our cab rattled through the streets, Holmes completed his transformation into his usual attire.

'But what of Mlle La Victoire? I thought you were more interested in helping the lady than in this art theft.'

'This morning's task was merely a footnote which I have taken care of at the behest of my brother,' said he, with a note of resentment. 'I shall catch Vidocq up on the facts as it suits me.'

'Oh, *that* should sit well,' I said. There was evidently a strong sense of competition between the two. I suspected Holmes had actually leapt to his night-time exploration for the express purpose of besting his French counterpart.

'My efforts are probably the reason Mycroft summons us here this morning.'

'But how did he know you were successful?'

Holmes did not bother to answer this.

CHAPTER 13

Mycroft

e awaited Holmes's older brother in the Stranger's Room in Mycroft's gentlemen's club, the Diogenes. The room was richly panelled in antique walnut, carpeted against all noise with a plush Oriental rug of greens and golds, and featured a bowed window looking out over Pall Mall. This was bracketed by shelves containing books and an array of beautiful antique globes. Here, we were well away from all others, and would be allowed to speak freely. Members were bound by the bylaws of the peculiar club to remain silent in each other's company while in the common rooms of the establishment.

I ordered coffee from an attendant, made myself comfortable in a chair near the fire, and lit my morning cigarette, trying to relax. My companion paced continually in front of the tall window.

'Do sit down, Holmes,' I entreated. He ignored me and continued to pace.

I became aware that an enormous man had arrived with the silence of a cat, and stood soundlessly at the door, eyeing us with disdain. Mycroft, taller and much heavier than his brother, and seven years his senior, glided into the room like a stately battleship. He was impeccably tailored, shoes polished to a mirror gleam, and exuded an unmistakable gravitas. He lowered himself slowly into an armchair by the fire, and sat unmoving. Intelligent eyes burned from his leonine countenance as he regarded his younger brother with a hint of what one might interpret as disapproval.

'You have been successful,' he said. It was a statement, not a question.

'Yes, the Nike is in London,' said Holmes casually.

'Changed from Liverpool,' said Mycroft. 'Odd.'

'It is, and inconvenient for them, if she is headed where we think. But they must have their reasons. She departs tomorrow. Well guarded, by the way.'

'I thought as much,' said Mycroft. 'She has already cost the lives of four men. Sit down.'

Holmes ignored him and continued to pace. 'Don't underestimate the men hired to protect her,' he said. 'Their Mafia connection has been confirmed by my American friends in New York.'

'Yes, yes, formidable, I know. And so is the collector who probably set this in motion,' said Mycroft. 'That is why I am placing you on the case, Sherlock. You and Dr Watson will leave for Lancashire by the noon train. You will be at Pellingham's estate when the statue arrives, which may be as soon as late tomorrow, and – while he is ever so private about his secret collection – he has in this case already issued *you* a personal invitation to witness her installation with your own eyes.'

Mycroft picked up a long thin letter on elegant stationery from the table next to him and extended it to Holmes. I could swear that he was smiling as he did so and yet there was no trace of charm.

Holmes had stopped pacing and stood silently by the window, ignoring the letter. His back was to the light and I could not discern his expression, but his tone was icy. 'I have done what you asked, Mycroft,' he said. 'Now what have you found about Emil?'

'The boy is safe, for the moment. I have located the house in London where he is hidden – and by friendly hands, I might add. But the game plan has changed. I am sending Vidocq to recover Emil. I'll give him the information shortly. *You* are being transferred to the Nike case.'

'Mycroft! Tell me Emil's location. It was our agreement.'

'Aren't you curious about this invitation? Of course you are.' He waved the letter once again.

Holmes held fast.

Mycroft nodded. 'But, all right, the carrot, then.' He replaced the letter with a sigh. 'Sit down.'

If there was a carrot, then there most certainly was a stick. I did not like the tone of this discussion. At last Holmes sat down.

'I fully understand that the art theft is not your interest, little brother,' said Mycroft, soothingly. 'The plight of missing or abused children appeals to your, er, all of our, sensitivities. But while you are in Lancashire doing this for me, you will also look into the murder of three children who disappeared from the Earl's factories. All three were orphans, and I believe conscripted illegally. The factory in question lies in a remote area and has avoided intense scrutiny. Money has changed hands.'

Holmes remained impassive. Mycroft sighed, studying his brother.

'The Earl has been out of our reach, and this is what you must understand,' continued Mycroft. 'Once we have the Earl on an art theft of international magnitude – and its attendant murders – only *then* does the door open to a complete investigation of his affairs, including the fate of these three boys and his own missing child. Until then, he is shielded by friends in Parliament. If we recover little Emil publicly before that time . . .'

Holmes was silent, his hands clenched.

'Do you see?' asked Mycroft.

'Of course,' said Holmes. 'And Lady Pellingham? What information do you have about her?'

'Her role, if any, is unknown. That is another of your tasks. We must understand the situation in Lancashire to ensure the boy's safety. Vidocq and the lady will be here shortly,' continued Mycroft. 'I will provide them with the address where Emil is hidden, and protection for them during his recovery. It is possible, after the Earl's arrest, that the lady will return with her son to France, and then their safety will be a matter for the Sûreté.'

Holmes stared out the window as if he were not listening.

'It will be left to you, brother, to discover why he was hidden and from whom,' Mycroft pressed on. 'Your clue about the weapon being specific to the tanning industry was key; thank you for that. Emil is, in fact, in Bermondsey, at the home of a Charles and Merielle Eagleton. Mr Eagleton is a tanner. Mrs Eagleton is the sister of the Earl's valet Pomeroy, who has been the go-between with Emil's French mother.'

'Why not send the police right now?' I blurted out. Both swivelled to face me. Mycroft looked at me with pity.

'The chessboard, Dr Watson. First of all, the police would feel compelled to return Emil to his father. He might not be safe. Consider the possibility that he was removed by friends because he was endangered at home. And second, Vidocq must make the rescue. It is critical to decoy him briefly from the statue or he may attempt to claim it for France.'

He turned back to Holmes. 'Content yourself with this. As to Vidocq and this Mademoiselle La Victoire, my sources tell me they are in love.'

'She distrusts him,' said Holmes. 'And your plan is dangerous to her and the boy. Vidocq cares less about the child than his reward.'

Mycroft stared hard at Holmes. 'Possibly. But there is another issue. You have developed feelings for the lady. A capital mistake, little brother.'

'Don't be ridiculous, Mycroft,' snapped Holmes. 'You know me better.'

'And yet Dr Watson would agree, wouldn't you, Doctor?' Mycroft swivelled to face me.

'No, I would say no such thing,' I stammered.

Mycroft assessed me briefly. 'And yet it is true,' said he, turning back to his brother, daring him to look away. My friend held his gaze. Mycroft shrugged. 'She is a remarkable artist, and intelligent,' said Mycroft. 'I understand your momentary weakness. But consider your rival. Vidocq, handsome, and a reputed ladies' man, has probably won her heart. In the French manner, he is not so much duplicitous as . . . complex. If he is attracted to her as well, he may attempt to have his brioche and eat it, too,' he added with a chuckle.

Holmes turned abruptly away from his brother. 'Have you a cigarette, Watson?' he snapped. I fumbled to supply him one and struck a match to light it. For a moment I thought I saw his hand shaking. His back was to his brother.

Mycroft eyed us coolly. A small smile floated on that impassive face. I wanted to throttle the man.

Holmes took a long drag on his cigarette, and then resumed his languid demeanour. 'I have no personal interest in the lady, other than that she has entrusted her safety to me. The Frenchman can be careless. With only Vidocq between Mademoiselle La Victoire and danger, the boy remains vulnerable,' he drawled.

'I will permit no danger to reach them,' said Mycroft. 'It is a promise.'

There was a silence. Holmes smoked. Mycroft poured

himself a small brandy and took a sip. It was nine in the morning. Where was my coffee?

'Now to the specifics. My plan is a fait accompli, and plays on your greatest strengths,' said Mycroft. 'The Earl has been in correspondence with a certain Fritz Prendergast, of the British Museum, a leading expert on the Nike legend and all artwork pertaining to her. I have intercepted this correspondence and have been laying this trap for over two years – *the long thin wedge*; you know my methods.' He took another sip of brandy.

'The Earl has fallen into my snare by inviting this man to a very private viewing of something he cannot wait to share with the one and only person who will truly savour the coup.' At this Mycroft tapped the envelope on the table beside him. 'Even the most private and obsessive of men has need of an appreciative audience. Now *that,* you do understand, Sherlock,' added Mycroft, smiling once more at me.

Holmes grunted.

'However, the Earl and Prendergast have never met, and you will be impersonating this man, dear brother, when you and Watson arrive at the estate tonight. There will be a grand dinner and tour of his rarely seen collection.'

I started in alarm. 'I can't! I mean, I am not an actor!'

'Certainly true, but set aside your fear, Doctor,' said Mycroft. 'Fritz Prendergast is confined to a wheelchair and accompanied at all times by his private physician. You have only to assume a new name. Your person remains the same.'

Holmes exploded. 'This is ludicrous! Even if I agreed to

this, I can't investigate from a wheelchair. Couldn't you have concocted an able-bodied—?'

'No. Fritz Prendergast is a very real person, and has corresponded for some time with the Earl, though they have never met face to face,' said Mycroft. 'Paralysed from the waist down due to an accident at age twenty. He is well within your range to impersonate. Look.'

Mycroft pulled a photograph from a folder on the table and showed it to us. Staring from it was a slim, ascetic-looking man a few years older than Holmes, with long sideburns, small gold glasses and a keen expression.

There *was* a resemblance. Clever!

Holmes glanced at the photograph and set it down. 'How did you arrange . . . where is the real Prendergast now?' he asked.

I am not sure, but I thought I saw a flash of discomfiture from Mycroft, gone in an instant.

'He is currently incommunicado, in Vienna.'

'Doing what?'

'He is in therapy with a private doctor there. Recovering, I believe, from a relapse of a cocaine addiction.'

Holmes stiffened. He took a long, slow drag on his cigarette. I felt a prickle of alarm.

'How convenient,' he remarked.

'Very,' said Mycroft.

'This relapse,' said Holmes. 'How did it happen?'

'These things work in mysterious ways,' said Mycroft. He stared at his brother with intention. I did not understand what passed between them, but before I could ponder it,

Holmes rose to his feet so fast he knocked a side table to the floor. He was shaking in a level of fury I had never seen. 'Damn you, Mycroft! Come, Watson.'

I stood, surprised at the vehemence of this reaction.

'Dr Watson,' said Mycroft. 'A word before you go.'

I paused, trapped between them. Holmes rang impatiently for our coats.

'Doctor,' said Mycroft. 'My brother is aware, but you may not be, of the considerable effort I have gone to recently in order to keep him out of gaol.'

'Gaol!' I exclaimed in spite of myself. 'The Ripper case? Weren't those charges proved false, and dropped?'

Holmes snorted. 'The charges were falsified. You know this perfectly well but let me languish for a week!'

Mycroft sighed. 'Politics have never been your forte, Sherlock. You are fortunate to be free as we speak,' he added. 'That is only because the highly placed person whom you offended has need of your services on this case. It is a chance for you to regain his good graces; a chance which you must not miss.'

'Who is this person?' asked Holmes in a shrill voice.

'Probably you have already deduced, and I will not speak his name. But among the highest in the land,' said Mycroft. 'What you do not know is that he holds a particular personal grudge against Pellingham. And yet the Earl has remained out of reach because of his own high connections.'

'And why should I trust you?' asked Holmes.

'Because, dear brother, you have no choice,' said Mycroft. He turned to me, his face a mask of concern. 'Doctor, I presume you continue to look after the wellbeing of my brother? He appears to be suffering from some fatigue. And evidence of recent cocaine use, hmm?'

I stood frozen, unwilling to reveal my friend's condition. But like his brother, Mycroft read me with ease.

'Ah, I see I am correct. Doctor, if the unnamed party were to hear of my brother's refusal, I have no doubt that some reason would be found to put him back into gaol – for an extended period of hard labour – from which it might be impossible, even for me, to retrieve him.'

Holmes did not move. I felt sick. Mycroft turned to smile gently at me. 'How do you think my brother might fare?'

The sun had moved behind more snow clouds and the darkened sky mirrored my friend's spirits as we left the Diogenes. Under my arm was the thick portfolio and letter from Mycroft, now wrapped in waxed fabric against the threatening sleet. It would be a long train ride and much work to absorb the information we'd need from within this tome.

I had never seen Holmes in a blacker mood.

Eyes on the pavement, his mind churning, Holmes was the picture of repressed fury. As we left Waterloo Place and reached Pall Mall, he absentmindedly walked straight out into the bustling traffic – just as the wheels of a fast-moving carriage bore down.

'Holmes!' I shouted and seized his arm, pulling him back on to the pavement. The carriage thundered by, the driver shouting a curse at us as he passed.

Holmes recovered and we proceeded without a word. There was much more to the story between the brothers, but I knew better than to ask. As a single man, without close family except for Mary, I had often wished for more relations. After today, I thought perhaps I should count my blessings. Mycroft's stick had turned into something more like a bludgeon.

As we continued down Pall Mall, we encountered Vidocq and Mlle La Victoire on their way towards the Diogenes. Flamboyantly dressed in an expensive coat and colourful cravat, the cocky Frenchman swaggered towards us, the lady clinging to his arm. She was elegant in deep burgundy wool, trimmed with fur cuffs and black soutache, her face hidden behind a veil.

On seeing us, Vidocq frowned, but Mlle La Victoire paused, and lifting her veil in a graceful gesture she smiled expectantly at Holmes.

'Monsieur Holmes, I understand we are to see your brother who knows where is Emil. But will you not join us?'

I glanced up at Holmes to discover all traces of his mood were erased. A consummate actor, Holmes appeared to have total control of his expressions. He smiled at Mlle La Victoire, expressing a sad regret, and gallantly kissed her hand. 'Alas, it is not possible. But my brother has good news. You will be reunited with Emil quite soon. I must apologize to you,' he said. 'I have promised you that I would personally find Emil but am called away.'

'Called away?' she gasped. 'But—'

Behind her and unobserved, the Frenchman flashed a grin of triumph at Holmes. He put a protective arm around the lady's waist. There was something distinctly proprietary about the gesture.

'*Attendez*, Mademoiselle. The good news is this,' said Holmes. 'Emil is safe and here in London. You will hear the details from my brother, who will provide Monsieur Vidocq with the information he needs to return Emil to your care.'

Holmes turned to Vidocq. 'Which is, I understand, your whole purpose in helping Mademoiselle?' he said. Vidocq did not respond.

'Then you are deserting us, Mr Holmes?' asked Mlle La Victoire, searching his face for an explanation.

'Not deserting, my dear lady. I have urgent business and must travel this afternoon. Again, please understand this is for the best. I will ensure success by keeping in close touch with my brother. And I intend to return shortly. If you are not satisfied,' and here he shot a look at Vidocq, 'rest assured I will step in to assist you at that time.'

'But we may not have the luxury of time,' she said quietly. Tears of anger welled in her eyes. I was in half a mind to insist we stay in London despite the danger to Holmes.

'You are in excellent hands with a man who . . . loves you truly,' he said, with more than a touch of irony.

Vidocq stood back, observing Holmes closely. 'What urgent business takes you from this lady, whom you promised to help?' he asked.

Holmes paused. 'I'm afraid I am unable to tell you,' he said. 'But do not tarry, Vidocq. It is a dangerous world. The sooner Mademoiselle regains her son, the safer he may be. May I suggest you learn what my brother has to say. Good day.'

CHAPTER 14

Armed with Lies

olmes and I made it to Euston Station five minutes before our train was to depart. Once there, we settled into our first-class compartment, arranged by Mycroft, so that Holmes could study his art texts and I my brief on 'Dr Richard Laurel of Harley Street' in complete privacy.

I had packed in a hurry, returning to my home where all my wife's little homely touches of domesticity – the basket of knitting, the floral teacups and the antimacassars gathering dust in the waning afternoon light – screamed out to me that I was some kind of madman, ricocheting once more off normal sane living and into the wilds of my former life with Sherlock Holmes.

I was strangely happy.

There had been no time for dinner. As I sat in the relative comfort of our luxurious train accommodation, a bit out of breath and wishing for a carafe of water, or better yet some stronger liquid, my thoughts were answered by a sharp rap on the glass door of our compartment.

I opened it to see a porter, carrying a tray with water, sandwiches, biscuits, and fruit. 'Courtesy of Mr Mycroft Holmes,' said the young man as I took the tray from him. 'Oh yes, and something else you may need.' He pulled from behind him an unusual wheelchair, elaborately constructed and elegantly decorated with a simplified floral motif, almost Japanese in feeling, and fully padded with red velvet cushions. It featured a mechanism by which it folded in on itself, like an accordion, and thus fitted easily, even in our small compartment.

'Hmm,' said Holmes, as soon as the young man had departed. 'If a world-renowned art expert were to have need of such a device, then this is the very one he would have.'

'Your brother leaves little to chance,' I mused aloud.

'This wretched thing will hamper my investigation.'

'Mycroft seems to do quite well without moving around much,' said I. His brother was notoriously sedentary.

'My brother quite literally has the Army, and sometimes the Navy at his beck and call. I will have only you.'

'Then I shall be your eyes and ears when needed,' I said.

Holmes raised his eyebrows but said nothing. He began to unwrap the folder from Mycroft.

'What exactly do you hope to find?' I asked.

'I am not yet certain. For Mycroft, obviously, the Nike.' He waved a letter attached to his folder of information. 'I am to cable his men, hidden in Sommersby, a village twenty miles to the south of the Earl's estate, when it arrives. They will then sweep in to make the arrest.'

'Twenty miles away? Why not involve someone closer, the local law, for instance?'

'There is suspicion that they may be complicit,' said Holmes. 'It is true, in these far-flung towns, that the local law – sometimes the constables, all the way up to the magistrates, can come under the financial sway of the prevailing landowners of their region. That is less the case in recent years, but in the North, and along the Scottish border . . .'

'Yes, in the North, things are different,' I said.

'It is possible they have been paid to look the other way,' he said, scanning through the first pages like a hawk looking for mice.

'But in our own case, what do you expect?'

'We must discover why Emil was sent away, and what his past and future there hold. Only then can we advise our client. If the child has been endangered or mistreated, which I suspect, we must root out and neutralize that danger.'

'If the Earl is arrested for the art theft, won't that suffice?' I asked.

But Holmes was engrossed in his reading. In a few seconds he looked up, realizing my question hung in the air.

'He will most certainly stand trial,' said he. 'And it is Mycroft's intention to confront the Earl with a number of transgressions including cruelty and child labour violations at his mills. I read here that his fortunes have rapidly declined in recent years; perhaps that has motivated these acts. Whether he will face punishment is another matter. You have begun to get a taste of how that works.'

I shuddered. If Holmes could be imprisoned so casually, it followed that the law was more easily manipulated than ever I suspected. I'll admit this had shaken me to the core. At thirty-five, I often found my idealism clashed with reality. It would be many years before this changed.

Holmes would probably say I never fully relinquished my optimism about human behaviour.

'There are other factors, Watson. The Earl is said to have a very long reach. We know little of his character. If he views Mademoiselle La Victoire as an enemy, then she, and perhaps Emil, may remain in danger as long as he is alive. And there is Lady Pellingham to consider. Little is known of the lady and her role in the matter. There are simply too few facts at hand.'

'I have been wondering about Lady Pellingham. What do you know of her at this point?'

'Other than that she is American, her dowry was large and based on her industrialist father's textile factories in New Jersey, that this dowry brought the Earl back from the edge of bankruptcy, that she is remarkably beautiful, has set quite a style during her London sojourns with her Parisian-designed silk gowns, and has proved, sadly, to be barren after an initial miscarriage, I have little information on the subject of Lady Pellingham,' remarked Holmes without irony.

'Ha!' I said.

'But I know nothing of her character, and upon that, much rests.'

'Well,' said I, 'we do know that she seems to love Emil like a son. At least that is what Mademoiselle La Victoire tells us. This speaks of a good heart.'

'It is entirely unclear whether this is true. Lady Pellingham has reason to despise the boy and feel threatened by his presence,' said Holmes. 'At this point we lack enough data to fully understand the situation. Now, let me pursue my studies, Watson.'

He continued to flip through the papers Mycroft had provided.

With trepidation, I turned to my own, opening the file on 'Dr Laurel'. I was greatly relieved to find him to be very close to my own history and description, save only for the name. I grew more confident that I could pull off the ruse.

An hour later I closed the file, feeling proud of my accomplishment. This pride was short-lived; in the same amount of time my companion had already completed his study of the Earl and his own 'persona' Fritz Prendergast, and had moved to a thicker set of documents on Greek statuary. He flipped through the pages at great speed.

Among Holmes's many skills was the capacity for memorizing large volumes of facts, retaining and organizing them as if he were a human encyclopaedia. Many of these facts were odd and obscure, including details of cigar and cigarette ash, of military uniforms and decorations, of types of mud and earth, of spoken inflections and regional accents, perfumes and cosmetics, and many more of which I was unaware at the time.

His present study on Greek statuary and the Nike legend proceeded at such a pace that he had completed the task only an hour after I had completed my own. He set them aside, and then stared morosely out of the window.

'I presume you are now well acquainted with Prendergast and his subject?' I wondered.

'Of course. He is an expert on Greek statuary and the Nike legend particularly.'

'But what of the man himself?' I asked. My Dr Laurel would of course be familiar with his patient.

'Not a great deal. Unmarried. Not a club man. Few friends. Apparently somewhat acerbic when off his main topic.'

'That should not be a challenge.'

A few moments passed. Our train rumbled on. Outside the waning light had turned the snow-clad countryside blue.

'What was the cause of his paralysis? It is not explained here,' I said, gesturing to my own meagre folder. 'As your doctor, I would know.'

'The cause was a fall from a carriage at age twenty, during a country ride with a young lady. There were no apparent romantic liaisons after. He is now aged forty-four.'

'Ten years older than you. May I see the photograph again?'

In it, the gaunt Prendergast peered haughtily over gold-rimmed glasses. I observed a Napoleonic 'hand in waistcoat' gesture, giving him an imperious air.

'He appears quite the pedant,' I said. 'Or Francophile, perhaps. The classic Napoleon pose.'

Holmes smiled. 'Pedantic, yes, but you mistake the second point, Watson. He is not imitating Napoleon here. That stance is derived from the ancient Greek, where it was thought bad form to orate with one's hand outside one's robes. He is merely reflecting the subject of his passion.'

'Mmm. Thin. Emaciated, almost. The cocaine, possibly,' I sighed. 'You have not touched your sandwich, Holmes.'

He abruptly stopped smiling and turned back to his studies.

'How convenient that Prendergast cannot easily be contacted,' I added, frankly prodding. I was still puzzling over Holmes's extreme reaction to the news of Prendergast's therapy in Vienna. Had Mycroft actually gone so far as to orchestrate this?

'I am sure you are curious about the silk industry,' said Holmes, changing the subject.

'Not very.'

'Well, neither am I, but I must now familiarize myself further with the minutiae of the Earl's failing business. Let me continue, please.'

Holmes returned to his studies and I turned to the window. Flat land with a wide, white sky above gradually transformed into rolling hills with fields bounded by snow-covered hedges. It became slightly hillier as we travelled north, drawing closer and closer to the Lakes and the border with Scotland. Barren old oaks rose around us, their black arms twisting grotesquely into the solid white of the air.

As Holmes continued to read, he grew troubled. Finally, he gasped and flung the papers aside, staring out into the darkness, turning his head away from me. If I did not know my friend better, I would have said he was hiding tears.

'Holmes, what is the matter?'

He turned, startled, as though he had forgotten my presence. His face was a mask of sadness.

'The tale is darker than I feared. Take a look at this,' he said. He handed me three photographs.

They were images I will never forget. Three children, all dead, their tiny bodies crumpled into unnatural positions, one in the corner of what looked to be a horse's stall, and two outside, partially covered by debris and leaves.

Bile rose in my throat. 'Good God, Holmes! What is this?'

'The labour infractions at the Earl's mills involved illegal child labour, apparently boys conscripted from an orphanage, including the three boys in these photographs. Each went missing, and their bodies were discovered as you see them. A fourth child, in addition to these, has since disappeared.'

'Who took these photographs?' I asked.

'Unknown. But these made their way to Mycroft anonymously, posted from a village some forty miles down the road.'

'The children look as though they have been . . . discarded. Almost like rubbish!' It was difficult to form the words.

Holmes's face hardened. I have often thought that while he appeared to be a cold, reasoning machine, it was not precisely true. Rather, Holmes was a man of very deep feelings, yet able to compartmentalize his emotions when the situation demanded it.

The horror of these children's fate seemed to energize my friend. From his valise he withdrew his theatrical make-up kit, laying out needed items on the seat beside him. He quickly began the subtle physical transformation into Prendergast, art historian *célèbre*.

In under an hour, he was unrecognizable. Masterfully, his disguise included details such as a colourful pocket square and shoes with unused soles. With hair whitened at the temples and rearranged, teeth slightly yellowed, and gold glasses on his nose, Holmes completed the ruse by subtly altering his posture and expression.

It was no longer Sherlock Holmes before me, but another man entirely.

'Remarkable, Holmes,' I said, attempting to shake off the disturbing images that had burned into my mind. 'One of your finest disguises.'

Outside the shadows descended and the blue-white snow passing by our now frigid train compartment seemed to rise into the air in a perfect miasma of bone-chilling fog. I could not help myself; I shuddered.

'Steady, Watson,' said Holmes. I turned to face him and he leaned in to me, speaking softly. 'There is great evil where we are going; you sense it and you are correct. Be at all times on your guard.'

I fingered the revolver in the pocket of my tweed coat. 'I am ready, Holmes,' I said.

He sat back, and with a strange smile, transformed once again into Prendergast. 'Good man . . . *Dr Laurel*,' he said, in a nasal voice.

Our train steamed onward as darkness fell.

PART FIVE

BELLY OF THE WHALE

'Artists who seek perfection in everything are those
who cannot attain it in anything.'

Eugène Delacroix

CHAPTER 15

Arrival

ur arrival at Clighton, Pellingham's grand estate, went smoothly, with nothing out of the ordinary about it, if visiting an earl's enormous estate in Lancashire could be deemed ordinary. While Holmes had travelled in such circles on many occasions, I had far less experience with the landed gentry.

Originally we were to change trains at Lancaster for a small local to take us to the nearest village, Penwick. However that local had been stalled in the recent snowfall. This information had apparently reached Clighton, and so when we disembarked at Lancaster, we were met there by gloved footmen and ushered into an ancient but handsome carriage, finely appointed and comfortable inside, with velvet cushions and lap blankets to protect us from the cold. Prendergast's wheelchair was handily strapped behind, and we made off at a gallop for what turned out to be a full hour's ride in the waning light.

The weather was fiercer in the northern reaches of Britain, and I was glad of my heavy overcoat and woollen scarf.

Lancashire as an area was largely unfamiliar to me. Bounded on the west by rugged sandy beaches, it was forlorn in fog and cold ocean winds. Our journey took us past mill towns, collieries, and several factories, spewing waste into the icy air. The depressing, meagre settlements surrounding them gave way eventually to hills dotted sparsely with trees.

These began to grow in number until they formed deep forests, lending an air of timeless medieval England. The dark smoke of the factories faded to a thin fog which wisped through the black trees as our carriage rolled onward to the Earl's estate.

Finally we emerged from the trees to find ourselves at the base of a bare hill – a pure, dark blue-white expanse of snow, probably a grassed and cleared area in warmer weather, at the top of which sat a grand house, Clighton. Palatial in size, and with windows glowing gold in the night, it seemed to be an amalgam of Gothic, Tudor, and Victorian styles. It exuded wealth, history, and idiosyncratic taste.

A long drive lined with elms formed the approach, and as we drove up through them in the darkness I was surprised to see – at this hour, and for only a visiting art historian – a small array of servants lined up by the door to greet us. Dressed only in their indoor livery, they stood shivering and conferring among themselves.

'The Earl must have quite a high regard for you,' I whispered to Holmes.

'I neglected to mention, Watson,' said Holmes, keeping his voice low as well, 'Prendergast himself is a baron, hence the Earl's trust in a peer. At least it helped, one might presume.'

'A baron!' I exclaimed.

'Bestowed four years ago, for his services to the culture of the Empire,' said Holmes. 'Unfortunately, this means that, even as my physician, you must address me as "my lord".'

'Good of you to mention,' I said. 'Had you forgotten this?'

'Of course not,' he said with a grin. 'Why rankle you longer than necessary?'

'Oh, it rankles,' I said. 'And only because you will enjoy it so.'

'One takes one's small pleasures.' He smiled. 'Ah, I note a clandestine romance among the staff. No, two. But one has recently ended.'

'How the devil—'

'Watson, it is only too obvious. Do you see the blonde chambermaid with the curls, there, and the dark-haired valet two down from her in the row? He slipped her a note as he took his place in line, and she— ah!'

Our carriage had rolled to a stop. A liveried young man with an open face and eager expression ran up and opened the door. He greeted us with a deep bow: 'Welcome, my lord. And Dr Laurel. Jeffrey, at your service. May we assist you from the carriage?'

With help from several footmen in carrying Holmes in his wheelchair up the steps, we made it to the imposing oak doors. There we were met by a tall, elegant butler, who introduced himself as Mason. 'Welcome to Clighton, my lord,' he said, inclining his head slightly.

Mason managed to be both respectful and intimidating at the same time and I sensed he was making a quick and thorough study, his eyes sweeping discreetly over our faces, clothing, demeanour – all without seeming to do so. I was heartily glad that my false persona was so similar to my own. My dress was correct, then, down to my shoes.

Holmes and his brother had taken great care with Prendergast's clothing, and I was profoundly grateful. As Holmes had often remarked, to the careful observer, clothing is a reliable signal of class, profession and attitude. In the eyes of the upper classes and their servants, it fairly shouted its messages.

I next wheeled Holmes through the imposing entrance and into the grand reception hall. One entered by the old portion of the estate and into the great hall, where a sense of history struck one like an axe. It was in medieval style, possibly dating to the late 1400s, and was huge, with timbers resting on a low stone wall. The flagged floor was uneven in places, though worn smooth in the well-trod areas by hundreds of years of foot traffic. Overhead five hammer beams crossed the space, ending in carved angels which stared down on the activity below with cherubic amusement.

There was a dank smell to the place, and although every

inch was polished clean, hundreds of years of fires in the vast fireplace at one end, and hundreds of dinners and balls filled with unwashed bodies lent a strangely haunted and smoky air.

'This portion of the house is over four hundred years old,' said Mason. 'It is little used now, except for large gatherings. I will have Jeffrey escort you to your rooms in the newer wing, where you will find a small refreshment after your journey and may change at your leisure. Supper will be served in one hour in the Grand Dining Hall, and Jeffrey will return to collect you then.'

'Oh, a Titian!' exclaimed Holmes as I wheeled him behind Mason into the newer wing. 'Stop here!' He regarded the painting with avid interest. 'A magnificent example. Similar to *The Man with a Glove*, acquired by the French after our unfortunate Charles I lost his head, only this one is better. A few years later, I observe. Very few portraits by Titian are extant. I expected no less of the Earl,' he remarked. 'Where is he, by the way?'

'He is presently resting, and will greet you at dinner,' said the butler, refusing to elaborate. 'But that acquisition was his father's, the late Earl,' added Mason stiffly. He, too regarded it with admiration. 'What you will observe in the older house and in part in the later wing is the father's collection. The present Earl has placed all of his own, newer acquisitions in the Palladium Hall, under lock and key.'

I thought I caught the slightest hint of resentment there and wondered why.

'Your lordship will be the first person outside the family to view the collection in its entirety.'

'An honour,' exclaimed Holmes in the nasal, high-pitched voice he had created for Prendergast. 'I anticipate it with great pleasure. And now, I require a short rest before supper.'

The butler rang for the footman. He then said in a low tone, 'I believe you have signed an agreement with the Earl not to disclose what you see here? I feel it my duty to ask, my lord. The Earl has much on his mind of late.'

I wondered at the propriety of a butler asking such a question of his respected guest, and Holmes rose to the occasion. His face instantly became a mask of disdain. 'That is a private matter,' he said coldly. 'I wish to retire and rest now.'

'As you wish, my lord,' said Mason.

In a moment we were escorted into adjoining rooms, the footman Jeffrey assisting us with our belongings.

Holmes positioned himself by the window, staring out into the darkness, the elms of the long driveway barely visible against the blue field of snow. Jeffrey and I unpacked the valises and hung our garments in each of the two bedrooms.

'Anything else, my lord, or . . . sir?' he asked.

'No, thank you,' I said, eager for him to leave.

'Boy,' Holmes said. 'There is one thing. I need expert assistance. My good boots have been damaged during travel. Who among the staff is best fit to help me?'

'My lord, I can polish them for you,' Jeffrey offered.

'No!' cried Holmes and the boy jumped. 'These are very

fine boots from Italy. I require an *expert* in the care of leather.' The boy looked nervously about him, not knowing what to say.

But Holmes knew how to put a servant at ease. He wheeled forward. 'Young man,' he said kindly, pressing a coin into the boy's hand, 'your assistance would be very appreciated. Surely there is one man, above all here, who knows leather best?'

'The Earl's valet, Pomeroy, does,' said Jeffrey. 'It is a special skill, yes, my lord. I'll send him to you the moment he is free.'

'Excellent,' said Holmes.

As soon as Jeffrey had left, he turned to me in triumph. 'We bring our suspect right to us,' he smiled. 'The man who used a tanner's knife to threaten our client surely knows his leather.'

CHAPTER 16

Repairs Needed

 few minutes later, a shy rap at the door revealed a dark-haired, pale young man, meaty in build, not quite thirty and with an honest face. Clad in formal livery, he exuded a solid reliability. He introduced himself as Pomeroy. We welcomed him and Holmes presented him with a single very fine boot, which he'd purposely damaged with a buttonhook.

Pomeroy took the boot in his hand and examined it closely.

'It is unfortunate, my lord,' he said. 'This is a deep scratch. But I may be able to help you.'

'Watson, lock the door,' said Holmes. 'And now Mr Pomeroy, kindly place the boot on the floor. We have called you here for another reason entirely.'

Pomeroy looked up in surprise.

'It is in regard to Emil,' said Holmes, 'the Earl's son. We understand you were to bring him to Brown's this Christmas for the meeting with his mother, Miss Emmeline

La Victoire – whom you possibly know by the name of Cherie Cerise – but that the reunion was cancelled.

'I— I—' stammered the valet, backing away.

'We have been told the boy has been "away" for some time.'

'I know nothing of this, sir!' the valet managed. His voice rose in pitch to a whispered wail. 'Please!'

'Put your mind at rest. If you tell us what we need to know, we will not reveal your secret. But we know you are complicit. Where is Emil?'

'Who are you?' he stammered.

Holmes sighed. 'My name is Sherlock Holmes, and this is Dr Watson. We are here to help you . . . and Emil, and on behalf of Mademoiselle La Victoire. *But reveal us at your peril.* Where is the boy now?'

'Emil?' said the man stupidly. 'Sir, really, I know nothing.'

Holmes's demeanour changed. 'Dammit, man! Where were you last Wednesday evening?'

'I . . . I . . . was here!' Pomeroy attempted to bolt for the door. I stood in front of it, blocking his escape.

'Will your young lady confirm this?' asked Holmes.

Pomeroy blanched.

'Yes, the chambermaid with the blonde curls?'

Ah, so Pomeroy and this girl were the two Holmes spotted on our way in.

'Nellie! How did you—? Oh, please, sir—'

'I believe you were in Paris, were you not? Does this look familiar to you?' With that, Holmes withdrew a strange implement, a "ladle with a sharp edge" as described by

Mlle La Victoire, and held it to Pomeroy's face. A tanner's dry scraper. He must have procured it in London with this moment in mind.

It was a touch dramatic, I thought, but it had the intended effect.

Pomeroy groaned and his knees buckled. I caught him as he sank, and sat him down.

'You threatened Mademoiselle La Victoire. Why? And what have you done with her son?'

'I would never hurt the lady,' said the man, his eyes filling with tears. 'She is . . . a lovely woman. And she loves her boy. I only wanted to warn her.'

'As I thought. Why?'

'She is a strong person. I was afraid she would try to find Emil. And if she did – I only wanted to help them both. She loves him so!'

'You meant well,' I offered, patting his shoulder.

'Watson, please!' said Holmes. 'And was it your idea to hide the boy in London? To kidnap him, so to speak?'

'No! I would never! It was his mother's idea.' Seeing our confusion, or at least mine, he continued: 'Lady Pellingham, I mean. She asked me to help.'

'Both Lord and Lady Pellingham seem to rely upon you to a remarkable degree,' remarked Holmes dryly. 'How is it that you were entrusted with the welfare of this child ten years ago? You must have been, what, eighteen, or nineteen?'

Pomeroy hung his head. 'I rescued the family dog from a snare and nursed him back to health,' he said.

Holmes stared at him harshly.

'And a few other favours. Since that time, I—'

'Yes, yes. Were either the Earl or Lady Pellingham privy to your yearly visits with the boy's real mother?'

Pomeroy blanched. 'His lordship, only,' he replied. 'The Lady was told it was to attend to personal purchases, clothing, Christmas gifts, and the like.'

'She allowed a baby, and then a toddler to travel to London on a shopping excursion?' asked Holmes in disbelief.

'Er . . . that was later. His lordship said that he also wanted the boy to be examined each half year by his London physician.'

'Hmm. But why hide him now?' I asked.

'We are getting to that, Watson,' snapped Holmes. He turned to Pomeroy, 'Where is the child?'

Pomeroy's face worked through a variety of emotions. Finally he spoke. 'He is in London, sir. Safe.'

'Where exactly?'

'With my sister and her husband.'

'Charles and Merielle Eagleton?'

'Yes. How did—'

'The knife. A tanner's. In Bermondsey?'

'Yes.'

'Why did Lady Pellingham ask you to hide the boy?' demanded Holmes, raising his voice.

'Shh!' I hissed.

'She . . . my lady . . . told me there was danger here. Nellie and I feels it, too.'

'Danger of what sort? Details, man!' said Holmes.

'Lady Pellingham did not say. It is not my place to question her, sir.'

'Obviously. But you have observed something. Describe it.'

Pomeroy began to shake. Holmes stood over him, leaning in, willing the answers.

'Nellie noticed it first. Emil has, well, changed recently. He was always a sunny child – chatty, friendly. A reader. But lately he stopped smiling. And he . . . stopped talking.'

'Did the Earl remark upon this?' asked Holmes.

'I am not certain that he noticed, sir,' said the young man. 'He has much on his mind—'

There was a rap at the door. Pomeroy jumped and we all froze.

'My lord?' It was the butler. 'Is the Earl's valet with you?'

'He is,' called Holmes in his high-pitched Prendergast voice. 'I called him about my boots.' Then, *sotto voce*, he said to Pomeroy, 'We will continue this after dinner. Speak not a word of this, or we will reveal you.'

Pomeroy nodded numbly.

'I trust he has been of assistance?' came Mason's voice.

Holmes waved, dismissing the terrified valet. Pomeroy wiped his tears and took a shaky breath. He started for the door, forgetting the boot. I caught his sleeve and handed it to him. He took it with relief and opened the door. Mason glared down at Pomeroy.

'Well?'

'Yes, sir,' Pomeroy said. 'I can help the gentleman, sir.'

145

The butler eyed him carefully, and then let him pass. He lingered at the entrance to our rooms. Seeing we were not yet dressed for dinner, he raised an eyebrow.

'I am instructed to escort you to dinner. Do you require assistance dressing? I can send someone.'

'Thank you, we can manage,' I said.

'I shall await you in the hall,' said the butler. 'It is quite easy to become lost in this house,' he added.

He closed the door behind us. 'Dammit,' whispered Holmes. 'After dinner, we must lose this insidious butler and continue our conversation with Pomeroy. Now, quickly, get dressed; then come have a look at something.'

'He's waiting for us, Holmes!' I said.

'Remember that I am "paralysed". Dressing takes time. But hurry!'

'This Mason – he is glued to us,' I mused, as I began to corral my evening dress. 'Do you think he suspects?'

'No. The white tie, Watson, not that one. He is a natural watchdog, loyal to the family above all. The Earl is vulnerable in the subject of his art acquisitions. I will be the first to see them. He is being wary, that's all.'

'I guess . . .'

'You may guess but I do not. Hurry, man. The "bull terrier" awaits.'

I moved into my adjoining room and changed rapidly into my evening wear. But Holmes was faster, and when I returned to him, he was dressed and ready, with a large paper unfolded across his bed, gesturing for me to look. It was a detailed plan of the house.

'How did Mycroft obtain this?' I wondered at the resourcefulness of the Holmes brothers. 'Nothing must have been safe in your parents' home!'

Holmes did not bother to reply. 'It truly is a maze,' he said gesturing at the map. 'Look closely, Watson.'

'How can this help us now? You can't be seen walking about.'

He sighed. 'No. But you can.'

I turned my attention to the page. It was a warren of passageways and odd rooms. We studied it for a few minutes, Mason be damned, and then headed down to dinner, with the butler in the lead.

CHAPTER 17

In the Bosom of the Family

hortly after, the butler accompanied us through many twists and turns to the grand dining hall. The old house did not easily accommodate the wheelchair and it took some time.

Arriving at the dining hall, Mason turned to me and announced, 'I will take care of Lord Prendergast for you, Doctor. You may dine with the staff, or if you wish, I will send supper to your room.'

I was considered a servant, then! I felt my jaw clench.

'Mason,' said Holmes sharply. 'The Doctor is not my servant, but my trusted friend and colleague, and a decorated war hero. What you suggest is unthinkable. He will dine with me, or we will not dine at all.'

Mason swallowed his surprise and bowed graciously. Prendergast, after all, was a baron.

'As you wish, my lord. I will so inform the Earl.' He turned and gave quick orders to one of the staff to set one more place at table.

The dining room was enormous, with deep wood panelling, and a row of paintings on both sides. The table was laden with enough china, crystal and silver to equal in value a medium-sized villa in Mayfair. Six places had been set. Candles were lit and the flames sent flickering highlights across the glittering display.

We were invited to wait at one end of this room, where drinks were set out. A servant poured us each sherry. Holmes noticed a tall, rather disturbing portrait behind the sideboard. 'What a lovely Géricault!' he wheezed excitedly. 'Reminds one of the portraits he completed in the insane asylum. One in particular, *Portrait of a Kleptomaniac!*'

The servant pouring our drinks started and moved away quickly, conferring with the butler. I leaned in to Holmes and whispered, 'You strain credibility! And for what purpose?'

'I assure you, everything I say is real,' he said with a sly smile. 'There is in fact such a portrait!'

The eagle-eyed butler moved around the table, adjusting the settings with precision, while throwing us an occasional glance. He was probably counting the silverware. *Portrait of a Kleptomaniac* indeed.

We continued to wait, with drinks in hand, for the Earl.

Five minutes passed. More servants entered and aligned themselves against the dark panelled walls. Behind them additional gloomy portraits hung, all staring dolefully into the room. Footsteps were muffled in the thick carpet. The wealth of many generations hung in the air like a layer of fine dust.

In spite of my curiosity about the Earl, I feared it would be a long evening. I stifled a yawn.

The side door to the dining room opened with a bang, startling the servants, who rearranged themselves immediately. A short but powerfully muscled and well-padded man, perhaps fifty, ruddy of cheek, and with an open, friendly face, blew into the room with the force of a small gale. 'Baron!' he shouted. Approaching Holmes he extended his hand, a broad grin making him look like an overgrown and enthusiastic child. 'Welcome to our humble little abode,' he boomed, and laughed at his own joke.

An American. Lady Pellingham's father, no doubt.

'Mr Strothers, I presume,' said Holmes faintly, with the remoteness of a baron who spent his days in a museum. 'A pleasure, I am sure.' He shook the man's hand, limply.

'You've got that right, I'm Daniel G. Strothers, of New York and New Jersey. My friends call me Danny. Came over for the wedding.'

'And you have decided to stay, then?' said I.

'My daughter insisted. Made myself useful too, and by golly if I don't love it up here! My son-in-law has been trying to educate me in the finer things of life. But it's a losing battle, I'm afraid.'

Holmes smiled politely.

'I hear you're a real expert on art,' Strothers continued. 'Guess you have plenty of time to study being stuck in that chair. What happened?'

Holmes regarded him with a weary tolerance. 'An accident. Long ago. A carriage. But I am well adjusted.'

'Happened to a friend of mine. Damned shame! You paralysed then?'

'Mmm,' said Holmes, looking away.

It was going to take more than an art education to smooth off Strothers' rough edges. But this did not bother me; his direct gaze and genial smile put me immediately at ease. And to Holmes, class was invisible when not relevant to a case.

'Sorry,' the American said, sensing he'd overstepped. He then turned to me. 'And who are you, sir?' he asked with a grin. Americans were nothing if not straightforward.

I hesitated for only a fraction of a second and Holmes quickly answered for me. 'This is Dr Laurel, my doctor and also my friend.'

We shook hands. Strothers' was warm and powerful.

'Well, Laurel, are you an art expert, too?' he asked with a smile.

'Hardly,' I replied.

'Hunter then? Sportsman?' he said hopefully. It struck me that Lady Pellingham's father was as much out of place in this stifling room as I was.

'I enjoy shooting,' I said.

'Good man!' he exclaimed. 'Great area for it. I netted three birds, just this afternoon! And in this weather. Imagine. Maybe we can have a go tomorrow.'

Things were looking up.

A Mr Frederick Boden was announced and we were joined by a stiff, well-built man in his late thirties, whose erect bearing and crisp tailoring spoke of a military background.

His face was handsome, with strong dark eyebrows and moustache giving him a stern air, made marginally cruel by a duelling scar down one cheek. This had been a serious wound to my medical eye, and not a recent one, but skilfully repaired.

He was offered a drink but declined. His high tenor voice contrasted strongly with his masculine demeanour.

Moving away, Holmes engaged Strothers in a one-sided talk on Géricault. I attempted to strike up a conversation with the other. It proved arduous; the man was as interested in idle chat as was Holmes, and so I shifted the topic to the army, based on my assumption of military service. Boden finally mentioned he had been at the Battle of Abu Klea.

'Ah, the Square! A remarkable feat!' I exclaimed. The British forces there, massively outnumbered, had been victorious by forming into an impenetrable square. The battle was famous; Boden must have seen exciting action. But he could not be lured to expound on the topic.

'We served when needed,' he said coolly, to my question. He then smiled stiffly, almost as an afterthought.

There was something odd about the man; I decided to try drawing him out. His accent was refined, a man of privilege and education. Feeling Holmes would be proud of my inferences, I went on: 'What brings you then to Lancashire?' I inquired.

He looked sharply at me, and then in what appeared a conscious gesture, masked the expression. 'I was engaged to oversee the Earl's six factories,' he said.

An employee, then? And yet distinctly high-born. Who was he and why would he be invited to a dinner such as this at the Earl's?

As if he read my mind, he added. 'As a favour to the Earl, of course. My family owns land elsewhere.'

A second son, I intuited – to the manor born, but without the attendant fortune. Such men often found their way through the military, inducted in as officers and retaining their privileges throughout their service; with favoured positions awaiting their return.

'I understand you have been successful,' I said. 'The Earl's silk is reputed the finest in the country.'

That was a mistake. His tone grew icy. 'Mr Strothers is a man of great business acumen. Employing his successful strategies, I have returned the Earl's interests – silk among the smaller of them – to their original state. Thus the Earl is able to continue his patronage of the arts as his father and grandfather did before him.'

'Er, very good then,' I mumbled.

'Neither Lord Prendergast nor yourself would be here, were it not so.' He paused, seeming to expect thanks.

I remained silent on this point. I wondered if this man might be connected in some way to the mysterious disappearances and deaths surrounding the silk mill. After several seconds had passed, I ventured again.

'How many factories do you now oversee, Mr Boden?' I asked.

'None. It was a brief favour only. I am now the local magistrate.'

Odd. But what was his current connection here? I was determined to find out. Perhaps he was the hunting companion and friend of the American, though their personalities were night and day. But then, that could be said of many friendships.

'Do you hunt, sir?' I asked. 'It is a particular interest of mine. Mr Strothers mentioned the area is rich in game.'

'Yes, I hunt. In a manner of speaking,' he said, and then added, 'Deer mainly. Unlike Mr Strothers, small game is of no interest to me.' He smiled at this, and then abruptly turned away. 'I have changed my mind,' he barked at one of the servants. 'Pour me a sherry.'

While there was nothing untoward in his words, I was glad our conversation had ended. The man made me uneasy. He silently projected something I could not quite place, a certain coiled sense of violence.

I wondered if Holmes had noticed. He seemed deep into animated conversation with Strothers, attempting to explain some detail of another gloomy portrait nearby. But as Boden moved away from me to accept a drink, I saw Holmes shoot a penetrating glance at the man.

Several awkward minutes passed, with Boden and I continuing as silent audience to Holmes's art lesson – and still our host and hostess did not appear. While it may be customary to await a grand entrance in some circles, this now bordered on rudeness.

At last the doors to the dining room were opened wide and the room went silent. If a blast of fanfare had sounded, it would not have felt amiss. There, down a long hallway, our host approached, moving slowly, with a studied grandeur. He was alone.

The Earl was a tall, well-built man, golden-haired and still remarkably handsome in his late forties, wearing costly evening attire that was simultaneously fashionable and yet reminiscent of days gone by. His waistcoat was hand-embroidered, his evening coat a masterwork of London tailoring.

His slow approach gave us ample time to take in the splendour he clearly hoped to convey.

There was arrogance in the Earl's carriage, some combination of entitlement, snobbery and diffuse energy that characterized the worst of his class. His face was a mask of disdain, his languid movements seemed calculated to irritate. Or perhaps I was just ravenously hungry.

The Earl finally entered the room and the servants stiffened perceptibly. Strothers turned to face his son-in-law.

'Ah, here you are, Harry, my boy! Food at last! Let's get to it!'

'Daniel,' acknowledged the Earl with cool politeness. Then he addressed us all, his eyes staring into the middle distance above our heads. 'Lady Pellingham is indisposed. She may join us later,' he intoned.

He then slowly turned to address my friend. 'Lord Prendergast. Welcome to Clighton. I consider it a great pleasure finally to meet you.' He smiled listlessly. This is what apparently passed for enthusiasm among the peerage. I disliked him immediately.

Four servants moved to the table and held out our chairs,

as a fifth escorted us to our designated seats. Holmes was wheeled to the place of honour on the Earl's right. Boden was placed next to him and Strothers across. I was directed next to Strothers. Lady Pellingham's seat, opposite the Earl, remained vacant.

The Earl slowly took his seat at the table. The others followed suit one by one. I hesitated, unsure of protocol. 'Be seated – Laurel, is it?' said the Earl dismissively.

He turned to Holmes. 'We will not wait for Lady Pellingham. Frankly, knowing the subject we share so intimately, she may be bored at our conversation. We shall begin without her.'

With a wave to the servants to begin serving, he continued to focus on Holmes. 'I understand you enjoyed my father's Titian,' he said, his face finally lighting up. 'I have acquired two more, finer even than that one.'

'Finer?' exclaimed Holmes. 'I am eager to see! Of what period, then?'

The dinner proceeded with talk of nothing but the Earl's art collection and its splendours. The food was sumptuous and plentiful – turtle soup, followed by one seafood course, then a second. There was no need to make conversation; the Earl and Holmes dominated the table with increasingly animated talk of art – punctuated only by the clink of heavy silverware, and the servants' hushed movements.

As oysters were served as a fourth course, I glanced at Holmes. He detested the slippery things and struggled not to show it. Just then the doors opened again and Lady Pellingham entered the room.

All eyes turned to her. Attired in a deep-rose silk dress of the latest Paris fashion, accentuating her pale blonde delicacy, the lady's beauty rivalled our client's, though of a different sort entirely. Not robust like her father, instead she was a porcelain doll, with a wasp waist, delicate wrists, blonde curls and a gentle demeanour. She entered in a rush, standing briefly next to the Earl, with a murmured apology.

The Earl appraised her coolly, but not without some concern. 'Feeling better?' he asked, taking her hand and patting it.

She withdrew it sharply. Then, to cover, she smiled at her husband. 'Yes. Quite, thank you.' She quickly took her seat at the end of the table.

'My wife is like a fern,' said the Earl with a smile. 'She eats little and seems to subsist on air.'

'Always has done so,' said her father with a chuckle. 'Eat up, Annabelle. You'll float off.'

A pale blush coloured Lady Pellingham's cheeks at these words but she turned to Holmes, with a forced smile. Her accent was American, but far fainter than her father's. 'Lord Prendergast. Dr Laurel. Welcome. Please forgive my lateness. I am of course very pleased to see you. My husband has spoken at length of your great expertise, sir.'

As the dinner proceeded, I noticed two things. Lady Pellingham spoke but little and ate next to nothing. She appeared troubled. Both her husband and her father were solicitous, alternately eyeing her with concern, or encouraging her to speak, to eat, or to relax.

At one point, Holmes managed to ask her about her family. Her mother was dead, she admitted, many years earlier. A wave of grief passed over her father's face as she said this, but her own demeanour masked something more complex. Grief and . . . anger perhaps?

'I understand you and the Earl are the happy parents of a boy?' said Holmes, appearing to change the subject.

Lady Pellingham dropped her fork with a clatter.

'He is away at present,' she said, recovering.

'He was suffering from a chronic cough,' said the Earl. 'Annabelle has arranged for him to winter in a warmer climate, haven't you, my dear?'

'Hmmph. Weakens the lad,' snorted Strothers. 'Bad idea!'

'It's not tuberculosis, I hope?' I asked.

The Earl and his wife shot me a venomous glance. That had been a *faux pas* on my part. In these circles, tuberculosis was considered a disease of the poor, and yet I knew of many a titled sufferer.

'Of course not,' Lady Pellingham said. 'He has been well looked after.' Shortly after, she excused herself from the table and retired, presumably, to her room.

I sensed rather than observed Holmes's disappointment. But he carried on as if nothing were amiss. At the end of the meal, he managed to convince the Earl to give him a preview of the private collection – that very evening, right after dinner – as he could hardly wait.

To my surprise, the Earl acquiesced. He seemed as eager as Holmes.

CHAPTER 18

First Look

s the Earl set off with Holmes towards his private museum in the Palladium Hall, I was invited to join Boden and Strothers for a cigar and cognac in the smoking room. But as our brief talk of guns and hunting moved into industrial matters, I grew restless. Genial as Strothers was, Boden made me uncomfortable and the discussion of productivity and shipping issues quite bored me. Making my apologies, I feigned fatigue, and took my leave.

Thankful to be alone, I decided to do some investigating. In retrospect this was a mistake, my first of the evening. I hoped to encounter Pomeroy, and perhaps continue the conversation Holmes had started. After serving our dinner, the servants were probably gathered in the kitchen eating their own late supper, I reasoned.

Heading in that direction, I took a back staircase and which led to a far less ornate section of the house with dark wainscoting and simple plaster walls, lit dimly by intermittent gaslight, turned down low. I reached a rear door to the pantry when I struck gold. Nellie and Pomeroy were two feet away from me, hidden in a walk-in cupboard. They were locked in a tearful embrace and I slipped behind a door to listen. Holmes had been right about them.

'Freddie, Freddie,' the girl sobbed. 'Can't we leave tonight?'

'Steady, Nellie. Don't let Dickie threaten you. I need another day is all.'

'But he's about to tell them about us! I feels it!'

Pomeroy sighed. 'We'll be fine. It's Emil and the Lady I'm fearin' for.'

'Leave it, Freddie. You could go to gaol!'

'But the Lady is as scared as we are! I have to help her.'

Lady Pellingham was afraid? But of whom, and why? Suddenly I felt the awful prickle of being watched. I turned slowly. Mason stood at the end of the hall, staring at me. He was not close enough to hear, but he had certainly seen me listening.

'Hello there,' I said. 'I am looking for some warm milk. I am preparing Lord Prendergast's evening medications,' I said loudly, hoping to warn the two young people.

It went quiet behind the door. Mason approached me sternly. 'You may always ring for what you need.' A tiny pause. 'Sir.'

'Ah, you've found them!' came Holmes's shrill Prendergast voice.

Jeffrey appeared, wheeling Holmes along the corridor. It was excellent timing.

'And Mason, what an astonishing collection your employer has acquired. I am in seventh heaven!' continued my friend. 'I look forward to studying it at length tomorrow.'

'My lord,' said Mason stiffly with a small bow. He turned to Jeffrey. 'The Earl, Jeffrey?'

'He has retired, sir. I notified his valet.'

'I must attend one last time to the Earl,' said Mason. 'But before I do, may I escort you to your rooms?'

'The Earl mentioned an exquisite Vigée Le Brun in your front hall that I would like to see before I retire,' said Holmes. 'Dr Laurel is used to this obsession of mine. We can find our way back.'

'It is a difficult house to navigate in your condition, my lord. Jeffrey, accompany our guests with a light. And then to their rooms.'

They left to arrange things and Holmes leaned in quickly to me. 'Persistent devil. But we are in luck, Watson. I have managed to identify enough stolen art in the Earl's possession to open a wing in the British Museum, not to mention make a serious case against him. Lord Elgin's own collection cannot compete!'

'What about the Nike?'

'She will be delivered at noon tomorrow! Mycroft will have what he needs. And we will have a clearer path to pursue the mystery of Emil and the other children.' He grinned in triumph. 'The Earl is a lunatic on the subject. He is obsessed.'

'But what now?' I asked, thinking the line between aficionado and lunatic was a fine one.

'I am hoping to see the nursery. And if possible Lady Pellingham.'

But neither was to happen, or at least not in the way Holmes had hoped. Jeffrey returned with a light, and after a circuitous route through the darkened house, during which Holmes deftly set the young man at his ease with a steady stream of witty banter, we arrived at the charming portrait of a Russian noblewoman peering impishly out of the darkness at us.

As we studied her, Holmes piped up, 'And what of illustrations? Children's illustrations are a particular passion of mine.'

'Perhaps in the nursery, my lord.'

'Take us there!'

'Sorry, sir, but it is strictly out of bounds. None of us may even set foot, sir.'

Holmes turned on his considerable charm. 'No one need know, Jeffrey, and you will make this old baron a happy man.'

'I can't, my lord. I wish I could.'

'Too bad,' said Holmes. 'I adore children's art. And children as well. They remind me of my own happier, carefree days.'

'I know what you mean, sir,' said Jeffrey.

'Do you know the child?' ventured Holmes.

'I do, sir. All of us do. A very playful little fellow, cheery-like and always smiling.'

'Always?'

'Well, until recently that is.'

'What happened recently?' asked Holmes.

'No one knows. But he ain't talked in nearly a month.'

'Really? And why, do you think?'

Jeffrey grew quiet. After a moment he said, 'I have spoken out of turn, my lord.'

We could get nothing more from him and soon came back to the butler. Mason was waiting for us where we had left him, and I had a sudden stab of suspicion. Had he followed us throughout the house?

I dismissed my fear as fatigue. I would be happy when this day ended, thinking that perhaps I was catching some of my colleague's mania.

'Did you enjoy the Vigée, Lord Prendergast?' he asked.

'Oh immensely, Mason,' exclaimed Holmes. 'Her portraits have such animation, it is as though they might speak at any moment. I shall sleep well, dreaming of what I have seen tonight.'

If only that had turned out to be true. As it happened, we would both witness something so horrible that the image of it would be burned forever into our brains. It would be a long time before either of us slept well again.

PART SIX

DARKNESS DESCENDS

'Our main business is not to see what lies dimly at
a distance but to do what lies clearly at hand.'

Thomas Carlyle

CHAPTER 19

Murder!

nce again, Mason accompanied me as I wheeled Holmes towards our rooms. Moving to the grand staircase, we passed by the library, the rows of gleaming leatherbound books visible through the open door. A sudden sound took us all by surprise – a heavy book dropped perhaps? And then the raised voices of two people in the middle of a row from the far end of the library.

I recognized the first; Lady Pellingham's voice was nearly a shout. 'Your insensitivity is—is—intolerable. No matter your passion for art, you are blind!!'

A baritone male voice answered in hushed angry tones; we could not make out the words, but it sounded like the Earl. 'Why can't I make you see?' came the lady's shrill response.

Mason closed the double doors to the library. The next sound was muffled but it was unmistakeably the voice of the Earl, shouting now.

Mason hurried us away, down another corridor, and finally to the base of the long staircase leading up to our rooms on the third floor.

'Wait here,' he said, 'I will ring for two footmen to carry Lord Prendergast and his chair.' A high-pitched female scream of terror, strangely cut off, echoed down the hall.

'My God!' I exclaimed.

The butler gripped my arm like a clamp. 'Do not move,' he nearly shouted in my face and ran off down the hall.

Holmes immediately sat up. 'Quick, Watson. Turn down this hall and run with me, like the wind.'

'But—'

'Do it! That scream came from the library. I know a back way!' Without hesitation I grabbed the chair and wheeled Holmes at a run down another corridor. Directed by Holmes we turned right, left, then left again. In a moment we faced a new door, which led into a darkened anteroom filled with bookcases and a couple of desks. Beyond this small chamber, another door was open to the library where bright lights blazed.

I wheeled Holmes into the anteroom, nearly slipping on a stack of papers that had been knocked off a desk on to the floor. 'There!' whispered Holmes, 'nearer that door!'

A door at the other end of the small room was partially open; through the crack we could see into the library. Servants rushed about in a panic in the bright gaslight. Several were clustered around something beneath them. Then the crowd parted and I glimpsed a bright rose dress spread out along the floor, a pale hand resting next to it. It was Lady Pellingham!

'We are too late! What a fool I have been!' hissed Holmes. 'See to her, Watson!'

But I had already leapt past him and ran at once into the room. 'I'm a doctor, let me help!' I cried. 'Stand back!'

The cluster of servants surrounding the prone figure of Lady Pellingham made space for me. I kneeled by her side. She was not breathing. I felt for a pulse in her wrist, but found none. I leaned in to check more closely, but Strothers rushed in and pushing me aside, gathered his daughter up in his arms, hugging her close to his body.

'Annabelle!' he moaned in agony. 'My child! Oh, my God!'

'Sir, let me examine her!' I cried. But the man was blinded by his grief and could not let go. He began to sob. Gently I tried to pry the limp form of Lady Pellingham from his fingers. I managed to get Strothers to release her and I gently laid her on the floor.

And then I saw her face. Its beautiful features were contorted into a mask of terror, eyes bulging open, lips twisted in agony, tongue protruding. And stabbed deeply into her upper chest was a silver letter opener. Small dribbles of blood surrounded it, staining her rose-coloured bodice.

Knowing she was dead, I nevertheless went through the motions. I felt again for a pulse. There was none. I withdrew my handkerchief, and with shaking hands, unfolded it gently across her face, blocking the terrible sight from view. I looked up. A ring of horrified faces hovered above us.

'I am so sorry,' I said. 'There is nothing I can do.'

Behind them, Holmes had wheeled himself into the room and was scanning it carefully.

Sobbing, Strothers once again threw himself across his daughter's body.

'Step away from the body, everyone.' Boden's high-pitched tenor voice cut through the general murmur. Everyone turned to see the magistrate standing at the door with the Earl and Mason, who had evidently fetched them both. Silence. Mason protectively supported the Earl's arm.

'There has obviously been a murder,' Boden said, easily taking command. 'Everyone step away and touch nothing.'

'Indeed,' Holmes snapped, temporarily out of character. Boden looked sharply at him.

Then the Earl stepped forward, uncertainly. 'Annabelle?' he whispered. 'Annabelle?'

Servants moved aside, giving him a clear view of the body. I knelt beside her on one side, Strothers on the other.

The Earl now had a full view of his dead wife, and sank to his knees with a moan. Mason and another servant caught him as he fell.

'Doctor!' said Mason, struggling to lower his master to the floor.

I could do nothing for the lady, and so rushed to the Earl's side. He lay unconscious on the heavy carpet, his eyes fluttering, his pulse racing. Shock? Grief? Whatever the cause, he was deeply in distress.

'Brandy!' I called, loosening his collar. It was supplied immediately.

'Clear the room now!' commanded Boden. Then, to Strothers, 'Daniel, if you please . . .'

Strothers looked up from where he had once again raised his dead daughter's body to his bosom. With a moan of grief, he gently laid her back upon the carpet.

'I am so sorry for your loss, sir,' said Boden. 'But this is a crime scene. Everyone must step back. *Now.*'

Strothers moved as if in a trance, helped out by two servants as another wheeled Holmes into the hallway. Boden approached the body, and flicked back my handkerchief to reveal the horrific face again. 'Sad,' he said. 'Very sad.'

He scanned the room. Only the butler, the Earl and I remained. The Earl was sitting up now, staring in horror at his wife's distorted face. He began to gag and I walked between them to block his view.

'Doctor, help Lord Pellingham out of this room,' said Boden.

'Mr Boden,' I began. 'It is possible that the lady did not die of—'

But Boden overrode me with vehemence. 'Unless you are a seasoned policeman, Doctor, leave the investigation to me. Do as I say. Now.'

We were all removed to a nearby hallway, and the Earl was placed in a chair. Resentfully, I continued to attend him. He had regained consciousness but was now gasping and moaning. Strothers, by contrast, sat opposite, silent, raining tears.

Holmes stayed back from the rest, observing carefully.

I administered a strong sedative to the Earl, and his breathing slowed. 'Annabelle. Annabelle,' he repeated sense-lessly as he began to fade.

A young footman, tow-headed and reed-thin, ran towards the library. Mason spotted him and called out, 'Richard! Get back to your post!'

'Sir, said the young man breathlessly. 'Mr Boden summoned me.' I sensed Holmes's slight reaction off to my side.

Mason hesitated only a brief second, and then nodded his assent. 'Go then, Dickie,' he said. The blond footman entered the library, closing the door behind him.

Dickie!

The sedative I had administered was working and the Earl nodded. 'He'll need to be carried,' I said.

As Mason directed two men to carry off Pellingham, I turned to Holmes. He sat still in his chair, but I knew he must be nearly beside himself with regret and frustration.

'Steady,' I whispered.

The door burst open. Boden emerged, followed by the blond footman. 'Where is the Earl? I have solved the case.'

Holmes and I exchanged a look of surprise.

'The Earl is sedated,' I volunteered. 'He has been taken to his room. I'm afraid he'll be insensible 'til morning.'

Boden stamped his foot. 'Mason, bring me the valet, Pomeroy. Get him here at once, and do not let him escape. He may try!'

Beside me, Holmes was on fire and unable to act. Mason signalled for some footmen as I stepped forward to check

174

on Strothers. The old man's face was tear-stained and he was shaking in grief. He gripped my hand, hard.

Abruptly Holmes wheeled to face the suffering man.

'I . . . I'll be all right,' said Strothers. 'I . . . I . . .'

'Sir, would you like a sedative?' I asked.

'Perhaps he simply needs to talk,' said Holmes gently.

Strothers started, then wiped away tears. 'Neither, but thank you. I need to . . . I need to . . . What would Annabelle have wanted me to do?'

At that point, two burly servants entered, dragging a terrified Pomeroy between them. He was brought before Boden.

'Here is the villain,' announced Boden. 'At least Mr Strothers may know his daughter's killer tonight. Pomeroy, you are hereby formally charged with murder.'

Holmes and I exchanged a quick glance of disbelief.

'Sir! I had nothing to do with—' began the terrified valet. Boden stepped forward and backhanded him hard across the face.

'Mr Boden!' exclaimed Holmes in Prendergast's high-pitched whine. 'Must you be so rough?'

'I have the proof. This man was seen entering the library with a silver salver bearing a letter and the murder weapon – the letter opener – only a minute before the murder. The lady was alone at the time, and the salver was discovered near the body.' Boden slapped Pomeroy again, hard. 'What have you to say for yourself?'

The valet was frozen in horror. 'N-not true, sir! I did not enter the library at all!'

'You were seen,' said Boden. The blond footman named Dickie stepped forward with a small smile and a nod. 'You had opportunity and means. I will soon learn your motive.'

He turned to the rest of us. 'It is time for all to retire and let the local constables handle this. We will call them and the coroner. Mr Strothers, justice will be found for your dear daughter. I will ensure it. Mason, please see everyone to their rooms.'

CHAPTER 20

The Chambermaid

inutes later we were back in our rooms, the door latching shut behind us. Holmes shot from his wheelchair as if propelled, and wringing his hands, paced back and forth in a fury.

'I'm an idiot!' he groaned. 'This is a disaster! They are framing Pomeroy. I need to get into that room!'

'Holmes! Your shoes!' I said.

He stopped, confused. Then abruptly slipped them off. 'Thank you, Watson.' It would not do to have wear marks on the bottom of a paralysed man's shoes! And until the Earl's arrest he must maintain the disguise. He continued to pace in his stocking feet.

'Damn! I need another look at the body!'

'We can't risk it, Holmes,' I said.

'Had I thirty more seconds we would know the murderer now!'

'You don't think it was the Earl?'

'Data! Data! We do not have all we need! If it is the Earl we must have incontrovertible evidence!'

He growled in exasperation. Then, slumped down on a chair, he sat staring at the dim fire in the small fireplace, rubbing his chest, a look of exhaustion and pain apparent. The room was cooling fast. The fire had been allowed to die down.

He was exhausted, and so was I.

'Holmes, let us turn in. There is nothing we can do at this hour.'

'The night is not over yet, Watson. Pomeroy's alliance with Lady Pellingham must have been noted. Whoever or whatever forces which aligned against her – her murderer – or not – are now conspiring to take him out of the picture.'

A knock at the door sounded and we both jumped. 'Who is it?' I called. Holmes quickly sat back in his wheelchair.

It was Nellie. The little blonde chambermaid Holmes had noted at our arrival was pale with terror, her cheeks stained with tears. I let her in and closed the door behind her. She stood before us, trembling and unable to speak. Holmes approached and gently took her hands.

'Mr Pomeroy sent you here, didn't he? And your name is Nellie?'

She could only nod in reply.

'I know you are Mr Pomeroy's young lady,' said Holmes softly. 'What can I do for you?'

'M-Mr Holmes is it?' she stammered.

'Ah, he told you that,' said Holmes with a frustrated look at me. He stood up from the wheelchair. 'What is it?'

She nodded. 'Freddie. He didn't do it!' she said.

'I didn't think so. But can you prove it?'

'It could'na been my Freddie. He was with me when the Lady screamed. Right with me!' She sobbed.

'Whom did you tell?'

'Only Janie, the scullery maid. Well, I didn't tell. She saw, too.'

'Why not tell Mason?' asked Holmes.

'Freddie said never to tell about us. We'd've lost our jobs.'

'Any idiot could see that you— never mind – but who is this "Dickie", and why would he lie about your young man's presence in the library?'

'Dickie, he fancied me once. But Freddie and I . . . and then Freddie reported him for stealing some port, and so you see—' She broke off and began to sob, loudly.

'But of course,' said Holmes. 'I understand. Calm yourself. I will see that justice is done. Tomorrow I will present your evidence.'

'Tonight! Sir, you must go tonight!' Her sobs rose in volume.

Holmes threw up his hands in frustration. 'Watson, fix this.' He moved away and began to pace.

I took her arms and gently raised her up to standing. 'There now, Nellie, take courage.' I patted her hand. 'You must understand, there is due process of law. Mr Holmes is very good at what he does. He will see that your young man is exonerated.'

'Is wot?'

'Set free. I promise. But you must keep our secret.'

She nodded her assent. I dried the girl's tears and sent her on her way. I felt uneasy and turned to my friend.

'I'm wondering, Holmes, if the time has come to reveal ourselves and join in the investigation?'

'Not until the Nike is delivered,' snapped Holmes. He turned to me. 'I wager this will still take place in the morning, despite this unfortunate interruption.'

'Surely the Earl wouldn't—'

'Do not underestimate the man's obsession. The delivery *will* proceed as planned.'

'But what of Pomeroy? Do you believe the girl?'

'I do. I know for certain that Pomeroy is being framed,' said Holmes.

'How?'

'The silver salver.'

'What about it?'

'It was not present in the room at the time of the murder.'

'You were in the room for less than a minute! How could you—'

Holmes silenced me with a look.

'Since it was placed there later, and not in our presence, it must have been brought in by someone after we left the room. Only Dickie entered the room after it was cleared.'

I said nothing. He was, of course, right.

'It is possible that other small arrangements were made. And now, Watson, I must ask you to do something,' he said, and hesitated. 'It is dangerous.'

'What do you need, Holmes? You know I am ready.'

'Return downstairs. You must get to the body and examine it.'

'They will never let me near the body. It's probably been removed already.'

'You must try! Do it in secret if you must! That stab wound was post mortem, of that I am sure; there was too little blood.'

'Agreed. And her face!' I said.

'Exactly. The eyes, the tongue indicate either poison—'

'—or strangulation!' I said.

'Precisely. I must know which. I need to return to the library. Oh, damn this chair and this whole ridiculous charade!' He swatted at the chair in frustration.

'Holmes, calm down. I can be your eyes and ears.' I started to go; then turned with a sudden worry. 'You will not venture out into the house yourself while I am doing this, Holmes? Because you will surely be caught.'

'I'm not an idiot!' he snapped. 'I'm sorry. I promise you this. I will not venture one step beyond that door. Count on it.'

'I want your word.'

He sighed in resignation. 'You have my word. And be very careful, Watson. The murderer could be still within the house.'

After a quick consultation with Holmes's detailed floor plans, I returned to the library taking our back way. With Pomeroy's arrest, most of the household had settled into stunned grief and there were few about. But the library was now locked from both ends.

Breaking the lock was out of the question. Surely they had someone standing vigil with poor Lady Pellingham. And offering my services would get me nowhere, of that I was sure. This was a senseless plan and unlike Holmes to suggest it.

I next tried the kitchen and succeeded only in acquiring the biscuits and hot milk that were my excuse, and the information that the coroner, one Hector Philo by name, was also the town doctor, and was busy with a difficult childbirth and would not appear to collect the body until the morning.

Lady Pellingham's body had meanwhile been laid out in the larder, which was kept very cool, and was guarded by two servants. I also learned that Pomeroy had been removed to gaol, and Dickie was nowhere to be found.

I made my way carefully back to the room, slipped inside our door and bolted it behind me in relief.

CHAPTER 21

On the Ledge

pon entering, I noticed the room was dark and freezing cold. Something was wrong.

'Holmes,' I called out in a loud whisper. There was no answer. I could not make out anyone in the bed. I set down the biscuits and milk and moved to the nearly extinct fire, and turned up the gaslight above it. The room was empty. The window was wide open and the curtains were flapping in the wind. In a panic I checked my room; he wasn't there, either. I locked my outer door and ran to the open window in his room.

There was a small Juliet balcony outside and I stepped on to it. The icy air assailed me, so cold it was hard to breathe. 'Holmes?' I whispered tentatively. My voice was lost in the wind.

Maybe he had lied to me and had gone off into the house. But the wheelchair sat behind me in the room. Would he have taken such a foolish risk?

Then I heard a faint cry. 'Watson!'

I stared into the darkness but could see nothing on the ground below. 'Holmes? Where are you?'

'Right below you!'

And then I spotted him – several feet down and spread-eagled flat like a spider against the side of the building. His toes were balanced on a drainage pipe and long fingers clenched vines growing up the side of the ancient structure.

'At the risk of stating the obvious, I am a bit stuck,' he said, smiling crookedly up at me.

I extended a hand down to him but could not reach. I leaned further out.

'You are not secure, Watson! Knot the blanket around the balcony rail and throw me the end.'

I did as he said and in minutes he was safe in the room, locking the windows behind him and drawing the heavy drapes over them. He turned to face me, stomping his bare feet and rubbing his hands.

'My God, the fire is dead! Can you get it going, Watson? I can't bear to call anyone else in here tonight.'

I stared at him without moving, furious. He had endangered himself, and the entire case, with this ridiculous game. 'Holmes, you've been an idiot,' I said. 'Light it yourself.'

He danced around in pain from the cold. If he had not just jeopardized everything, it might have been funny. But his face was white and his whole body convulsed in shivers from the exposure. He had a manic quality, and concern overrode my anger. I approached and grabbed his hands. A quick examination of his fingers revealed no frostbite. He had been lucky; remarkably so.

He yanked his hands away and shouted, 'The fire, Watson, build the fire! Come on!' He tore a blanket from his bed and wrapped it around himself with a moan. 'Yes, yes, a mistake! And not my only one.'

I got the fire sparked, then stepped to one side to let him closer to it. He sat down, and as he pulled on heavy socks, I surreptitiously removed the packet of sedatives from my pocket and slipped some of the powder into the milk I'd brought up from the kitchen.

'Warm milk. Drink this.'

'Tell me what you found,' he snapped.

I related it to him as he sat there, shaking. He did not take the drink and I pressed it into his hands.

'You sent me on a fool's errand. Drink this, now. Come on, Holmes, you've risked frostbite and a fall, and for what? Here, I'll fix the fire.' I leaned in to poke the kindling.

'Through the windows, I discovered the body is in the larder, the coldest room in the house,' he recounted. 'It is well guarded. And the library has been rearranged, as I suspected!'

'I learned nothing in addition to that. Holmes, we have lost this round and we are done for the evening. You are overwrought, and it is time to rest.'

The kindling ignited the logs and the warmth began to spread through the room. Holmes sat down on the edge of his bed, the picture of dejection. It was rare that he was beaten during a case, and he never took it well.

I put one more log on the fire so it would last. I felt a growing concern about his judgement and evident mania.

Perhaps sleep would change things for the better. I turned to look at him.

My sleeping draught had evidently taken effect, and he had collapsed backward on to the bed, snoring lightly. Momentarily proud of this minor success, I rolled him to the centre, threw the rest of the covers over him and turned to leave when something caught my eye.

He'd dumped the drugged milk into a bowl on the nightstand.

I sighed and retired to the next room. My own rest came slowly. I was deeply troubled by the violent death and by our evident failures here tonight. A woman had been murdered as we visited her home, her child still missing, and an innocent man framed. Our original client was doing God knew what in London with a questionable ally, and we were helpless, right now, to do anything about any of it.

But even worse, I had begun to doubt our own abilities. Holmes and I had made one mistake after another. Had the few months of my new marriage made such a difference? Had I gone soft? Or had Holmes recently suffered so in gaol that he'd been damaged in some way?

To quiet my disturbed thoughts, I willed myself to think of my sweet Mary. Sleep came at last. But Lady Pellingham's horrifying dead face with its bulging eyes haunted my dreams – and would for many nights to come.

CHAPTER 22

A Terrible Mistake

n the circus, there is an expression, 'the show must go on'. It describes a certain ethos which can no less apply to the upper classes in England, for whom any outward display of a ripple on the water is a mark of weakness.

And so, the next morning, precisely as if the mistress of the house had not been murdered the night before, a sumptuous breakfast was laid out on the sideboard of the large, chilly morning room. Holmes and I sat at the table, staring out the windows at a vast expanse of snow and black trees in the distance.

We were alone in the room. 'Watson,' Holmes whispered, 'you must go up to town. Make some excuse. Cable Mycroft that the statue is nearby and will be delivered tomorrow near noon. I shall remain, if allowed, to see what I can discover about the murder. Meanwhile, you must intercept the coroner and get in his good graces.'

'What about our client?'

'We must trust that she will be safe in Vidocq's hands; Mycroft will see to it. Emil is likely to be with her by now. But until I unravel the situation here and see the Earl behind bars, we risk having the boy wrenched from our protection and legally returned into the jaws of danger. He is especially vulnerable now that Lady Pellingham is dead.'

'Then the Earl *is* the danger, is that your theory?'

'I do not have enough data to be entirely sure. That is why I must stay.'

'Do you think the murder is connected to the child? Or the art?'

'It remains unclear.'

'Surely the Nike will not be delivered here in the circumstances.'

'It cannot be stopped, I wager,' said Holmes but before we could continue, a footman entered with coffee and began to refill our cups. Mason, too, entered the room and approached the table.

'Gentlemen,' he began. 'I beg your pardon for the interruption, and for the news I bring you. In light of the recent tragedy, the earl will be unable to host you further. He begs your forgiveness but asks that you return to London this morning.'

Holmes's disappointment was real. 'Certainly, Mason,' he replied. 'I shall write to him soon, but please convey our deepest sympathy and gratitude for his hospitality.'

Whether what happened next was intentional or an accident I may never know. But at that instant, the footman who had been pouring coffee for Holmes stumbled and splashed a quantity of the boiling liquid onto Holmes's leg. Unable to control the reaction, he jumped and then immediately realized his unavoidable mistake.

Mason stared at Holmes in surprise which quickly became a cool fury. 'Leave us,' he barked to the footman. He turned to Holmes. 'I do not know what your game is, sir, but you are an impostor. Were it not for our current tragedy, I would see you gaoled within the hour. But I must attend to other things. You two will be on the next train for London or I will personally see you arrested. Trust me, there *will* be consequences.'

Within minutes we were escorted from the estate, loaded into a rough wagon with our jumbled luggage, and after a tumultuous ride during which Holmes and I sat silent, deposited at the railway station in Penwick. Our luggage was dumped on to the roadway next to us, where mine broke open, spilling its contents on to the frozen slush.

As I began to gather my things, Holmes pulled some clothing from his own and barked, 'Hurry, Watson. Store our things in the station while I change; we must be off to the gaol! Pomeroy may be able to help us, and we him.'

At that point he ducked into a lavatory, and emerged minutes later, with Prendergast completely eradicated, and Holmes now in his place. The speed of my friend's transformation was astonishing. But there was no time to ponder this.

Rushing down the street, we were unsure of our directions and paused to ask one of the few people about this early.

It was a young man of our own age heading purposely down the High Street. He was slender, well dressed and copper-haired, with round gold spectacles, an earnest, open face – and carrying a doctor's bag. I asked him directions to the gaol, and to my surprise, he said he was going there himself. His name, he offered, was Dr Hector Philo, and he was the town doctor.

'Ah, then you are the coroner as well, correct?' said I.

'Why, yes, I am,' said the young man. Holmes and I exchanged a worried look. Why was he headed for the gaol and not for the estate? I was bursting with questions but Holmes warned me with a glance. He adopted a pleasant, casual tone.

'We are going to the gaol, also,' said Holmes. 'Do you mind if we accompany you?'

'I would be relieved, actually,' said the young man. 'It's never a comfortable visit there.'

The gaol was some distance from the station and as we made our way through the icy streets, past shuttered stores and markets beginning to open for the day, Holmes continued his conversation with Dr Philo. But the young doctor grew nervous and more reticent. Finally, to redirect the questions from himself, he inquired after ourselves – our names, professions, and from whence we came.

To my great surprise, Holmes told him. 'My name is Sherlock Holmes, of London,' said Holmes pleasantly, 'I am a consulting detective. Perhaps you have heard of me.'

At that the young man stopped dead in his tracks.

'My God!' said Philo in amazement. 'I have indeed! My

wife Annie and I read of your adventure! He turned to shake our hands with enthusiasm. 'And you must be Dr Watson! Oh, I can't tell you how happy I am to see you both . . . your scientific method . . . the remarkable way you . . . but . . . what are you doing here? Now?'

'Later,' said Holmes. 'You say you admire my methods?'

'Oh, most definitely. While I'm a country practitioner primarily, I've become the *de facto* coroner in these parts, quite against my preferences, but I tell you, Mr Holmes, there has been many an instance where I wished to discuss my findings surrounding a death with someone of your and Dr Watson's experience!'

'Have you come across a suspicious death then, Doctor?' Holmes asked.

'Yes, and more than one. But . . . ah . . . we approach the gaol. We cannot speak freely here.'

'And why is that?'

'The magistrate, Boden. He . . . he is a dangerous man. Judge and jury all in one. He's set himself up as the final word around here, and woe betide the man who opposes him.'

'But there is due process,' I exclaimed. 'How is this possible?'

Dr Philo looked at us both in a high state of anxiety. 'We are remote from London. I believe money has changed hands, to overlook . . . but, I shall give you my theories later.' He then looked over at the gaol and paused, uncertain.

'What is it, man?' I asked.

Philo stood there with his eyes closed. 'God forgive me,' he said. 'I fear that I'm to write the death certificate for some poor soul arrested last night – died, no doubt while imprisoned.'

It was as though an electric shock passed through Sherlock Holmes. 'Inside, at once!' he cried and barged into the gaol. I had no idea of his plan, for even if Boden did not recognize him out of disguise, he surely would recognize me. And perhaps word of our fraudulent identities had already reached the magistrate. Philo and I ran in after Holmes.

At the desk we learned with relief that Boden had gone home to sleep off the night's activities. Facing us was a large, ponderous, straw-haired man with a thick, waxed moustache and lumpy face. Bottoms was his name, and had he an ass's head he would not have appeared more dense.

He peered at us with suspicious small eyes, but Philo told him that we were consultants of his and had been invited there by Boden. Bottoms blinked a few times considering this, asked us to sign a kind of visitors' ledger, where Holmes and I supplied pseudonyms, and then ushered the three of us to a dank cell. It was so cold inside this chamber that our breath was visible.

There, to our horror, we discovered Pomeroy lying on his back on a wooden bench, motionless and deathly still. He was in shirtsleeves despite the freezing temperature. Philo rushed to him and took his signs. 'Alive,' he said, 'but barely. He is in shock.' Then, to me, 'Doctor, help me examine his back.'

Gently we both sat the poor valet up and, despite my wartime experience, even I felt a wave of revulsion.

The back of Pomeroy's shirt was black with blood, sliced into ribbons with the shreds embedded into a series of deep gashes. The man had been whipped, severely, with his clothing still on.

'What the devil has happened here? He's been here less than six hours!' I said, as I sat and cradled the poor man's head while Philo prepared an injection of a stimulant. 'Has he been sentenced and punished all at once, in the night?'

'Exactly,' said Philo. 'And he is not the first.'

He plunged the needle into the limp figure. The man remained still as death for several seconds. Then young Pomeroy breathed a deep sigh and was still. 'We have lost him,' said Dr Philo. We laid him gently down.

I had been so preoccupied with our patient that I had not noticed Holmes. He was off to one side, in an agony of remorse. He spoke in a whisper. 'I am such a fool. A fool! . . . God forgive me!'

'Holmes, no one could have predicted this!'

'We were warned. It all fits. The two people who conspired to hide Emil are dead. This Boden is part of a larger plan. Come! We must leave at once!'

Outside, and once again well away from the gaol, we walked quickly, taking a circuitous route through the town, careful that we were not followed. Holmes barraged the doctor with questions, and Philo answered them all.

'Yes,' said Philo, 'there were a series of deaths, here in town and in the surrounding area.'

'Have any of the deaths been children?' Holmes asked.

Philo started. 'Why yes! That is, three children have gone missing from the silk mill fifteen miles away. Three bodies were found but I cannot say the cause of death, other than each was beaten and possibly assaulted.'

'How old?'

'Perhaps nine or ten. No one knows exactly; they were orphans.'

'When?'

'Over the last six months. They were, I am sure, illegally conscripted from a local orphanage.'

'How did you come by this information?'

'I have a friend at the orphanage,' said Philo, ashamed. 'I regret that I could do so little.'

'And here, in the gaol – how many prisoners have been punished without trial?'

'I cannot say. I am only called as coroner. But four have been killed in a manner similar – well, one hanged himself – since Boden took office here. A number of men in this town live in fear, and it is thought that I am complicit. Which,' he added sadly, 'in a sense I have been.' Here he paused, and swallowed.

'And why is that?'

Philo looked down in shame. 'My wife has been threatened, and I, too . . .'

'Yes, of course. But why have you not cabled London about the deaths? About the children?'

'I have cabled Scotland Yard three times with no response.'

Holmes took this in. 'Yes, and you mailed photographs, correct?'

Philo nodded in shame.

'The situation is dangerous; I understand your position. But you have found your allies and we will not let you down. We must be off. I trust you have urgent business at Clighton. Take care there.'

Philo was puzzled. 'What business at Clighton?'

Holmes looked at him in surprise. 'You have not been called to the manor?'

'Is someone ill?'

Holmes paused. 'Watson, come with me at once. Our cable cannot wait. Then we must locate the body and examine it!' He spun on his heel and took off back towards the High Street at a run.

Dr Philo turned to me, imploring. 'Whose body, Dr Watson? Tell me!'

'Lady Pellingham was murdered last night.'

'My God!'

'The cause of death is unclear, Dr Philo,' I added, quickly relating the details I had observed regarding the stab wound and the lady's expression. 'We were hoping to examine the body more closely but have not been able.'

'If allowed, I will do so,' said Philo sadly. He handed me his card. 'Here is the address of my home and surgery. Pray visit me shortly, and we can talk more freely. I have more to tell you, and in fact need your help.'

I took the card. 'I will see that Holmes gets this,' I said and hurried after my friend.

I had to run to catch up with Holmes, whose long strides had him half a block away. 'Holmes,' I cried, running after him.

He whirled and barked at me, 'Quiet, man! The entire world need not know we are here.'

'But what next?' I asked, catching my breath. 'The place is lawless. We cannot do this alone!'

'I'll inform Mycroft and Scotland Yard. The post office, quickly! I noticed it on the way here. We have no time to lose. By now Boden will have been alerted to our presence. I will have Mycroft's men standing by on our signal, tomorrow morning,' he continued. 'In the meantime we must attempt to view the body, and lie low as much as possible.'

As we moved towards the post office into the dull winter sunlight, I caught a glimpse of something which nearly stopped my heart. In front of a tobacconist to my left was a newsboy, hawking the morning London paper.

There, on the cover, the headline shouted, 'Blood on Baker Street! Sherlock Holmes and Paramour Feared Dead!'

I grabbed the paper and read. 'Missing and feared murdered, the famous detective Sherlock Holmes was apparently living in flagrante with a female companion, believed to be French and of a theatrical profession. Chaos, destruction and a large quantity of blood was found in the detective's residence on Baker Street, discovered by the local policeman, who was alerted to an incident by a passer-by. Inspector Lestrade of Scotland Yard . . .'

I read no further but caught up with Holmes outside the

post office. 'Read!' I gasped. As he did, his pale face grew even whiter.

'Watson, you must return to London at once. Oh, this is a disaster on all fronts! Our client, if she is still alive, is in peril. Who knows if they have located Emil? Oh, I have been an idiot on all counts. An idiot! Go and meet Lestrade. Find out what happened at 221B and find Mademoiselle La Victoire. Get Mycroft's help if the answers are not clear.'

'But, Holmes! Why not return to London yourself? What can you do here?'

'Watson, I must see about the children at the mill, and discover Lady Pellingham's murderer. Don't you see? It is all connected. If Emil is dead it will not matter; but if he is alive, he will not be safe until I unravel the mystery here! I must arrange for the Earl to be taken as promised. Everything points to the manor, don't you see?'

'It is all too much,' I argued. 'We must get help.'

'Watson, there is no choice. I will take care; see that you do the same. Look, the ten sixteen for London has pulled into the station. Run!'

I handed Holmes Dr Philo's card. 'Here is an ally at least. I will send a telegraph in our code, care of him.'

'Good man. I shall wire you at Baker Street. Now go!'

PART SEVEN

TANGLED THREADS

'Life and death are one thread, the same line viewed from different sides.'

Lao Tzu

CHAPTER 23

Terror Looms

he train to London was moderately full, and as we steamed southward in the bright morning light, I found a seat by the window in a first-class compartment. There I stared at the passing scenery, ice crystals on the train windows adding another wintry dimension to the vast expanse of white beyond. My mind was in turmoil.

The plight of our client and her son weighed heavily upon me. Whatever had transpired at 221B had certainly caused injury, though to whom and to what extent remained to be discovered. As I often did on a case, I carried with me my medical bag.

I would need every ounce of strength and concentration for the task ahead. I once again willed myself to rest, and sleep overtook me. I did not awaken until the train pulled in to Euston.

While I slept, however, my friend was tirelessly active, yet another instance of his legendary stamina during a case.

I shall depart here from my normal narrative to relate his doings over these next hours, exactly as Sherlock Holmes later recounted them to me.

'After seeing you off at the station, Watson, I retrieved my valise and effected a quick change into the guise of a Scottish labourer, red-haired and bearded. If the rumours were correct, and orphans were being conscripted into the Earl's nearby silk mill, I needed proof. And if those were the children whose bodies were later found and featured in the horrific photographs given to us by Mycroft, then there was no time to be lost.

'The events surrounding this strange and privileged Earl held more than one mystery to be solved. I could not shake off the feeling that Emil's disappearance, the missing children, the stolen statue, and the two recent murders were all tied together somehow. The secret lay at Clighton, but the two people most likely to shed light on the matter – Lady Pellingham and the go-between Pomeroy – were now dead. Until the Earl could be caught red-handed receiving the Nike, he remained out of reach.

'More evidence, more data was needed. If our suspicions of misconduct were correct, visitors to the mill would be most unwelcome. However, as the humble and hungry "Bill MacPherson", desperate for work and ready to be exploited, I was readily admitted to make my application. Cap in hand, and suitably cowed, I found myself presently in an anteroom off the foreman's office awaiting my interview.

'Seated on a wooden bench in this dusty waiting area, I

could glimpse part of a more luxurious foreman's office through one open doorway. A second door looked into a large work area, and I could see a sliver of its vast collection of complex machinery.

'It was a remarkable array of mechanized arms, spinning, separating, winding and weaving the colourful threads to make up the luxurious cloth which – from the sweat of the men and women who tended these machines – would soon grace the figures of the well-to-do worldwide.

'But at what cost to human suffering? I shuddered to view these slaves to machinery rushing to feed, pedal, push, pull, wind, thread, and frankly nurse these infernal devices at a speed that would tire a champion athlete. The work required numbing repetition for which the human brain was never designed.

'I would sooner walk the treadmills in Pentonville Prison, my dear Watson, than toil daily at this mill. The groaning roar of this great room leaked into the small area where I sat, and the rhythm of the machines shook the very floorboards.

'If there were children at work, they were not visible from my position. They would most probably be kept hidden. Children had formerly been worked to exhaustion, housed in chilly garrets, and denied schooling – treated little better than slaves. But that is illegal now. Children of school age can be no more than "half-timers", receiving schooling for part of the day. But here, far into the countryside, and protected by the cloud of immunity which seemed to surround this Earl, anything might be possible.

'I needed to find the children, if any, and question them. I left my designated bench and made my way on to the main floor. There, I passed unnoticed for several minutes, so engrossed was each man and woman in their time-critical ministrations to these hungry machines.

'Hair was tied back in caps and ribbons, clothing was tight on the arms and body, or wrapped to be so to prevent fatal entanglement, or God forbid, any delay to the production. Despite the frigid outdoor temperature, the heat from the many bodies, and from the whirring and clacking machinery, made the atmosphere at once dank and stuffy.

'As I walked down a central aisle, I observed the ashen faces of these slaves to machinery. One young woman, no more than twenty, ran up and down the row of a complex set-up of skeins unwinding twisted thread onto bobbins, her actions driven by the need to feed successive bobbins rapidly. One misstep and she could easily have become entangled. As I watched, she stumbled and cried out, quickly regaining her balance and running again to the end.

'Near her, an old man, his wrists braced by leather cuffs, fed threads into a whirring loom over and over, his face a mask of pain, his hands no doubt the source.

'The sound was a dull roar, punctuated by the occasional shout from a foreman or team member, and ranging in pitch from a piccolo whirring sound to the deep boom of equipment – the complexity of the tumult enough to trouble every ear.

'It was a kind of mechanical, steam-driven, Sisyphean hell.

'As you know, Watson, I am no enemy of technology and progress, in theory – nor indeed in all of its practice. A telephone, for example, may very well be in our future at Baker Street.

'And in all fairness, not every worker seemed distressed. Some handled their work with a detached ease, apparently suited both physically and mentally to their tasks. As I moved among them, it happened that I grew briefly distracted.

'I had read of the Jacquard loom, of course, but here was a close view of the complex workings of this brilliant invention. Cardboard cards, approximately three by ten inches, with holes punched in them, and sewn by threads into long sequences, were fed into a machine, one by one. Each card then dictated, by means of its code, the placement of threads of specific colours into the warp and woof of the fabric being woven, so as to create patterns of great complexity. A rich paisley of blues and reds was forming before my eyes, directed by the mechanical guiding force of the punched cards.

'I pondered this briefly. If a man could harness this technology for executing a pattern, I thought, what other actions or processes might be enhanced by such a collection of cards with holes in them? Could a complex action or decision be broken down in such a way as to write this code to recreate it? To perhaps solve a puzzle or mathematical challenge that required many iterations of minutely changing calculation?

'Certainly in my own work, the most complex situations

were often untangled by attention to tiny details and their aggregate meaning. But if not deduction, might not induction be replicated with inorganic materials powered by steam? Perhaps eventually one might even simulate human thought and action.

'Fascinated by these ideas, I nearly missed seeing what I had come for. A child's cry drew my attention to one corner of the room. There, tucked away from the others, four boys stood in front of rows of large spools, busily engaged in silk throwing. They ran long threads between bobbins to twist them into weavable form. One boy stood back, crying, his finger spurting blood.

'A heavy-set man nearby turned to the child and, grabbing the injured hand, yanked it forward, inspected it and then leaned in to the boy with a sneer. "Trying to get some attention and time away, are we?" he intoned fiercely. "We'll see about that!"

'With a snarl, the man produced a filthy handkerchief from his pocket. To my disgust, he bound up the cut finger so tightly that the boy cried out again. He flung the child towards the rows of spools, where the boy landed on the floor. "Back to work, you little worm. And no supper for you."

'Repelled, I made a mental note that once I had taken care of Boden and the Earl, I would make London aware of conditions at this mill immediately.

'"You!" came a high-pitched shout above the clattering roar. "You there, MacPherson!"

'I looked down the long aisle past the clamouring wood

and metal beasts. The foreman and the clerk who had asked me to wait were at the far end, pointing at me. I shrugged apologetically, trying to appear lost.

'But the foreman gestured in fury, and from behind him, two large workers charged towards me. It was not the time to negotiate. I turned and ran.

'At the end of the large work chamber were two doors. The first was locked, and as the men drew nearer, I quickly opened the second, which led to a small narrow stairway.

'As I clambered down the steep wooden steps, they creaked under my weight. I came to a door, which was locked from my side. I drew the bolt and dashed inside, knowing I could easily be trapped. But the alternative presented even lower odds.

'It was a kind of storage room. Huge bales of raw silk, bound in linen sacks lined the chill, damp room. I slammed the door behind me, jammed a chair against the door latch and looked about for a means of escape. A filthy pane of glass glowed dimly at the far end and I ran to it, down a narrow aisle between the stacked bales. Dust blew around me as I hurried past.

'My pursuers arrived at the door, and I could hear their struggles and shouts. The chair rattled at the bolt.

'The window was sealed shut. Looking around for something with which to break it open, I was astonished to notice a small boy tucked back into the shadows, sitting on a pile of shabby blankets and watching me with curious interest. He was no more than ten or twelve.

'"Hello," he said. "Unlock me, please."

207

'The door continued to rattle.

'The boy held up a skinny arm. It was handcuffed to a ring on the wall. Next to him, I quickly noticed, were several other rings and a nest of similarly threadbare blankets and some straw. A dirty, torn stuffed animal made out of a sock was just visible under one of the blankets.

'Children were being kept here as slaves, or so it appeared. Watson, you know I am not a sentimental man, but this was unthinkable.

'The door shook again and I could hear the voices recede.

'The child stared up at me. "I can help you," he said boldly. A long shank of filthy brown hair partially obscured his eyes.

'Whether or not this was true, I would not leave the child like this. I approached him, withdrawing a small lock pick from my usual kit.

'"Are you being punished?" I asked.

'"We sleeps here. But today, yes."

'"Why?" He did not answer. In seconds I had him free.

'"Can I have that?" he asked, having watched in fascination.

'More voices returned and louder beating at the door. Keys were tried. *Idiots.*

'"Perhaps. Later. Is there another way out?"

'He surprised me with a grin. "Might be."

'A splintering crash at the door told me they had brought something to ram through it.

'"This is not the time for bargaining."

'The boy stayed silent and continued to stare.

'"What do you want?"

'"That little fingie."

'"Fine." I gave him one of my picks.

'"And . . . somefing else."

'Another splintering crash sounded. I was being out-manoeuvred by a ten-year-old.

'"What?"

'"Take me wif you when you leave."

'It was my intention anyway, but I nodded as if he'd won. Quickly the boy led me to one corner of the room. There he slid a large box across the damp stones, pulling back a dirty canvas to reveal a crude hole in the wall. Squeezing through it after the boy, and barely through a narrow passage, I arrived at an outdoor alley.

It was blocked at both ends with high gates and barbed wire. The boy gestured up to a rusty ladder leading to the roof. He clambered up like a monkey, and I followed.

'This was evidently a well-used route for him. The ice on the slanted roof was treacherous, but we managed to traverse it in the growing snowfall, only to arrive at a four-foot chasm between our building and the next. Facing us was a newly constructed wing of the mill.

'The boy turned and smiled at me. "You game, then, sir?"

I nodded. He nimbly made the leap with the ease of a spring hare, and then looked back at me. "You sure?" He grinned, daring me to take a chance.

'To his great surprise I easily made the jump with space to spare. "Not bad for an ol' man," he said.

'"Old is a relative concept," I replied.

'A trapdoor in the roof opened into another larger storeroom, which looked to be the despatch room. Boxes and boxes of finished fabric were stacked high. Here the insulation was more efficient and the room a liveable temperature.

'We stopped to catch our breath and to warm our hands next to a vent from which a draught of slightly warmer air wafted from the floor below.

'The boy motioned to me and I followed him to a cramped, secret space behind a pile of boxes, where straw, blankets and a meagre stack of food items were secreted. Several books and magazines were there, as well as a few candle remnants.

'But this was no secret hideaway of a dreamy child who wished to read and think alone. Instead, it had the feral aspect of a wild animal's bolt-hole.

'We sat and could hear the hue and cry for us in the distance.

'"They won't find us here," the boy said. He sighed, and pulled a piece of dirty bread from under a cloth. Green mould covered one side. He carefully broke off that section, and took a piece from the other. He chewed hungrily.

'We regarded each other. He held out a clean piece to me. The bread was revolting, but the gesture was touchingly generous.

'I took it and smiled. "Thank you." I pretended to take

a bite. His sharp eyes missed nothing and he looked askance at me. I took an actual bite.

'"Freddie," he said. "S'my name. You wants to know."

'"Orphan?" I asked.

'He laughed bitterly. "Course not. Me mum will be by directly, wif tea and cake."

'And to protect you from your tormentors, I thought. "Were you taken here from the Willows Orphanage?" I asked.

'"Who is it wants to know?"

'I sighed, debating my next move. Then I noticed a dog-eared, stained issue of last year's *Beeton's Christmas Annual* edging out from under a blanket. I recognized it instantly as the one containing the first of your – forgive me, Watson – rather lurid accounts of our adventures. "Are you a reader, then?" I asked.

'He followed my glance and tucked the magazine out of sight. "I reads a little," he said guardedly.

'"The orphanage taught you?"

'"Me mum. Before the orphanage. Now I asks again. 'Oo are you?"

'"Freddie, you may have read of me. My name is Sherlock Holmes," I said. "I have come to investigate the disappearance of several children from this mill. Do you happen to know anything about this?"

'Freddie paused with a glance to where the magazine was stashed. He wanted to believe but could not. "You ain't no Sherlock Holmes. 'E don't look like you."

'But of course he was right! I was still "Bill MacPherson,

day labourer". I took off my cap and my wig of red, curly hair, revealing my own dark hair, and then pulled off my long sidewhiskers and moustache, sitting before him now as myself. Once again his jaw dropped open.

'"Cor!" he said. "You're 'im!"

'I suppose there are benefits to your accounts, Watson. "About those missing children?" I asked. "Be quick, Freddie, it's time to leave."

'Once the floodgates were open, Freddie proved a voluble witness. Three children had disappeared, the last a close friend. All had been from the orphanage, all boys, between ten and twelve years old.

'The abduction itself had not been witnessed, except for the first child, and that not clearly. But Freddie did notice someone he described only as a "very large man" silhouetted against the door to the main floor of the mill. This man had appeared twice around the time of the disappearances. Once he had pointed towards Peter, a small fair-haired child, who was the first to disappear. Peter had been plucked from the mill floor, bodily carried outside, and when he began to moan in fear, was promised "a sweet if he would come quietly". It was the last anyone saw of poor Peter.

'It was then I did something I regret, Watson. I pulled out one of the photos I had brought with me. I showed it to Freddie. He went pale and looked away, with a curse, trying not to cry.

'"You know him?" I asked.

'"It's Peter," he said, in a whisper. "Nice lit'l kid. You got more of those pictures?"

'I should not have shown him even the one. God forgive me, Watson, I denied having others. He turned to me, suddenly fierce.

'"I will kill who done this," he said.

'"No, Freddie. The law will prevail. I will see them punished, I can promise you that," I said. "Now I need you to help me." I questioned him further about the "large man" but Freddie could provide no other description.

'"Did nobody ask about these boys who had gone missing?" I wondered.

'"I did, once, about my other friend Paulie. S'why you see me locked up in there. Told me, 'Keep askin' an' you're next.'"

'"Freddie, we must leave now," said I. "Can you get us outside?"

'He nodded. I wondered why he'd not flown to safety before this.

'"But I gots nowhere to go, Mr Holmes," said he, as if in reply to my very thoughts.

'"Leave that to me," said I.

'So it was that Freddie and I departed for the town. The temperature had dropped even further. I noticed that the boy's threadbare clothing did little to keep his thin frame warm, and I stopped in a small shop and bought him a heavy coat, scarf, hat, mittens and socks.

'But we could not linger in town easily. By now, Boden's

men would have heard of both my charade at Clighton and our visit to the gaol, Watson. They would soon hear of the runaway mill visitor and make the connection.

'What I needed to do before the net closed in on me was to get to the mortuary to examine Lady Pellingham's body. But what could I do with the boy?

'It was then I remembered Dr Philo's card. We made our way to the small, comfortable cottage on the outskirts of town, which housed both his surgery and his home.

'I rang the bell. An impressive young Valkyrie, blonde hair pulled into a knot at the back of her neck, and clothed in the practical skirts and blood-stained pinafore of a wartime nurse, opened the door. She stood there with a questioning look. "Is this an emergency?" she asked, politely but with a tone that brooked no frivolity. "The doctor's hours are over and he's resting now."

'Freddie burst into tears, and immediately the woman softened. Annie Philo, for she was the good doctor's wife, dropped to her knees to face him. "What is the matter, my little man?" she asked kindly. He held his hand out as if injured, and as she took it and examined it closely, he winked up at me. The little devil!

'Dr Philo appeared at his wife's shoulder. "Annie," he cried, "this is Mr Sherlock Holmes, friend of Dr Watson. I've been telling you about him."

'Soon we were warming ourselves by the fire in the Philos' spacious kitchen, plied with soup, tea, and brandy. Freddie ate like a starving pup, making slurping sounds until I admonished him with a look. But our comfort was short-lived.

'When I asked Dr Philo what he had discovered about Lady Pellingham's death, he replied thus:

'"No call came from Clighton," he said. "And so I proceeded to the mortuary on some excuse, and enquired about any deaths within the last twenty-four hours. They had received no bodies but an old farmer who had died of exposure the night before. This astonished me, but it was no use pressing further. I next went to the graveyard, and to my horror I discovered that a burial had taken place only hours earlier.

'"No one would admit it, but I saw fresh earth in one area where the snow had been cleared. When neither coroner nor undertaker is called, one can assume that foul play is at work. Mr Holmes, I believe they buried the lady at three this afternoon!"

'Upon receiving this news, I was struck with an urgency about this case that would not let me rest. I told Dr Philo and his wife that I would depart for the graveyard as soon as it was dark, where I would dig up the body of Lady Pellingham and get to the truth of her murder. I was thankful only that she had not been cremated.

'Dr Philo understood me completely. "I shall go with you," he offered. "The earth will be frozen and hard to turn."

'His wife put a hand on his arm. "You will do nothing of the kind, Hector. You have a family to think of, and if Mr Holmes is caught he could hang for this."

'"But the lady! Justice must be served," he cried.

'"No," I interjected. "I will not allow anyone to accompany me. But if I do not return by morning, wire my brother Mycroft at this address with the enclosed message."'

At this point in his narration, Holmes allowed my interruption, replying, 'I am sorry, Watson, I could not wait for you. This had to be done immediately, and under cover of darkness. And yes, it is true: had you been with me, things might have gone differently. But let me finish—'

I did, and Holmes resumed.

'Doctor Philo set out to provide me with the shovel and pick I needed, as well as a waterproof mackintosh and boots. As Freddie dozed by the fire, Mrs Philo covered him with a blanket and came to me. "I am sorry," she said. "But I hope you understand."

'"Yes. You are pregnant, I perceive."

'"My God!" she exclaimed. "But how did you know? I have not yet told Hector!"

'"Rhubarb on the table, magnesium there, and oranges out of season on your windowsill. You are troubled in the morning with sickness," I said.

'"Oh . . . well, that is obvious now that you mention it!" said she. As usual, Watson, when I give away my methods they seem trivial.

'"Your secret is safe with me, Mrs Philo. In any case, I would not allow him to come. This is my work alone. But I should very much like to rest before it grows dark. Have you a place?"

'As Annie Philo prepared an impromptu bed on a sofa in the study, I stood at the window, looking out. The winds had picked up and a flurry of snow began. A storm was promised for the evening, and I knew that a grave challenge lay ahead, in more ways than one. I was concerned about breaking through the frozen ground, and I hoped I was up to the task.'

CHAPTER 24

Watson Investigates

Arriving at 221B, I ran up the stairs to find the door wide open and Lestrade and his men still there – hours after being called in.

I stared around me in alarm. A violent fight had evidently taken place within our rooms. While 'a large quantity of blood' was not in evidence, furniture *had* been upended, papers were scattered, the vases of flowers overturned and broken, their water adding damp stains on the rug and couch. One of the drapes had been torn.

'My God, what has happened here?' I exclaimed.

'Dr Watson! Ah, what a relief to see you, man! That is what we were hoping you'd tell us,' said Lestrade, rising wearily from the couch and approaching me with a look of defeat. 'We got your wire, and so glad to hear – we were worried about the two of you, Doctor.'

'Holmes is safe in Lancashire,' I said quickly, hoping that was still true. 'What have you found out?'

'That's good news, Doctor. I was fearing we'd be dragging the Thames for your two dead bodies,' said Lestrade.

'But no one else was here when you came?'

'Not inside. But it seems there had been a woman and two others at the time. French, it looks to be. A rather fancy lady, even.' He eyed me with a kind of admiring suspicion. I had no time for this.

'But outside? What did you find? Who called you in?'

'Someone in the street heard noises, and told the local. By the time we arrived, everyone had cleared out.'

'No dead bodies?'

'Well, there was the one. Out front.'

'A man? A woman? Not a child! Come on, Lestrade!'

'Sorry, it has been a very long day. T'was a man about forty, I'd say. Well dressed. Carrying a business card of Mr Holmes's brother, Mycroft Holmes. We think he may have been working for the elder Mr Holmes. We are inquiring—'

'But blood! The newspaper reported blood!'

'We cleaned it already.'

'Why? How can I tell what transpired here?'

'We thought you'd been killed. So in consideration of your Mrs Hudson . . . The good lady was beside herself at the sight of it. Fortunately, she was out at the time of the attack.'

'Thank heavens for that.'

'But of course we have taken our notes and measurements, Doctor. Calm yourself. Mainly it was a pool, right here.' Lestrade indicated a stain on the wood floor next to a window. It had been scrubbed.

'Have you touched or moved anything else?' I demanded.

One of Lestrade's men approached. 'More blood, sir, on the stairway. By the door.'

How had I missed that coming in?

There was a large, dark-red mark along the wall near the front door. I examined it and saw within it a splatter, and then a smear. Using Holmes's methods I deduced that someone had been struck a heavy blow, fallen into the wall, and then been dragged or slid along it, causing the smear.

I felt a frisson of panic. Had it been Mlle La Victoire? Or the child? No, the smear was too high on the wall. Perhaps Vidocq then, or one of the assailants.

I returned upstairs to examine the sitting room closely, attempting to use Holmes's methods. But as most scents are undetectable by humans but obvious to a hound, I am sure there were clues aplenty that were simply unreadable to me.

There was a slash in the couch. Knives. Our black-clad group, perhaps? I glanced around for bullet marks but saw none, except Holmes's previous target practice displaying a 'VR' on the wall.

Thankfully his Stradivarius was safe in a corner. But the chemistry table and equipment were in splinters.

'I fear for the fate of our guests,' said I. 'Tell me what else you've found.'

'First, who might those guests be?' asked Lestrade. 'Maybe that will tell us who came to attack them. The lady in particular, Doctor?'

He looked at me with a smile. His curiosity about 'the lady' bordered on the impertinent.

'A client,' I said crisply. 'Now, again, what have you found?' My friend's impatience with the police grew more understandable by the minute.

'French, I take it?'

'Lestrade! This is dangerous business, and there were three people here, including a child! Our client – and yes, she is French – her small son, and a man who was supposed to be guarding them.'

'All right then; that explains the mess,' he said. 'There was quite a struggle. I'm thinking several men went to it down here in your sitting room. No bodies here; we've covered the place top to bottom. But who left with whom, and under what circumstance, that is the question.'

It was then that I noticed a handcuff hanging from a post on one of our bookcases. What on earth had transpired there?

I ran upstairs to my old bedroom. Throwing open the door I was assailed by the strong aroma of Jicky perfume. A bottle was broken on the floor, along with a crystal decanter shattered nearby. The bed was a wreck, as though someone had leapt from it in a panic. The side table, which had held many a medical book and seafaring novel during my residence, lay on its side. Mlle La Victoire's valise had been overturned from a rack, spilling out delicate lace undergarments.

These were being examined as I entered by a burly young officer, with perhaps more interest than necessary.

'Any clues there?' I asked sharply.

He dropped the delicate item in embarrassment and squinted at me.

'Who are you, sir?' he blustered.

'Dr John Watson, and you are standing in my room. Or rather, what used to be my room.' My outrage at his actions temporarily overruled logic. His eyebrow raised suggestively and he smiled in what could only be described as envious admiration.

'Sorry, sir,' he said. 'Did not mean to pry.'

'A woman and her son were using this room. I'll thank you to keep to your business,' I said.

I looked around for blood but saw none. However, my relief was short-lived. Under the bureau, something caught my eye. I stooped and picked it up. It was a toy horse, its neck broken and lying at an odd angle. The child had been here and his toy crushed! My concerns deepened.

'Ah, we missed that,' said the young copper.

I sighed. If only Holmes were here, he'd have the entire picture in mind by now. I returned downstairs, feeling the strong urge to act, but lacked a direction. Mrs Hudson entered with a tea tray for Lestrade and his men. Upon seeing me, she nearly dropped the tray, but set it down instead on the dining table. She rushed into my arms.

'Oh, Dr Watson! It is too much! Too much!' she cried.

I embraced her warmly. Poor Mrs Hudson – first Holmes and his despair and fire, then these strange French guests and now this. 'But you are all right, Mrs Hudson! Thank heavens!' I said.

'And Mr Holmes?' she asked, still trembling.

'Safe in Lancashire,' I reassured her. 'I must find where our clients have gone or been taken. You heard nothing?'

'I was not here!' she said. 'I'd been called away to my sister's in Bristol, only to find it had been a false alarm. T'was something to get me out of the way, I think!'

I was relieved that Mrs Hudson had been out of harm's way. However, I was also, quite frankly, at a loss as to what to do next. The lady herself provided the answer.

'Come with me, Doctor, I have something for you,' she whispered.

I followed her downstairs to her apartment. She unlocked the door and I stood for the first time in our landlady's small domain. The bright floral wallpaper and cheery entry table bedecked in holiday greenery, coupled with the delicious smell of gingerbread from Mrs Hudson's kitchen, gave me a sudden nostalgic longing for my days spent here with Holmes. While Mrs Hudson was our landlady, not our housekeeper, she nevertheless looked after Holmes and me as a kindly aunt might look after a couple of late-maturing university toffs.

But these thoughts passed quickly. Our clients were in peril. Mrs Hudson approached with a letter from Mycroft at the Diogenes. 'It arrived by messenger two hours ago,' she said. 'How he knew you'd be here, I can't say.'

But Mycroft knew most things. I tore it open and read.

Dr Watson

My brother has no doubt sent you from Lancashire.

Be assured your client Emmeline La Victoire, her son

and Jean Vidocq are safe. My men arrived on the scene but a little late. M. Vidocq's small head wound accounts for the blood you have discovered. However, it is suggested that you join them immediately at the address below where Vidocq brought them to take refuge. At all costs, dissuade the lady and her son from proceeding to Lancashire. Danger may await them both until my plans are consummated.

Mycroft

The address below was a place I knew well.

I made my way by cab through the dusk down Baker Street and east on Oxford Street, cutting south through Hanover Square to arrive at Verrey's, on the corner of Regent Street. This elegant French eatery was a place where Holmes and I had once dined after a particularly well-paying case.

The restaurant was not yet crowded, as it was late for the ladies who frequented the place after shopping, and yet too early for the fashionable diners. The owner at first was reluctant to admit he harboured our client, but at the mention of Mycroft Holmes his manner altered immediately.

He left me at a small door at the end of a flight of stairs behind the kitchen. I knocked. There was movement within but no answer.

'It is I, John Watson,' I called out. 'Mademoiselle La Victoire, I have a message from Mr Holmes.' I heard some angry whispering; then the door was opened a crack, and Mlle La Victoire peered out.

Her face flooded with relief and she let me in. 'Oh, *Mon*

Dieu,' she exclaimed. 'Dr Watson, where is Mr Sherlock Holmes? Only a message? Is he not here?' She glanced at the stairs, in evident hope. Then she flung herself into my arms.

Thank God she was unharmed.

'*Ferme la porte!*' came a gruff voice from behind her. As she closed the door behind us, I noticed Vidocq lying back on a small bed, his head wrapped in a silk scarf from Mademoiselle's vast collection. It was bloodstained, and the Frenchman was pale. And then I got my first glimpse of the child.

Emil sat at a table to one side, slumped and still. His resemblance to his mother was marked – his pale skin, green eyes, and something of the nose resembled her closely, while his blond curls must have been his father's legacy.

But his demeanour concerned me. He was motionless and pale, and as I looked at him, his eyes drifted away, as if in doing so he might become invisible. He began to rock back and forth, humming softly. I'd seen such a condition in men overcome on battlefield. The boy was traumatized.

I looked at his mother. Her eyes were filled with tears. 'He cannot speak,' she whispered.

'*Will* not speak,' snapped Jean Vidocq from the bed.

I hesitated. The physician in me took precedence. The child's condition, while of grave concern, could not be immediately remedied. Mlle La Victoire had suffered no injury, but Vidocq, on the other hand, might well have been concussed.

At the lady's request, I examined Vidocq's head wound.

With no grace whatsoever, he allowed me to unwrap it and I began to clean, stitch up, and dress the superficial but lengthy cut.

'Who attacked you, Vidocq?' I asked. 'What did they want?'

'The same men who attacked us in Paris. They had come to kill your friend.'

'But not you, again?' I wondered, as I pulled out a needle.

'Ahh! Carefully, Doctor!' He winced but I'll admit I was not as sympathetic as I might have been. 'Your friend was clumsy. I believe he managed to show himself while investigating at the docks, and led the villains back to his own home.'

I doubted this. When Holmes wished to travel undetected he was rarely observed, especially in London where he knew every alley by heart. Even I had not recognized him disguised as an ageing seaman.

'Yes, the great Sherlock Holmes makes mistakes,' Vidocq said.

At this Mlle La Victoire interrupted. 'You are lying, Jean. You left for the docks yourself, and wearing Mr Holmes's clothing! If one considers the timing of this attack, it was you who attracted the wolves to the den!'

She and I exchanged a look of understanding. I let it pass. They were safe now, at least for the moment. Finishing with Vidocq, I returned to the child and knelt before him.

'Emil?' I said gently. 'I am Dr Watson. I am a friend of your mo— of Mademoiselle La Victoire, here. This lady who loves you so much. I am here to help you.'

The boy's eyes shifted and rolled; he would not meet my gaze. Instead he squirmed and began to keen, softly. My God, what had happened to this little boy? I needed to examine him but this was not the time or place. I stood and noticed Mlle La Victoire gathering her things.

'What are you doing?' I asked.

'I am going to confront this monster. His father will answer to me for whatever happened to my— to Emil,' she said. 'A train departs for Lancashire in forty-five minutes. Emil and I will be on it.'

Oh, no.

Vidocq sprang from the bed. '*Mais oui!*' he said. 'I will go with you, my darling.'

Idiot! Of course he would wish to go to Lancashire. The statue was due to arrive at any moment!

Not only had Mycroft warned me to dissuade them from returning, but I feared the child's reaction when he discovered the woman he loved as his mother had been murdered. Forcing the child to face this fact in his current state could be a disaster.

'No!' said I, facing Vidocq. Behind him, Mlle La Victoire was gathering her things. 'It is not safe for you to take Mademoiselle and Emil there!'

'And why is that?' asked Vidocq.

I was unsure what to give away at this point. Nor did I wish to reveal all with Emil in the room. I lowered my voice. 'Think of the child! He was sent to London for his own safety. He was not kidnapped. There is danger for him there.'

Mlle La Victoire moved close and put herself between us. 'Where is Mr Holmes now?' she demanded.

'He is seeing to the Earl as we speak,' I said. 'It is a complicated affair, and best left to a professional, Mademoiselle. The police will be called in shortly.'

'Will they? Monsieur Holmes has made many mistakes, *n'est-ce pas*? Perhaps this is another,' said Vidocq. I knew his thoughts were still with the Nike.

'Please,' said I, addressing the lady. 'This is a complex matter. There are other children involved.'

'Other children?' demanded Mlle La Victoire. 'Have other children been . . .' she glanced at Emil and did not wish to continue the sentence.

'Worse, Mademoiselle,' I said. She held my gaze.

'I see,' she said. 'Then if what I fear is true, Emil may never be safe until the evil is put to rest. You say Mr Holmes is on my case? And Vidocq here will journey with us. What of you, Dr Watson? Will you come? With three such men as you, I feel Emil and I will be protected.'

I hesitated. My concern for Holmes was burning in my mind and I was eager to return to Lancashire myself.

'In any case,' said the lady, 'come or stay. I will depart on the next train.'

'And I will be with you,' said Vidocq.

Dashing a quick note to Mycroft, I departed with them for Euston. Within the hour we were seated in a first-class compartment headed for Lancashire. Emil was asleep in his mother's arms instantly, she dozing over her young son. Vidocq and I remained awake. As the train pushed northward into the gathering storm, I gestured him to join me in the corridor outside the compartment where we could speak freely.

'Vidocq,' I said, offering him a cigarette. 'I need some information.' He took it and paused, expecting me to light it for him. I ignored this and he shrugged and lit his own, carelessly tossing the match to the floor.

He then reclined casually against the window, his insouciant smile and scarf bandage giving him the distinct air of a theatrical pirate. He took a few drags, and eyed me through the smoke. 'What do you need?' he asked. God, the man was irritating.

'Tell me what transpired in London while we were gone. What have you learned of the people who took Emil? What have you noticed of the child? Tell me anything else you think may help us in Lancashire.'

He paused, inhaling the smoke and savouring it. Then, stubbing out his cigarette on the floor of the train, he began his tale.

CHAPTER 25

Vidocq's Story

s Vidocq and I stood in the corridor outside
the compartment, dusk descended early beyond
the icy windows of the train. Mlle La Victoire
and Emil dozed within our snug compartment,
visible from where we stood through small openings in the
curtained windows. While I cannot vouch for the accuracy
of our French colleague, I can be sure of my own; I made
notes immediately following this conversation. I believe the
broad strokes, at least, to be true. Here, then, is what Jean
Vidocq told me, in his own words.

'As you well know, Cherie and I visited your friend's
brother Mycroft after our meeting with you in the street.
Neither of us was pleased with his plan; I was instructed
to give up my pursuit of the Nike (thus confirming Cherie's
suspicions that the Nike was my priority, and hardly
endearing me to her!) Mycroft Holmes ordered me to go
to an address in Bermondsey where his men had positively
located Emil. I was informed that your friend had located

the statue at the London docks, but Mycroft Holmes assured me that he had arranged with the Sûreté that the Nike would be returned to France and that I would share credit in her recovery – in return for my cooperation now.

'I fully realized that I was being pushed aside so that Mycroft's noxious brother – no, I will not mince words regarding your friend – could publicly recover the Marseilles Nike, while I was saddled with my darling and her missing son. I will admit that this did not, how do you say, "sit well" with me.

'While I am, of course, not immune to my dear lady's fine sentiment and painful emotions, nevertheless it seemed only logical to ignore this meddling poseur Mycroft Holmes. And, as you might have done in my place, I decided to pursue my most pressing mission first.

'My thinking was this: the statue would no doubt be leaving London in the immediate future for its final destination, while the boy was thought to be safe, and not likely to be moved soon.

'With this priority in my mind, I caused us to return to 221B where I asked Cherie to pack our things for a "hasty departure to Paris" while I would set out alone to retrieve the boy and return him within a few hours. My plan, of course, was a quick visit to the docks first, but naturally I did not confide in her.

'But *hélas!* My darling Cherie would not hear of this. She wanted to go to Emil herself. She had wished to go directly from the Diogenes, and even our return to 221B made her wildly impatient.

'But I suspected another agenda from my dear one. I read a deep fury in her – a seething rage that would not be, how do you say, mollified with the mere rescue of Emil. He was her first priority, but . . . she wanted to know the what, who, and why of his condition. And if the child had been harmed in any way, I knew she would never leave England without revenge.

'A woman's emotions, ah! They are not helpful in our business, *n'est-ce pas?* She stood by the door in your friend's apartment, furious, irrational, refusing to let me go alone. I knew at once that she could easily jeopardize my own mission, as well as the rescue of her son. I made a sudden decision.

'"Cherie, my darling," I said. "Come! Look out the window here. Is there someone in the street below, who has followed us? We may have to take evasive measures to retrieve Emil!"

'She approached the window and looked down. "Oh my God," she said. "There *is* someone there! I saw this man outside the Diogenes not twenty minutes ago, Jean! It cannot be a coincidence."

'But . . . what was this? I had enticed her to the window with a ruse, in order retrieve something from my valise – which I now hid behind my back. But was there *vraiment* someone?

'Concealing the object in my pocket, I joined her and drew back the curtain. My darling was right. There, across the street, was a man huddled under the eaves, attempting to conceal himself. As we regarded him, he looked up at the window. *Alors!* But perhaps I could use this. I closed the curtain and took Cherie's hand in mine.

'"Darling," I said, "it would be safest if you remain here. I can lead him away and evade him myself more easily, and it will be in Emil's best interest."

'It would have gone better for us both had she acquiesced. "Never!" she said. "I will go with you to Emil. He will not come away with a stranger."

'Alas, I disagreed. With a quick move, I removed the pair of handcuffs I had hidden in my pocket and secured my darling lady to the post of a large bookcase in your *salon*.

'In the South of France, we have a special kind of wind. It seems to arise from nowhere and hits with a fury that can take down a small house. It is called *le mistral*. And that was precisely the response of my delicate flower.

'With a kick aimed at my most vulnerable area followed by a sharp right from her free hand, I was knocked backwards on to the floor, a pot of her damned flowers crashing down upon my head.

'"*Salaud!*" she screamed, which I will not bother to translate. There followed a barrage of words and wild struggling. Arising from the floor, I picked up a chair and gently extended it towards her, as one would approach a circus lion. She obliged me with a roar.

'My intention was only to give her a place to rest as she waited for me, but she wrenched the chair from my hands and flung it across the room. It barely missed some old violin – I'm sorry, but what is "a Strad"? In any case it took down a small table covered with chemistry equipment which shattered on the floor. Some bubbling liquids went everywhere. The smell!

'Foiled in this attempt to give her comfort, I grabbed two pillows from the divan and, from a distance, threw them at her. 'Sit!' I shouted over her screams. 'I will be back – with your son!'

'I noticed that my greatcoat and hat were dangerously within her range, so I left them there, and instead grabbed a hat and coat from a stand by the door, and dashed out.

'Once in the snowy streets. I looked around me but the man hiding in the shadows had apparently given up and gone. Perhaps it was not a follower, merely someone taking shelter. But I had better things to do.'

At this point in his narration, I interrupted. 'You left Mademoiselle La Victoire handcuffed and alone? With treachery about?' I demanded. The man was an irresponsible cad!

Vidocq shrugged. 'Ah, Dr Watson. Mr Holmes said it himself; those threatening us are after the statue, and me, not Mademoiselle.'

'But you could not be sure!'

'Reasonably sure. In any case, no one came for her. Let me continue – that is, if you would like to hear of Emil's rescue?'

I acquiesced. It is true, she was not harmed. But I was filled with outrage at the man's callous disregard for the woman he professed to love. I urged him to continue nevertheless.

'*Mon Dieu!* Your London air is freezing,' he exclaimed,

picking up his tale. 'Once on the streets, I put on the clothing I had taken. In my haste, I had grabbed the coat and rather fine top hat that Holmes had worn in Paris. I put them on now; the coat was constricting on my larger frame, and altogether too grand for my next mission. Ducking into an alley, I dented the hat and bent its brim, and smeared some mud and slush on both garments, to age and conceal their finery. I did not wish to be conspicuous in the dockyards, *eh bien?*

'Satisfied with my work, I made my way to the docks. There, proceeding to the address I had read – upside down – during my meeting with Mycroft. It is one of my special talents – what, not so special, you say? In any case, I easily located the Nike herself, covered in layers of canvas and held up by wooden supports. She was well guarded.

'I recognized two of the men from our adventure at Le Chat Noir. I had only to wire Paris now with the Nike's location, thus ensuring my credit in her recovery, as the French could be said to have located her as easily as the English. If the Sûreté had men in London, she would be in our hands by nightfall.

'Departing to send off my cable, I felt that I was being followed, and took evasive action. But I never saw anyone, and completed my mission uninterrupted.

'Now that the statue had been located I could attend to the matter of Emil. I next proceeded to that vile industrial area of London called Bermondsey. *Mon Dieu*, the stench!

'The sweet baking aroma of your Peek Frean's biscuit factory (why you English persist with these tasteless biscuits in face of our far superior patisserie is beyond imagination) combined with the acrid smells of the many tanneries made it difficult to breathe. As I saw others do, I tied a scarf over my nose, and proceeded to the address provided by Mycroft.

'There in a dim little house behind another off the main road, I discovered my quarry. Mycroft told us that Emil had been hidden with a sister and brother-in-law of one of the Earl's servants – a tanner by trade, who had taken in the child and housed him. Whether this action constituted a kidnapping for ransom, or a rescue from some ill treatment at his former home with the Earl, remained to be seen. Who knows?

'I saw through the window a sad little boy, sitting alone at a table, cradling a small toy horse. I recognized him from my darling's description. He was slight, with curly blond hair, introspective – and with that recognizable patina of wealth. This glow, whether it be from an abundance of good food, the lack of physical labour, or even, I think, from not having to worry where one's next *saucisse* would be coming from, was obvious.

'But there was a kind of – how do you say? – deep sadness as well. I saw no physical injuries. And yet something was not right. The child sat with his toy, rocking back and forth mechanically, his face frozen in a blank, sad stare. Something bad had happened to him.

'Few comforts were provided. Aside from his horse, there were no other toys, and the boy's breath was visible in the room. A small bed was made from several straw mattresses in one corner with a few threadbare blankets folded neatly on it. Embers in the kitchen fire were low. The boy must have been suffering.

'There was no time to waste. I circled the house from the outside, peering in at the windows to see who else might be present. It appeared he had been left alone, though for how long I could not guess. I was lucky but needed to act fast.

'Returning to the kitchen, I easily unlocked the window and climbed through it.

'"Emil?" I asked. "Emil? I have come from your mother. I am to take you to her." I forgot that my face was masked against the odours by the scarf. That and my foreign accent must have frightened the boy. I should have realized this.

'The child screamed and backed away from me. He picked up a chair and held it between us. He was his mother's child, certainly.

'I tried reasoning with him. He would not reply either in English or French, nor would he make a move to accompany me.

'"Please, Emil, will you come?" I begged him. Although why indeed would he follow a stranger who terrified him?

'But then I heard the sounds of someone returning through the front door, I gave up being polite. I seized a large canvas bag lying in the corner of the room and threw the child into it.

'*Calmez-vous*, Dr Watson; I did so carefully; I am not a monster! I carried him bodily back to 221B Baker Street. What? Yes, in the bag.

'Now, for my troubles, was I greeted with gratitude and

love upon returning to my darling? *Mais non!* You cannot imagine! I entered your apartment and set down my struggling parcel. Cherie saw the bag move and knew immediately it was Emil.

'The *mistral* became a virago! I was forced to reveal the boy at the opposite side of the room before I dared to approach and unlock her.

'The second she was free, it was as if I had disappeared from the earth. Cherie ran to her son and gathered him in her arms. He hugged her back. There were tears.

'"Emil, *mon cheri!*" she said.

'The boy did not speak and suddenly he backed away in confusion. She was not, after all, the mother that he knew. But a family friend was certainly better than this masked stranger.

'"Ah, my little one. You do know who I am, *non?*" she asked. He nodded. He did recognize her but was still confused. "You are safe, *mon petit*, come to me." He hesitated, then fell again into her arms amid a flood of more tears from them both.

'She covered him with kisses, checked him all over for bruises or signs of injury, and took him upstairs, where she called for a warm bath for the boy.

'Thus abandoned, I discovered a rather choice brandy on the sideboard and settled down to read the evening papers and smoke a very fine cigar I found in a box on the mantelpiece. In this way we spent our evening. She did not speak to me until the child had been safely tucked away in her own bedroom, and was fast asleep.

'There is something to be said for the comforts of your English sitting room, and I was dozing by the fire when she returned downstairs. She entered sheepishly, or so I interpreted it. "Jean," she began, "I cannot get Emil to speak. Was it difficult to rescue him? What condition did you find him? Who was guarding him? Did you suffer danger or injury? What happened?"

'When a woman questions one in such a fashion, there is no use in simple honesty. "No. Silent. No one. No. I threw him in a bag," would never do.

'And so instead, I will admit to a touch of embroidery. Is not a finely embroidered silk *abécdéaire* more beautiful than a piece of plain linen? I was careful to be accurate in my description of the child and his condition, perhaps only a few details gained in the telling. A woman enjoys a good story.

'*Eh non*, Dr Watson, do not look sceptical; this story I tell you is the real one. I assure you.

'I continue. Now grateful, she seemed to forgive me completely on the matter of handcuffing her to the bookcase earlier. Any strong feelings she may have had vanished in the face of her new worry – what had happened to Emil to make him so silent? Even she could not get him to speak, and she was beside herself with concern on this point.

'"I will kill him if he harmed the boy," she said.

'"You refer to the Earl?" I wanted to be sure.

'"Yes. He either hurt Emil, or overlooked something that happened to our child. I will discover what that is, and he will pay. I will make him pay!"

'"*Calmes-toi*, Cherie. I am sure Emil will speak eventually," I said to her.

'"We must leave at once for Lancashire. I will get to the bottom of this!"

'At last we were united in our agenda! Lancashire was exactly where I wanted to be. The statue could very well be heading there in the morning.

'Yes, yes, and of course to help the lady. Dr Watson, do let me finish.

'I needed to delay her, however, to make certain it actually left London. I said, "*Ma Cherie*, shouldn't Emil rest the night here? He is asleep, *n'est-ce pas?* What is best for the child?"

'Seeing reason, she agreed to travel in the morning, but without even a kiss goodnight, she retired to our room where she had put Emil to sleep in our bed and closed the door. Then the door opened and she threw my sleeping clothes out and down the stairs, closing the door again.

'This left me either the *salon* or Sherlock Holmes's room for my own repose. I entered it and looked around. *Mon Dieu!* So cold and empty, the bed so hard and narrow, the books and papers everywhere, wax from many a night-burning candle, an ashtray overflowing with cigarette butts, a small, cold fireplace with no wood nearby, a large tin box, and strange photos of criminals lining the walls. I would sooner sleep in a demented monk's cell!

'Returning to the sitting room, I collected various cushions, a soft red blanket which hung over a chair, and made myself infinitely more comfortable on the couch. Sleep came easily.'

At this point I could not contain myself. In spite of the urgency of the tale, I was infuriated at Vidocq's casual violation of our, or rather Holmes's, private sanctum.

'Have you no propriety, man?' I exclaimed. 'Except to attend to illness or injury, and once to search for . . . er, something, I have never ventured into Holmes's bedroom, nor would I consider examining it in this way.'

'Perhaps you should,' Vidocq said. 'It pays to really know with whom one associates. Holmes's asceticism borders on martyrdom, you know.'

I objected to this, citing the many pleasures Holmes takes in his violin, the opera, museums, and . . .

'And his drugs,' said Vidocq.

'Finish your story,' I said.

Vidocq continued with his tale.

'It was most fortunate that I was in this room and not upstairs with Cherie, as I am convinced we would both be dead had this been the case. I was awakened in the night by the sound of a sudden cry. It seemed to come from outside on the street, and very close by. Then I heard the lock being picked downstairs. I was on my feet in an instant and, seizing a poker by the hearth, I hid behind the door when they entered. There were three of them, black-clad and masked, yet I recognized them as the men we fought at Le Chat Noir.

'I knocked one down, but the second and third caused me considerable – how do you say? – problems. But hearing noises, one left the fight and bounded upstairs, returning with Cherie and Emil at knifepoint as I struggled with the third in the *salon*.

'I will not detail the disaster that followed, but one of them shouted out your friend's name. Evidently they mistook me now for Sherlock Holmes all along! This was his home, after all. And I was in nightclothes. We are both tall. I don't know. I am the more handsome—

'All right, I continue. The men were professionals. I was hampered by the close quarters, the need to protect both the child and his fearless mother, and my lack of hard shoes.

'I managed to take them, killing one, but received a cut on the forehead. Head wounds bleed a lot, and my own blood, mixed with two of the others, was everywhere. I apologize for this mess, but of course you understand.

'Cherie, the boy, and I barely made it alive from the place. We took our clothes and ran. In our haste, we nearly tripped over a body at the entrance. It was the man whom we'd seen waiting in the shadows earlier, who had followed me to Bermondsey. Mycroft Holmes's man, I thought, but had no time to check – no doubt it was his death cry I'd heard at first.

'We escaped into the night. Through the dense fog, I saw the two remaining attackers escape down a side street with the body of their comrade.

'Not too far from Baker Street is the restaurant *français*, Verrey's. It is owned by a friend of mine. Cherie, Emil and I ran and took refuge there. My friend, he keeps a small room upstairs for guests. Cherie did her best for my poor head; then she and Emil fell asleep as I warmed my frozen feet by the small fire. It was there you found us, Doctor.'

Vidocq finished his cigarette and stubbed it out on the floor, grinding it into the carpet without a care. As if in complaint, the train groaned to a halt.

We entered the compartment where Mlle La Victoire and Emil slept on, unaware. Swirling snow and nothing else was visible outside the windows. The purser arrived shortly and informed us that the storm had made all progress impossible, and that we would be stranded, midway between London and Lancashire, until the tracks could be cleared. It would probably be many hours.

Blankets and tea were brought round. Vidocq shrugged and settled in but I returned to the corridor, attempting to calm my worries with a cigarette. I wondered how Holmes was faring. If he needed my help, there was nothing I could do about it here.

Had it been a mistake to travel to London? I'd recovered our client and determined who had attacked 221B, and possibly why. I could now deliver Mademoiselle and her son to Holmes's safekeeping. Perhaps that was a small consolation. But I felt I'd done little to unravel the mystery surrounding the boy, and wondered if bringing him north at this point was in his best interest. With these uneasy thoughts I retired for the night.

PART EIGHT

THE WASH OF BLACK

'A painter should begin every canvas with a wash of black, because all things in nature are dark except where exposed by the light.'

Leonardo da Vinci

CHAPTER 26

Man Down

ometime in the early hours of the morning our train restarted, and we reached Penwick shortly after dawn. We were awake and ready to descend as the train pulled into the station. However, our little group was in disagreement over precisely what we would do upon arriving.

My first concern was to locate Holmes. Mlle La Victoire wished to find a safe place for Emil, then proceed to Clighton to confront her one-time paramour. However, I'd informed Vidocq of Lady Pellingham's murder and for once, he agreed with me. Mademoiselle's plan was unsafe, and together we convinced her to find Holmes first, and travel as a group, backed up with Mycroft's men, to the estate.

However, none of this was to transpire.

As we descended from the train, a tall, handsome blonde woman in a state of high anxiety rushed up to us. She was accompanied by an emaciated small boy with a fiercely intelligent expression on his young, careworn face.

247

'Dr Watson, I presume?' the woman gasped, out of breath. 'I am Mrs Philo, the doctor's wife. Please come with me quickly. Your friend and my husband are in grave danger!'

With this she turned to Vidocq. 'And you! Are you a friend of Mr Holmes?'

'Sometimes he may think me so,' said Vidocq with a smile, ignoring the lady's apparent distress, or perhaps thinking his Gallic charm would distract this hysteric. Instead it provoked the woman.

'No time for this,' she snapped. 'Friend or foe? Lives are at stake!'

'We are his friends,' said Mlle La Victoire quickly. 'How can we help?'

'What has happened?' I demanded.

'Follow me; I shall relate as we go,' she said. She took off at a run. Leaving our bags with a porter at the station, I ran after her along with Vidocq, but Mlle La Victoire paused. Emil stood rooted to the spot, confused. He was shaking.

The other little boy, who I later learned was the orphan Freddie, instinctively took his hand. Emil looked at him and some understanding passed between the two boys.

The five of us hurried after Mrs Philo.

The bright winter sun came in low over the horizon and slanted through the town, blinding us at certain turns as we pressed on through mounds of snow and along the icy cobblestone streets. The town was nearly deserted, exactly as it had been the morning before. I recognized the route – we were heading to the gaol.

My God, the gaol.

'Fill us in, Mrs Philo. Please!' I gasped, catching up to her.

'Mr Holmes was arrested last night while digging up Lady Pellingham's grave. He did not give in without a valiant fight. This little boy, Freddie, witnessed it. My husband discovered this and went to the gaol to try to help him. Neither has returned. Freddie . . . an orphan . . . I will explain later . . . followed my husband to the gaol. He heard screams.'

''orrible screams,' said the child. 'I don' know whose. But awful.'

Mrs Philo did not need to exhort us further. Within minutes we were approaching the gaol. Standing in front of the building was the magistrate himself. Boden was talking and laughing with two of his men. I gestured urgently for everyone to stop and duck out of sight behind a building. I found a carriage to hide behind and approached to where I could overhear them.

'Go and sleep it off, Wells. Too much entertainment tires a man,' said Boden with a laugh. The other laughed shrilly, as though uncomfortable. 'Take care of the mess, would you? But go have a pint on me first – make that a coffee, and a good breakfast too. It's been a long night for us all. And Carothers and Jones took a bit of a beating from that London toff. See that they're looked after.'

We needed to get inside the gaol at once. But I willed myself, and the little group, to wait until Boden's men left. In the meantime I instructed Mrs Philo to leave with Mlle La Victoire and the two children, and to return with a conveyance that could transport the prisoners – in whatever state they might be.

Any other woman would have insisted on rushing to find her husband. But she knew where he was, and displayed a cool logic I would soon admire. 'They may need medical assistance. I am a nurse; I will prepare what you need at his surgery,' she said. She departed with Mlle La Victoire and the boys.

Turning our attention to the gaol, Vidocq and I saw three men come out of the building, two limping piteously. 'These men are murderers,' I said. 'Have you a pistol?'

In response, Vidocq pulled a French MAS 1887 from his jacket, an elegant weapon and no less deadly than my own trusty service revolver.

We approached the gaol from the back. The door opening on to the alley was locked. Frustrated, I yanked at the door. Folly; it rattled loudly.

'*Ah, non!*' said Vidocq. 'You work too hard.' He withdrew a lock-pick kit almost identical to Holmes's own and quickly undid the lock. '*Eh, voila!*'

I ran in, drawing my pistol. Vidocq followed, brandishing his own. We made our way down a darkened corridor past several empty cells, and came to the large room at the front of the gaol that served as reception, courthouse, and office, all in one. A single man stood at the front desk, sleepily filling out some paperwork. Like the previous attendant we had encountered, he was immense and appeared slow-witted. He sported an enormous cut across the forehead and a rapidly swelling bruise over one eye.

I raised my gun and entered. Vidocq did the same. 'Where are the prisoners?' I demanded. The man looked up, confused.

'Who are you?' he said.

I cocked my gun. 'Now!'

'Do you mean the doctor? He's right down there,' said the man, fearfully, glancing between Vidocq and me. He indicated a second hallway.

'And the other? Tall, very thin man. About thirty-five. Dark hair.'

At this the man paled. 'Uh. Uh . . . I don't rightly know, right now that is, but the doctor, maybe he . . . he saw . . . he, uh . . . I was here the whole time. At this desk. I swears.'

Vidocq, to my surprise, ran up and grabbed the man by the collar, and jamming his gun to the man's head dragged him towards the second corridor. 'Show us,' he growled. 'And bring your keys.'

We arrived at a small cell in which Dr Philo, in shirt-sleeves and with his head in his hands, sat alone on a scarred wooden bench. He looked up in surprise, his eyes red-rimmed and desperate. He leapt to his feet as the guard unlocked the door. He appeared uninjured.

'Dr Watson, thank God! But I fear you are too late!'

'What has happened?' I asked. 'Where is Holmes?'

'Boden arrested him last night at the cemetery. There was a "trial", and Boden convicted him for grave-robbing and witchcraft.'

'Witchcraft? What insanity is this? Where is he?'

'Downstairs, I think. If he is still alive. The sentence was eighty lashes and—'

'Downstairs where?'

'There is a special cell where Boden does his work,' said Philo, a look of horror on his face.

The little boy with Annie Philo had heard screams.

'Take us,' I shouted to the guard. With Vidocq's gun jammed in his neck, the gaoler led us down a darkened hallway to some stairs at the back of the building. As we descended to the basement, the temperature dropped twenty degrees and the air grew damp and frigid. The image of Pomeroy floated before me, dying bloodied in his cell. I began to shake uncontrollably from the cold, and the fear of what we were to find in this lawless hellhole.

We were blocked by a locked door. The guard fumbled for keys.

'They strung him up,' said the young doctor. 'There is an old rack, over a hundred years old, and they tied him to it.'

The guard was still fumbling. 'Vidocq!' I said. Vidocq sprang forward and wrested the keys from the man, sending him reeling with a sharp kick in the groin.

'Your friend is a proud man, and brave. He refused to show fear and called the magistrate a coward and a bully.'

Vidocq could not find the right key, either. 'Kick the door down, man,' I shouted. I turned back to Philo, 'What then?'

'Boden just smiled at this. But when Mr Holmes predicted the magistrate himself would die on the gallows, a disgrace to his family, the man went insane. He attacked in such a fury—' Philo hung his head. 'I did not see it all. They dragged me away. It was more than an hour ago.'

But Vidocq had at last found the key and we ran through the door and into a large room, icy cold and stretching off into total darkness. It seemed to be some kind of holding cell. Facing us was a wall of bars, bolted and locked. Vidocq signalled the cringing gaoler to open it for us. This time he did not hesitate.

We barged in. We could see nothing in the pitch-blackness.

'Quiet!' I said. No one moved. Silence except for the small sound of a liquid dripping.

'A lantern!' I cried. But Vidocq was ahead of me on this, collaring the man and jamming the gun under his throat. 'Light us. Now,' he said.

The man nodded stiffly and proceeded to find a lantern in the corner and lit it. It cast a feeble glow in a small circle around us. We moved further inside.

'Holmes?' There was no answer. I turned to the guard. 'Where?' I demanded.

The guard indicated with a nod an area off to our right. 'Show us.'

He would not move, but stood there gripping the lantern in shaking hands. 'Hold him,' I said to Vidocq and, taking the lantern, Dr Philo and I proceeded further into the darkness. My foot slid sharply on the slick floor, and I looked down to see that I was standing in a pool of blood.

'Oh my God. Holmes!' I cried. 'Holmes?'

'Over here!' said Philo.

I turned and shone the lantern on to a sight I will never forget.

Sherlock Holmes was spread-eagled, shirtless, and tied

against a wooden frame shaped like a gigantic artist's easel. His body faced in towards the frame, his face averted. His upper body, neck, and all four limbs were secured to this frame with thick leather straps holding him against red leather pads. His legs had given out and his thin body hung limply from the restraints.

He did not move.

'Holmes!' I cried, running to him.

His back was black and red with blood, and lacerated with too many wounds to count. Some of the cuts were deep, and still bleeding profusely. His breathing was shallow. Next to him on the floor was the cause of these injuries, the type of whip called a 'cat o' nine tails'.

'Barbaric. You English!' said Vidocq.

'Step aside!' Philo moved in to support Holmes, taking the weight off his arms.

'My God, Holmes can you hear me?' I cried. I felt for a pulse at his wrist. Faint, but it was there. Holmes was alive but in shock.

'Looks like more than twenty blows,' said Philo. 'They dragged me away after five, but Boden stops when he cannot revive them. It lacks appeal for him if there is no reaction.'

'Holmes! Can you speak?' I whispered.

I touched his face. It was white as death and very cold. But his eyes fluttered open. Seeing me, he smiled weakly.

'Watson. Good of you to come.' He passed out.

CHAPTER 27

Blood Brothers

inutes later, Vidocq, Philo and I had Holmes in front of the gaol, where, as Annie Philo had promised, a carriage was waiting.

In it were blankets, several foot-warmers, and to my surprise, Mlle La Victoire. As the carriage moved quickly across the snow and ice-covered landscape towards Dr Philo's surgery, the three of them, at my direction, rubbed our patient's hands and feet against the shock and hypothermia, while I checked Holmes for additional injury.

'What happened to him?' asked Mlle La Victoire.

Vidocq put an arm around to comfort her but she brushed him off, '*Pas maintenant*,' she said. 'Not now!'

In addition to the lacerations, there were a number of cuts and deep bruises. Holmes lay deathly still as we careered through the icy streets. Mlle La Victoire stared down at him.

'Will he live?' she asked.

I could not answer truthfully. My initial examination

revealed no broken bones, and yet the situation was dire. Hypothermia coupled with shock and blood loss was a terrible combination.

'Doctor?' she repeated softly. I glanced up to see her eyes filled with tears. I was strangely touched but could not bear to linger lest I be drawn there myself. Detachment was what I needed to function.

'We will try,' I said, turning away.

We carried Holmes in through the entrance to Philo's office on the side of the house. We passed through a small waiting room into his surgery, a large well-lit room which was ready and waiting for us. The adjacent kitchen was visible through another door.

Here, a fire glowed in the grate, buckets of warm water were standing by, and everything we needed was lined up near a large table – carbolic acid, bandages, suture and needles, sponges, painkillers and stimulants, all arrayed with professional precision. I recognized the technique of emergency triage, and learned that Mrs Philo had served in the Afghan War for two years as a Nightingale-trained nurse.

For the next several hours, Dr Philo, his remarkably competent wife and I applied ourselves in a prolonged attempt to save Holmes's life. Mlle La Victoire and Vidocq were banished from the room and sent to look after the two boys.

As the hours progressed we worked relentlessly and tediously with warm compresses to bring Holmes's body temperature up, hoping he would revive enough to take fluids. But he remained unconscious.

During this time Philo related the rest of the events leading to Holmes's arrest.

'When we told him of Lady Pellingham's sudden burial hours earlier, he was keen to examine the body that very night. Despite our entreaties, he insisted on visiting the graveyard alone as soon as it was dark to dig up the body. Snow was predicted; we tried to stop him.'

'Your friend does not back down,' said Mrs Philo.

Philo then related that Freddie, a little boy Holmes had rescued from the mill, took it upon himself to run after Holmes into the gathering storm to 'help' his new-found hero. Hidden behind a gravestone, he had witnessed Holmes being surprised and ruthlessly taken by Boden and four men – not without a heroic fight, apparently.

'But had he succeeded in examining Lady Pellingham's body?' I asked.

'I think so,' answered Philo. 'The Lady herself was laid out on the snowy ground. Freddie said he was bent over her, and in this concentrated state did not hear the others arrive.'

'Holmes!' I stared at the still, white face. What had he discovered? Would he take Lady Pellingham's secret to his own grave? I was nearly overcome with a mixture of grief and rage. Damn him! Why had he not waited for me? I thrust this thought from my mind and returned to my task. Carry on,' I said, as much to myself as to them. 'What happened next?'

Philo summarized. According to the boy, two men attacked Holmes. But the child said his hero Sherlock

Holmes had turned into a kind of wild dancer, and leaping and parrying with his shovel, had easily fought off both of them.

This was probably no exaggeration. Holmes had already considerable gifts as a boxer, stick fighter and, later in his career, master of baritsu.

But then Boden set two more men upon him, and against four, Holmes had no chance. Once they had him cuffed and on the ground, only then did Boden approach and apply his own hand to the shackled prisoner, striking him in the face.

Freddie then ran to tell Dr Philo and his wife of Holmes's capture. In spite of Mrs Philo's entreaties, Dr Philo ran to the police station.

I interrupted Dr Philo's story at this point. Holmes's body temperature was now close to normal and we needed to change tactics.

'Help me turn him as I attend to his back,' I said. As we worked to clean and dress our unconscious patient's lacerations, Philo continued his story, in detail as he'd thereafter seen it first hand.

'It was close to four a.m. when I arrived at the prison and burst in to find a mock trial in progress, despite the hour,' he said. 'Holmes was handcuffed and standing at a makeshift "dock" with Boden presiding as judge – but as though it were a celebration as well as a trial, a broad smile on the villain's face. His minions sat together in a row, making up a kind of jury.'

'"Ah, Doctor," Boden said to me in his most jovial manner.

"Had you not arrived I would have summoned you! This situation promises to require your services. Please bear witness as we administer justice to this heinous imposter, grave robber, murderer and blasphemer."

'Two of his men approached and literally pushed me on to a bench facing the scene. They stood by me, in case I had plans to leave. I'll admit to being terrorized, Dr Watson, but I would have run to summon help had I been able.

'The "trial", if it can be called that, lasted less than five minutes. In it, Holmes was accused of grave robbing, grand theft, and finally witchcraft. The man doubling as the clerk gently reminded Boden that he would need some more details, in case anyone asked what Holmes had done to constitute witchcraft.

'Boden then produced from his pocket a finger he had carved from the body of Lady Pellingham! I'll admit that even as a doctor who has seen a corpse or two in my day, I quailed when I saw it. Boden walked over to Holmes and brushed the finger gently over his face, then placed it in your friend's vest pocket.

'My God!'

'Holmes did not move. He said nothing. He was stoic to an unimaginable degree.'

I could well imagine it. 'What then?' I asked.

Philo continued breathlessly: 'Boden pulled out several tarot cards, crystals, a feather, and a small bag of some substance, perhaps ash. He placed the items in the pocket, along with the finger, then smeared ashes on Holmes's face. He had obviously planned ahead.

'"Looks like a kind of satanic ritual, I'd wager," said Boden. He turned to me. '"We, as men of science, Doctor Philo, know this to be pure hogwash, do we not? But to these men here, this is witchcraft. What say you, gentlemen?"

'His four lackeys nodded in assent. "I knows it when I sees him the first time," said one.

'"'E had the look o' the devil about him," said a second. They laughed.

'Holmes, his hands still cuffed behind him, stood silent. Whatever he was thinking, I could not discern it. His eyes had grown dark and his face unfeeling.

'Boden sentenced him to eighty lashes and life imprisonment. The second was superfluous; eighty lashes are lethal. Your friend knew it but said nothing as they led him away. Boden seemed to have a fresh idea. He turned to me. 'This time you will watch as we carry out the sentence."

At this point, Philo glanced at his wife, and back to me. He was ashamed.

'I tell you, Dr Watson, this terrified me and Boden knew it. To watch a man being flogged to death and yet be unable to stop it, I, I . . .'

'There was nothing you could do,' I said.

'Doctors!' said his wife, bringing us back to the present. 'His blood pressure has dropped. We are losing him.'

Holmes remained deathly pale and unresponsive. We had failed to rouse him despite all our efforts. It could only be blood loss.

'We must get fluids into him!' I said. But one cannot force fluids into an unconscious man.

'Transfuse, perhaps,' said Mrs Philo.

I had been thinking the very thing. But with what? At the time of this event, transfusion was in its infancy. Water and milk had been used with an almost zero rate of success and this technique had been discarded as unsafe. Animal blood was hardly better.

Mrs Philo stepped in. 'Person-to-person live blood transfusion. I have seen it work.'

'Where?' asked her husband in surprise.

'Afghanistan. Only once. But I assisted and I know how.'

'I as well,' I said. 'Three times. But all three men died. The odds are very poor.'

'Even so, they are better than zero,' said the nurse calmly. 'And we are at that point, Doctor.'

It was true. I looked down at Holmes. Death was near, if we did nothing. Mrs Philo took me aside to explain she wanted to volunteer but was pregnant, a fact which she wished not to reveal to her husband yet. Then Philo himself volunteered, but I refused.

The donor would be at risk as well. It would be *my* blood we would transfuse. I would hear no argument.

A cot was immediately set up and I lay prone on it as the connection was made. Across from me, Holmes was white and still as death. I closed my eyes as Philo inserted the long needle into my left forearm, connecting it with a length of rubber tubing.

As the blood flowed from my veins, I gave a sudden shiver and felt a coolness, and a strange 'drawing' sensation in my abdomen and legs.

Nurse Philo stood beside Holmes, ensuring that the blood flow into his arm was unrestricted; her husband watched that my own connection functioned properly, occasionally making adjustments to the angle and position of the tubing connecting us.

Literally the lifeblood was leaving my body. I looked across at Holmes. He lay there, unmoving, several cuts on his face showing up bright against his pallor. I am not a praying man, but I closed my eyes, willing my life force to reach out to my friend and not kill him in the process.

I am not sure how much time went by; I may have passed out. A groan sounded nearby and to my left. I opened my eyes. It was Holmes!

I sat up in excitement, and was overcome with dizziness. 'Easy, Doctor,' said Mrs Philo, handing me a brandy and crushed fruit. But her face shone with anticipation. 'It seems to have worked!'

Soon the apparatus was disconnected and we stood, surrounding Holmes.

His colour had returned and he stirred in discomfort. His hands and legs were warm, and we sat him up, managing to get some brandy and water down his throat. He sputtered and coughed. We persisted.

At last his eyes opened. He stared around in confusion, and then a wave of pain contorted his features, as the effects of the night's traumas overcame him. 'Ah . . .' he moaned. 'Some morphine would be most welcome,' he said to me, in the familiar, sharp voice.

He was attempting to direct his own recovery, now.

In an hour, we had Holmes seated and taking in some crushed fruit, and more liquids. He had begun to shiver, a good sign, and we sat him near the fire, wrapped in blankets. With a small amount of morphine in his system, his pain receded.

'Watson,' he whispered, as the others began to tidy the equipment at the other end of the room. 'It was as we suspected: Lady Pellingham was strangled, not stabbed. I need one additional piece to the puzzle before I can move in for the arrest.' He paused, and a look of alarm crossed his face. 'But what day is it? How much time have I lost?'

'A single night only. It is Tuesday. Holmes, you are going nowhere. You must let Mycroft's men confront Lord Pellingham. You can present your evidence later. Your recovery is paramount. You nearly died!'

Mrs Philo rushed in from the adjacent room. 'They are gone!' she cried.

'Who?' demanded Holmes.

'All four of them. The two French, and the two little boys. I believe the children left first. And the adults followed, in a rush it seems! The door was wide open to the elements. They have all gone!'

'But why? And where?' I wondered.

'Damn it, man, why did you let them come? They've gone to Clighton!' cried Holmes. 'Emil is running to his parents. Freddie, no doubt, offered his help. The two French will never stop them in time. We must hasten to the estate! There is no time to lose!' Filled with the adrenalized energy

I have seen so often, Holmes leaped to his feet, the blankets falling from him.

But he swayed suddenly, his knees buckling. I caught him as he stumbled.

'Sit down!' I commanded. He acquiesced and I stepped back.

'Let Mycroft's men take over, Holmes. Surely they received my cable,' I said. 'They will be there by now.'

Mrs Philo snorted. 'Did you cable them from the post office in town? You might as well have put your message in a bottle.'

Philo leaned in. 'She's right. Every message sent from there passes through Boden.'

'Then Mycroft's men are still are twenty miles away!' exclaimed Holmes. 'Those children are in danger. Give me cocaine. A seven per cent solution. Now! It will see me through.'

'Absolutely not!' I shouted. Turning to Mrs Philo, 'You have no idea—'

Her husband stood rooted to the spot, unsure. But his cool-headed wife was already preparing the injection. 'Of course we do,' she said. 'We have seen the needle marks on his arm.'

She held the hypodermic out to Holmes and before I could stop him, he grabbed it from her and slammed it into his own arm.

'No!' I shouted, but the nurse stepped between Holmes and myself.

She grasped both my arms, staring me in the face. 'I have

seen enough to understand this man. Your friend will go to Clighton with or without cocaine.' She paused. 'This way he has a better chance.'

I could not argue. I looked over at Holmes. He stood, breathing deeply, eyes closed, fists clenched, gathering his astonishing strength as the cursed drug coursed through his body.

Annie Philo was right. There would be no stopping him now.

CHAPTER 28

The Winged Victory

n minutes we were in a carriage, racing across the frozen countryside to Clighton. Meanwhile Dr Philo set off to send a protected cable from a neighbouring town, instructing Mycroft's men in Sommersby to proceed to Clighton at once. I hoped that this one would reach its target, and that they had not been decoyed elsewhere.

We approached the grand house as darkness settled, and a chill wind started up. The massive buildings loomed deep purple in the twilight, in high Gothic splendour, with few lights in the windows. At one end, still shrouded by trees, I could see a long, single-storey wing lit golden from within. The Palladium Hall. *The collection.*

The temperature in our carriage plummeted, and the rugs which covered our legs and backs were of little use. Shivering from the cold myself, I glanced at Holmes. He sat up, eager and ready, his eyes glittering from excitement and the effects of the drug.

Whatever evil awaited us at Clighton would be met by a powerful force for good. But my friend was all too human, and while this manic, drug-fuelled energy posed a formidable threat to the Earl, it did nothing less to Holmes himself. I greatly feared the cost.

He caught my glance. 'I'll be fine. Check your firearm and have it at the ready,' said he.

Holmes next signalled the driver to pull up behind a stand of trees, and we stepped from the carriage. He whispered some instructions to the driver, and slapping his horse, sent him off.

We made our way on foot along manicured paths towards the darkened house, finding ourselves presently in an elaborate French-style garden behind the Palladium Hall. Ice-tipped topiary glinted in the moonlight.

As we drew closer, the lights from within Pellingham's private art Mecca glowed ever brighter, casting a yellow haze through the dim garden and creating ghostly shadows among the trees.

Someone cleared his throat near us in the darkness. I drew my weapon. There, seated on an ornate iron bench, was Vidocq, slumped in the moonlight. He shrugged in the Gallic manner, holding up an arm. He was handcuffed to the bench! Vidocq's expression turned sardonic as he took in our little party 'You seem remarkably recovered, Holmes. It is good to have a doctor for a friend, *n'est-ce pas?*'

'Where are the children?' Holmes demanded.

'*Hélas*, we never caught up with them. But we tracked

them here.' He sighed theatrically, rattling his handcuff. 'The lady, she insist on continuing alone.'

'She means to kill the Earl,' said Holmes. 'You would only complicate things. Come, Watson!' He turned and melted into the darkness.

'*Ah, non!*' cried Vidocq. 'I will freeze!'

'Where are your lock picks?' I asked.

He nodded to where the small kit lay in the snow, out of reach. The lady was no fool.

I hesitated, then removed my own coat and threw it to him.

'*Merde*,' he muttered behind us as we ran.

On reaching the rear entrance to the magnificent hall we peered through the double doors leading into the gallery from the garden. Standing at the distant end of the room was Pellingham, his clothes awry, his gestures emotional as he spoke to someone not visible from our position on the terrace.

Numerous large sculptures were arranged along the centre of the hall, impeding our view, but at the far end and off to one side was an enormous statue that dwarfed the others. It was held temporarily in place by wooden buttresses and guy wires. The form was a female, bearing a torch aloft, her flowing robes wrapped around a figure of such exquisite beauty that even I was affected by her stunning grace.

'There she is – the Goddess of Victory!' whispered Holmes. 'That, dear Watson, is the famous sculpture that cost the lives of so many.'

It was the Marseilles Nike!

The doors were locked but yielded quickly to Holmes's expertise. We entered at the far end of the long hall unseen by Pellingham, screened as we were by the mass of statuary.

He continued to speak in low but strident tones to his unseen and silent listener. At this distance, the words echoed in the marble-floored hall and were unintelligible.

I considered the large statues between our position and the Earl. They were sculptures from many eras – originals, no doubt – worth not one fortune but many. On the walls, densely hung from floor to ceiling, was a collection of paintings to rival the Louvre.

Even from our darkened end of the long hall, I thought I recognized Titian, Rembrandt – and was that a Vermeer? Further on – Degas, Renoir . . .

'Watson!' hissed Holmes, snapping me from my awe. He had removed his coat and dropped it on the floor. 'Eyes forward.'

He began to advance carefully down the hall towards the other end, moving from statue to statue but remaining unseen. I followed his lead. About two-thirds down the hall, the voices became clear and we paused behind a large, multi-figure work.

And then we saw her. Mlle La Victoire faced the Earl, her face locked in fury. Holmes had read her intentions correctly: she held a gun aimed straight at her lover's heart.

Emil and Freddie were nowhere to be seen.

Pellingham moved slightly, blocking our view of the lady.

'Where are you hiding the children?' she demanded.

'I . . . what children? Emil is gone. What do you mean?'

'What did you do to our son? Something terrible. He cannot speak. Tell me now!'

'Nothing!'

'Where is he?'

'If only I knew. Cherie, my darling, I love our son. Y-you know that, don't you?'

'Where is he? Tell me, or I shoot you now!' she said.

Signalling me to stay hidden, Holmes stepped from the shadows. 'We shall find him, Mademoiselle. Put down your gun.'

Our beautiful client stood wavering, her gun hand shaking. Gesturing to the Earl, she said, 'This man is a liar. Always he lies!'

Holmes moved towards her slowly and extended his hand. 'Give me the gun, Mademoiselle,' he said gently. 'If you shoot the Earl, you will hang. Emil cannot afford to lose two mothers.'

She paused, and then lowered the weapon. Holmes quickly took it from her.

He turned and aimed it at the Earl. 'Now, sir, it is time to discuss the murder of your wife.'

The Earl turned white. 'The culprit was gaoled—'

'Your valet was framed, possibly at your behest. He died in that gaol, tortured to death. Hold out your hands, Pellingham.'

The Earl hesitated, uncomprehending.

'Lady Pellingham was not stabbed to death. Not by the valet or by anyone. I dug up the grave and examined the body. She was strangled, and the murderer wore a ring on the little finger of his right hand.

'You dug up her grave—?'

'Hold out your hands, I say. Or *I* will shoot you.'

Lord Pellingham reluctantly brought his hands forward. *On the little finger of his right hand was a signet ring.*

'It wasn't me,' cried the Earl. 'I loved her! So beautiful . . . and mine . . .'

'A part of your collection, then. But she disappointed you, didn't she?'

'No!'

'First, in the matter of an heir?'

'No . . . no . . . I loved her.'

'And later, why? Did she love Emil more than she loved you?'

'No! No! My darling Annabelle was not perfect. But I loved her every imperfection! She was, to me, like a great work of art. Perfect in its imperfection, she always—'

'Stop talking!' Holmes barked. He paused, thinking. 'But of course! It is not perfection we admire in art. It is something else,' he mused. He looked around at the collection surrounding us. 'Art, by its nature, is not an exact representation of reality. If it were a perfect depiction it would be a photograph. But, imperfect as it is, it transcends its flaws and is the greater for them. And *that* is why it is treasured.'

What? Was the cocaine wearing off? Had my friend lost his senses?

'Exactly,' whispered the Earl. 'So few understand. Annabelle was my special treasure.'

'You would not destroy your special treasure. No, in spite of the ring, I believe you,' said Holmes. 'You did not kill your wife. She was part of your collection.'

Granted, the ring was circumstantial evidence. But if the Earl did not murder his wife, then who and why? For once, I doubted my friend's reasoning.

A tiny movement caught my eye. I turned and saw a small figure back in the darkness, hiding behind a statue and watching all.

It was Emil!

I remained hidden, but waved my hand to catch Holmes's eye. He glanced my way and I mouthed Emil's name. Holmes turned back to the Earl, and I was not sure he had made out my signal in the dim light where I stood.

'I have been wrong about you killing your wife,' Holmes said, his voice growing louder. 'Wrong, wrong, wrong! But I do believe you *have* harmed your son. And you will pay for it! You will pay for it *right now!*'

He raised Mlle La Victoire's gun, arm extended theatrically, as if to shoot the Earl.

What the devil?

But Emil ran from the shadows and leaped into his father's arms, putting himself in harm's way.

'No, no! Do not hurt Papa!' the child shouted.

'Emil!' cried his mother.

Holmes paused, then lowered his weapon. 'Thus proving my theory!' He smiled and turned to our client. 'Mademoiselle, this man has done no harm to your son. You can see the love the boy has for him. I have been quite wrong on many points. The Earl is weak, and others near him have suffered because of it. But he has harmed neither woman nor child.'

The Earl and his boy clung to each other in tears.

The sound of a gun being cocked riveted our attention. Boden stepped from behind a statue, holding his gun to Mlle La Victoire's head. He grasped one of her arms and wrenched it hard, securing it behind her. 'Drop your gun, Holmes, or the lady dies. Now, kick it away from you.'

Holmes complied, signalling with the hand nearest to me for me to wait.

'Is there anyone else hiding in here?' Boden called out with a laugh. There was no sound. 'Good, then. And now, Sherlock Holmes, how is it that you are still alive?'

Holmes paused. Boden twisted his victim's arm and she cried out.

'Magic, Boden. You accused me of witchcraft, remember?'

'I shall have to finish you, you know. But not yet. Keep joking and I'll shoot this squirmy little wench in the stomach. You know what a slow and painful death that will be.' He slowly lowered the gun to her stomach and smiled at Holmes.

Mademoiselle La Victoire cursed under her breath. Her eyes met Holmes's. They were steady; the lady was strong.

'But first, back to the Earl,' Boden continued, turning to the stunned gentleman. 'The "great detective" has given me what I need to gaol *you* for murder – whether you did it or not! I have been hoping to bring you in for a little . . . conversation for a long while.'

'You work for me, Boden, you despicable vermin!' said the Earl.

'You only *think* I work for you,' said Boden. 'You are in my power now.'

'I think not, Boden,' said Holmes. 'London has been alerted to your games.'

Boden paused, his face darkening. 'My father is a duke. You cannot touch me!'

'Idiot!' said the Earl. 'I have provided you with anonymity and a new life as a favour to your father!'

Boden wavered; the Earl continued: 'He needed you far from Sussex. You were an embarrassment to the family after your *imbroglio* with the shepherdess and her young man. I simply obliged an old friend. A mistake.' The Earl regarded Boden with disdain.

'Ha! "*Imbroglio*" you call it!' exclaimed Holmes, turning to Boden. 'You're the Duke of Wallford's vanished youngest son, responsible for the Cullen–Cuthbertson double torture–murder of '86! The missing fingers – ha ha, I see it all now! No wonder my services were declined by your father. He already knew the culprit.'

Boden's face became a mask of cold fury. Still using Mlle La Victoire as a shield, he altered his aim to the Earl and Emil. 'You arrogant old fool. Say goodbye to your son.'

'*Non!*' screamed Mlle La Victoire. 'Not the boy!'

Emil stood, his arms wrapped around his father's legs. The Earl tenderly unpeeled the child from his embrace and pushed him away.

'Emil, stand aside,' said the Earl. 'You are in danger here.'

The little boy wavered uncertainly and tried to return to his father.

'Emil, no!' shouted both the Earl and Emil's mother in unison. The child froze.

'Yes, that's it, stay right there,' said Boden. 'It's your father who interests me.'

The Earl stood tall to meet his death with dignity. 'Shoot me if you must. But spare the boy. Please.'

Holmes smiled. 'Ah, Boden, the final piece is clear! The small fry don't appeal to you. You are a common or garden variety sadist, and adults make far more interesting victims.'

Boden turned to aim at Holmes. 'I've made you sob like a child, and I'll do it again,' snarled Boden. 'And this time finish the job. Where is your assistant, by the way? He has such concern for you! It will be a pleasure to have him watch.'

I would kill that man if it were my dying act. Still I had no clear shot.

'The game is up, Boden,' said Holmes. He turned to the Earl. 'Lord Pellingham, this man tortured and murdered your valet. As for your wife—'

With a roar, the Earl ran straight at Boden.

Thrusting Mlle La Victoire aside, Boden took aim with both hands at the charging Earl as one would at an elephant – but Holmes leapt between them, knocking the gun from his grasp as both fell to the marble floor. Boden's gun skittered away.

'Run!' screamed Mlle La Victoire to Emil. Holmes and Boden rolled on the floor, grappling for a chokehold. I leapt from my hiding place, saw my chance and took it. My gun rang out and Boden screamed. Holmes pulled free and the villain clutched his own leg.

My shot had hit an artery and blood gushed from the wound.

Boden stared with venom at Holmes and me. 'I will see you both in hell,' he snarled, and fell back with a moan.

I helped Holmes up.

'Nice work, Watson,' said he.

'There there, now. Come to Grandpa,' said a familiar American voice.

Everyone looked up to the doorway. Emil had run straight into the arms of Lady Pellingham's father, Strothers. The man now stood backlit in the entrance to the room.

Strothers grasped the little boy and held him up as if in joy. Then, in a move I will never forget, suddenly crushed him tight to his chest with one powerful arm. The child's legs kicked wildly and his screams were muffled, but he was pinned, unable to breathe. 'That's right, come to Grandpa, little one.'

From the back of his waistband, Strothers drew an enormous Colt 45.

'Ah, finally, the man of the hour,' said Sherlock Holmes.

'Daniel?' whispered the Earl.

'Nobody move,' said Strothers. 'Drop the gun, Doctor. I know you are a good shot, but I could take you.'

I dropped the gun. At Strothers' gesture I kicked it away. It ricocheted off a statue and landed near Boden. Damn. But the man lay unmoving. Dead, I hoped.

Strothers stayed back from us, holding the child as a

shield. 'I've been listening for awhile. You are pretty clever, Mr Sherlock Holmes, but you missed most of it. No match for good old American ingenuity.'

I glanced around me. Mlle La Victoire caught my eye and flicked hers briefly to the floor. Her gun lay four feet from where I stood, hidden from Strothers' view. I blinked my recognition.

'Quite possibly, Mr Strothers,' said Holmes. 'I know you are the mastermind behind the acquisition of this coveted prize.' He gestured to the Nike and smirked. 'This ridiculous piece of stone that three nations wanted and no one could capture. But *you* managed, didn't you? You brought her here with hardly anyone in France or England the wiser. I tip my hat to you.'

Strothers fairly preened under the praise. 'Well, you got that right,' he said.

I edged towards the gun. In synchrony, Holmes moved slightly away to draw attention from me.

'Loosen that child,' he said. 'Let him breathe, and I'll tell the rest.'

Strothers paused, but Holmes pressed on. 'Sir, you will kill us all anyway. The power is in your hands. Don't you want them to know how you did it, first?'

What was Holmes playing at? I felt the perspiration dripping down my back. The boy's struggles began to weaken.

'Monsieur!' cried the boy's mother. 'He cannot breathe! Please!'

Strothers wavered. 'Yeah, but you'll never guess. I want

to hear the famous detective make a fool of himself. Go on.' He loosened his grip and Emil gasped for air.

His mother moaned in relief.

Across the room, I noticed a movement from Boden. He shuddered, and a hand moved toward his wound. He was alive, and less than four feet from my own gun! I sensed that Holmes had noticed as well.

The Earl stood rooted to his spot.

'Strothers, I do know something of American criminal ways,' said Holmes. 'From the Marseilles reports, and later in Paris, I recognized the signature killing style of a certain Mazzara, a famous New Jersey Mafioso. I wired a colleague in New York, and he confirmed the connection of your New Jersey industrial interests to that particular branch of *la Famiglia*. However, I was wrong about you. I thought that you were simply paying back the Earl for some favours, or perhaps acting at his behest. But no, you were manipulating him, weren't you? You were the mastermind. You diverted his attention from his factories, his wife, his son, and focused it on the one thing he wanted above all else. Very clever, indeed.'

The Earl gasped. 'God, forgive me, I have been a fool twice over.'

'As your wife said: blind,' said Holmes, never taking his eyes from Strothers. 'Particularly strange for an art lover. This man had you cold!'

Strothers laughed. 'Ha, very good. Very good! Right on that account. I *am* the mastermind. I may lack your manners and vocabulary, but look out for us country bumpkins!'

Holmes sighed and threw up his hands. 'Exactly!' he admitted. As he did so I edged closer to the gun. 'A remarkable feat! And all the while you were controlling a number of puppets with your strings, Mr Strothers. It was quite enjoyable, wasn't it, hunting small game? And acquiring the sartorial polish of the English country gentleman? Your new look, by the way, is very impressive.'

I sensed in Strothers a hesitation.

'The ring on your left hand, in particular,' continued Holmes.

All eyes went to Strothers' hand, facing us as he gripped the child. He, like the Earl, was wearing a ring on the last finger.

Strothers laughed. 'I've been listening to you through the door, fool. Yeah, I'm wearing a ring. So you think I killed Annabelle? Why would I do that?'

'To keep her from revealing you as a pederast,' said Holmes.

Mlle La Victoire stifled a little scream, and the Earl made a strangled sound.

'One little problem. My ring is on the wrong hand, you idiot,' said Strothers.

'I think not. Right before the murder, you and Boden were in the smoking room. You heard, as we did, the argument between Lady Pellingham and the Earl. You had a motive: you knew she was close to the breaking point. And you seized your opportunity; the argument threw suspicion upon the Earl. The direct route to the library from where you were was through the small annexe. I also entered from there and noticed papers knocked from the desk. Someone had passed through in haste.'

'That's . . . that's . . . nothing!' exclaimed the American.

'Lady Pellingham was facing the other end of the library when she was killed,' said Holmes. He paused a moment. 'The ring is on the correct hand if, as I now know, she were *strangled from behind*.'

The Earl staggered. 'My God! Her own father!'

'That is not all. The children from the factory were murdered and worse. You are a fiend!' Holmes shouted.

'You can't know all that!' gasped Strothers.

'Ah, but I do. Your own daughter was the first you violated; probably when she was ten years old. But it is small boys who really excite you. While you waited for little Emil to be the right age, you satisfied yourself with the orphans procured for you by Boden here and delivered to the mill for your choosing.' Gesturing theatrically, Holmes moved closer to the Earl, drawing Strothers' attention from me.

I knew instantly what I was to do. I moved even closer to the gun near Boden. I glanced at him; he was pressing his wound in agony. Did he see me?

'Had the Earl been more involved in his affairs, he might have noticed, but you further distracted him with the Nike, thus leaving you to your playthings. Boden was your accomplice, a kind of evil twin with his own pathology. In return you bought him his office and his own playground.'

The room was deadly silent. I was two feet from the weapon.

Holmes continued. 'This might have gone on for a long time, had you not raised your game to murdering the children after you took your pleasure. This attracted outside attention. London has been aware for some time, though looking, I might add, in the wrong direction.'

Strothers had gone dead white. 'You are in league with the devil. Or . . .' He turned to Boden. 'Boden, you traitor. You told him everything.'

Boden looked up from his leg. 'I told him nothing!' he cried.

'Impossible!' shouted Strothers. He swivelled and pointed his gun at Holmes. 'You are the very devil, man! Nobody is that smart!' Emil began to thrash and Strothers changed his grip, with one large hand grasping the child's thin neck. 'Nobody could have figured—'

He suddenly screamed and his gun went off, the shot going wild. The orphan Freddie had emerged from the shadows and bitten him in the calf!

After that, everything passed in a flash. Strothers dropped Emil and aimed at Holmes. I dived for our client's gun and took a rolling shot from the floor, grazing Strothers, who fell back.

Boden lunged at the other gun and pointed it straight at the Earl.

Holmes leapt between them.

Three guns went off at once in an incredible explosion of sound that boomed throughout the hall and rattled the windows. I had hit Boden between the eyes, his own shot going wild. I whirled to see Strothers, who now lay by the door, a river of blood flowing from a shoulder wound. Vidocq stood next to Mlle La Victoire, his smoking gun aimed at the heinous monster.

Vidocq then strode over to the prone figure of Strothers. Wresting the gun from the old man's hand, he then returned to embrace his lady and Emil. Freddie stood by in mute admiration.

Holmes, remaining next to the Earl at the base of the Nike, nodded towards Boden's body. 'Good work, Watson. It looks like he's actually dead this time.'

He turned to the little group. Vidocq knelt by Mlle La Victoire and Emil, encircling them both in his arms and gently kissing her face. '*Ma cherie, ma petite!*' he whispered.

'In at the last, Vidocq,' said Holmes. 'As usual.'

'I would not miss it for the world,' said the Frenchman, drawing Mlle La Victoire closer. The beautiful lady's eyes were on Holmes, however.

'*Merci*, Monsieur Holmes,' she said softly. She turned to me. 'And Doctor Watson. *Ah, mon Dieu*, you are wounded!'

It was then I noticed the bullet wound in my bicep, now bleeding a bit faster than one might wish. It was not fatal, but I would need a pressure bandage and quickly. 'Someone give me a hand with this—' I began.

The boy, Freddie, approached me and offered his scarf.

'Mr Holmes! I mistook you. You have saved my life . . . and that of my son . . .' gasped the Earl. 'But my darling Annabelle! Our child! I cannot conceive . . .' Hands to his head in despair, he staggered backward.

As he did so, he tripped on a support at the base of the

Nike. Holmes leapt to catch him but missed. The Earl slipped through his hands and fell heavily against the base of the giant statue. For a hideous moment the Nike wobbled on her temporary perch. In horror I watched as the ropes holding her snapped. The goddess slowly toppled forward.

'Look out!' I shouted.

The statue crashed to the ground and splintered, pinning the Earl and Holmes under its largest piece.

PART NINE

221B

'Everything is simpler than you think and at the same time more complex than you imagine.'

Johann Wolfgang von Goethe

CHAPTER 29

London Bound

ust then Mycroft's men, along with Hector and Annie Philo, miraculously burst into the hall. The room swarmed with activity. Mycroft's men hastened to the shattered Nike while the doctor and his wife ran to my assistance as we pulled Holmes and the Earl from the rubble. Pellingham had suffered a broken arm and would mend without incident, but my friend Sherlock Holmes had fared less well.

He had suffered a serious fracture of the left leg. After quickly wrapping my own wound, the Philos and I attended him. Mycroft's men took charge of the rest, calling in the Earl's private physician, and relieving us all of any further dealings with Boden and the villain Strothers.

The next day we were London-bound through the snow on a privately equipped train provided by the grateful Earl.

Adjoining compartments held Holmes's sickbed and my own resting place. Down the hall, additional compartments accommodated Mlle La Victoire, Emil, Vidocq, and a member of Scotland Yard as protection.

The Marseilles Nike, or what was left of her, had been loaded on to an adjacent carriage. She was destined for the British Museum, unless Vidocq and the French government prevailed. I cared little at that point.

I spent the hours, worried, at my friend's side. The fractured bone threatened to break the surface and the risk of infection in such an injury as his was very high; I'd wrapped his leg in carbolic-soaked pads and wired ahead to a bone specialist in London who was to meet us in Baker Street.

Holmes drifted in and out of consciousness, but within an hour of London he regained his senses, as if knowing that he was close to home.

I called for tea.

'Emil,' he said wearily. 'Where is he?'

'He is here on the train, with his mother. The Earl will rejoin them in Paris soon.'

'Watson, you must see that he receives help . . . a counsellor, perhaps.'

'I will do so,' I said. 'Now rest.'

'And you, Watson? Your arm?'

'It is a flesh wound only. Not to worry, Holmes.'

He lay still, staring out the window at the snow-covered countryside.

'Pity about the Nike,' he said.

'It's only stone pieces now,' I said. 'But the British Museum is good at that kind of puzzle. You've solved the big one. Rest now, Holmes.'

He shifted uncomfortably and a groan escaped his lips. Distraction, I knew, would help ease his pain. 'Then perhaps you would care to elucidate some of the finer points of our recent adventure,' I said.

'Is it not entirely clear to you?'

'I do understand that Lady Pellingham's American father, Strothers, was at the heart of the series of crimes. Daring to pose as a philanthropist and champion of children's rights! But I do not understand his motives. Surely, if he wished to engage in his sick pursuit of children, and that alone, he could have his pick among the many orphanages he founded in the United States. There would be no need to follow his daughter to England, once she had successfully married an English earl.'

'Two things, Watson: Lady Pellingham, as a child, was probably his first victim. Those with this deviant addiction often begin with a single incident, close to home. Their first is special. Strothers, though he later preferred small boys, maintained a sick passion for his own daughter.'

I wondered at this insight. 'But still—'

'Posit for an instant that he travelled here simply because he *could not stay away*. Once here, a gold mine appeared. First, he had a tremendous opportunity for obtaining children through the factories on Lord Pellingham's estate. The sadist Boden, who was at that time the foreman, became a natural ally. Their relationship was complex, and eventually Strothers bought him off with the magistrate's position. This gave Boden unlimited powers to practise his particular brand of 'justice', and the privacy to do so.'

My stomach turned at the evil behind this tale. It was hard to conceive of such depravity. 'My God, Holmes—'

'Meanwhile, as time passed, Strothers saw something in the glamour, wealth and position of the Earl that he wanted for himself.'

'Well, isn't that the usual reason those American robber barons marry their daughters to the English aristocracy?' I asked. 'For the patina of respectability, and position?'

'Not all are robbers, Watson, but yes, partly,' he replied. 'And a chance to make money. Of course, American capital often goes a long way towards sustaining some of the failing great estates. Lord Pellingham's father had made several disastrous business decisions during the current Earl's childhood. The industry moved on, and silk fell out of favour among fashionable ladies. But father and son were stubbornly enamoured of the beauty of silk. Their fortunes plummeted.'

'Enter Strothers and his lovely daughter to save the Pellingham estate,' said I.

'Yes, exactly. But poor, young Annabelle Strothers! At first she thought she would be thousands of miles away from her abusive father, and safe in England. Lord Pellingham, while weak and preoccupied, was not a terrible man.'

'But surely he will be held accountable for all the murders surrounding the Marseilles Nike?' I asked.

'No. I'm afraid the Earl is guilty only of obliviousness and simple greed,' said Holmes testily. He shifted uncomfortably on the bed. I adjusted the pillows behind him.

'But if the Earl truly loved his American wife, then why dally with Cherie Cerise?'

'Probably a single transgression. Surely you have noted the lady's charms.'

'Well, hmm. But how could Lady Pellingham accept Emil as her own?'

'Children of abuse go one of two ways, Watson. Either they perpetuate the abuse heaped upon themselves as children, or the opposite. They protect their young as a female bear will kill for her cub. Lady Pellingham had a great need to nurture a child in the way she herself had *not* been treated. And Emil never knew—'

The train went over a trestle and swayed, jostling Holmes. He groaned in pain. I put a hand out to steady him.

'Some morphine, Holmes?'

'If you would be so kind.'

I removed a syringe from my leather satchel and found the vial of morphine.

'So she asked Pomeroy to hide the boy when Strothers began to show an interest.'

'Precisely.'

'What will happen to Pellingham now?'

'Nothing dire, I expect. He will retain the Strothers' money, I believe. As a peer, he will probably escape serious punishment as long as he returns the stolen artwork and makes some kind of public amends.'

Cleansing a spot on Holmes's arm, I injected the medication. 'And Mademoiselle La Victoire?'

'Do not worry about the lady. In any case, Emil will inherit as was planned before.'

'Then all will be well, in the end,' I said.

There was a long pause. Holmes's eyelids drooped.

'Except for yourself, Holmes,' I added. 'This case has cost you dearly.'

'I will be all right, Watson.' His voice had become slurred. 'I have, as you know . . . excellent . . . medical . . . care.' As the morphine took effect, he smiled and closed his eyes. Reassured by his steady breathing, I fell into a fitful sleep at his side.

CHAPTER 30

Renewal

t is said that doctors are their own worst patients. After settling Holmes in 221B with a specialist to attend to his leg, and a private nurse overseen by my colleague Dr Agar, I hurried to a friend on Harley Street to look after my wound. Upon returning home, I received the news that my dear Mary had taken ill.

And so it happened that in attending her for ten dramatic days, I neglected my own condition. As a result, my wound became infected and I was hospitalized myself.

Following this, my dear wife enjoined me with considerable emotion and a great deal of pressure to accompany her on a short holiday to Brighton where we might both regain full health.

There we spent a belated New Year with friends, partaking of the brisk seaside air and many good meals. Although I wrote and telegraphed Holmes daily during this time, I received no reply. Dr Agar, however, reassured me via letter that Holmes was healing well, though he never responded directly to my questions about my friend's spirits.

It was a full five weeks later, and late January when I finally returned to Baker Street. I slowly mounted the steps to our old rooms, fearing to find my friend once again in the grip of his addiction. I entered our former shared quarters with a mixture of trepidation and guilt.

But instead of the gloomy chaos I expected, the shades were thrown open and the room filled with light. A happy Mozart tune blared from a new gramophone, like the one in Lautrec's Paris apartment. Holmes sat on the couch by a cheery fire, leg propped up, poring over the agony columns as of old.

There were several other changes to the room. Crutches stood at one end of the couch. Over in one corner sat a curious mound of pillows and a candle placed on a thick rug. Above this, a colourful oil sketch hung on the wall, near the bullet holes spelling out 'VR' that he had once shot into the wall out of boredom. A Toulouse-Lautrec, if I was not mistaken.

'Holmes!' I cried. 'I am glad to see you looking so well!'

'Quite so, Watson. Dr Agar has worked his magic, and my nurses have been, er, nothing if not effective. I see you've noticed the new painting. Magnificent, is it not? I predict it will receive wide acclaim in future.'

He gestured to the framed work, which I now recognized as a picture of Mademoiselle La Victoire as Cherie Cerise, singing at the Chat Noir. Lautrec had captured both her beauty and something poignant in her expression – perhaps a reflection of her personal ghosts, like the ones he had observed in Holmes.

'Beautiful,' I said, though I could not say whether it was the painting or the subject which drew me most.

'It was a gift from Lord Pellingham. The man, for all his weaknesses, knows his art. Alas, Monsieur Lautrec has left Paris and is now struggling with his addictions in the South of France.' He regarded the painting for a thoughtful moment. 'His emotional artist's nature, I'm afraid, has overtaken his rational mind.'

It was the very state that had threatened my friend in the past, and in which I had expected to find him now.

'But the traces of Monsieur Lautrec, unlike our own footprints, Watson, will remain to please the ages. Though I doubt he is aware of it.'

As I moved closer to the painting, he looked me over carefully. 'I am glad to see you have recovered, Watson. I have heard of your setback from Dr Agar.'

'I was negligent, I'm afraid. Foolish of me!'

'Yes, foolish, and now sit!' Holmes busied himself with pouring tea. He handed me a steaming cup.

'Holmes, I am so sorry,' I began.

'No apology needed.'

'But you are well? How is the leg? And your back?'

He waved off my questions. 'Healing proceeds apace; let us speak of other things.'

'But I am your doctor as well as your friend.'

He ignored me, and taking a sip from his cup, he leaned back and smiled. 'You'll be pleased to hear that Emil is recovering, and divides his time between his mother in Paris, and the Earl. He has begun piano lessons, and has a gift, says Mademoiselle.'

My heart rose. 'He speaks, then?'

'Quite a lot, apparently.'

'Ah, that is good! Oh, but I have read that the Nike has been acquired by the Louvre. That scoundrel Vidocq takes all the credit for its recovery!'

'I care nothing about credit, Watson. You know that.'

'But you do care about justice. And the Earl has apparently once again evaded the law!'

'Not everything reaches Fleet Street, my dear boy. My brother, has somehow convinced the Earl that the right thing is to donate the entirety of his collection to the British Museum. He is now in the process of transferring both the works, and his, er, affection. I know for a fact that he is buying a chateau and a vineyard near Tours, France.'

'In France, you say! Near Mademoiselle La Victoire?'

'Not so very far,' said Holmes with a smile.

We sat drinking our tea. I could have used something stronger.

'Brandy. On the sideboard,' he said. It is embarrassing to be so known.

'The orphans and the mill?' I wondered as I poured a glass. 'Brandy, Holmes?' I asked.

'No, thank you, Watson.'

'And Strothers?'

'All has been set aright. The mill is being investigated from London, the orphans removed to a boarding school, their expenses borne by the Earl. Strothers is gaoled and will undoubtedly hang. I do wonder about little Freddie, the orphan, though,' he said. 'I have not yet heard what has become of him.'

'Ah! There I have some news! I have received a letter from Dr and Mrs Philo. They have adopted Freddie. Oh, and they expect a child!'

'That last I knew already.'

'How?'

'The windowsill.' At my puzzled look, he grinned in delight. 'Oranges. Morning sickness.'

'Of course!' I said. 'But there is one aspect to this case which troubles me, Holmes. It has to do with your brother, Mycroft.'

Holmes's face darkened. 'What about him?'

'He threatened you, Holmes. I don't wish to intrude, but—'

'Then don't. Here, pour us more tea.'

'But your own brother!'

'It is complicated.'

'*That* is an understatement!'

Holmes paused. I stood up and refreshed our teacups. Noting my consternation, he continued: 'Watson, I am always one step ahead of Mycroft, while he thinks the same of me. It has ever been so.'

For all his brilliance, I believed Holmes to deceive himself upon occasion. But he read my face and snorted. 'Let us change the subject to a more felicitous one. You are wondering how I managed all this time without you?'

'Well, yes,' I said. 'And without cocaine.'

'It is only the lack of work which troubles me. I am fine alone. Better, possibly.'

I did not believe it. 'Yes, yes, of course you are. So, how have you managed?'

'I have taken up a form of meditation which might best be described as "mindfulness". It is widely practised in the Eastern countries.'

'Meditation! But isn't that a spiritual practice? A kind of religion?' I could not fathom the rational thinking machine that was my friend being attracted to any kind of spirituality or mysticism – unless the horrors and suffering he had encountered during our last case had completely altered or unhinged him.

'It can be. For myself, it is not about faith, but a further exploration of the powers of the mind.' He smiled. 'A favourite subject, as you know.'

'What, or how do you do it?'

'I sit over there, my back straight as a green blade of grass, and there I stay unmoving for long periods of time.'

I followed his gaze to that strange mound of cushions. 'Is that all? As you do with a pipe when solving a case?'

'No,' said he. 'In meditation one directs the mind to narrow specifics. Not puzzles, as with a case, so much as minute observations – the breath, for example. It is a different kind of mind work.'

He must have been joking. 'You focus on your breath? Why not your big toe?' I asked.

'You fail to understand. By quieting and focusing the mind on minutiae, paradoxically grander schemes are revealed and a sense of equanimity created.'

I snorted. 'Preposterous!'

Holmes laughed. 'Dear Watson, you cannot know until you have tried it. Meditating in this way happens also to reduce pain – and hence my need for less, shall we say, external relief.'

If that were true, it would be a medical miracle, and something my profession should embrace. I wondered whether only minds such as Holmes's unique one could enjoy such benefits. Holmes seemed to read my thoughts.

'This technique has been used successfully in the East for a thousand years,' he said. 'By monks, warriors, artists—'

'Of course. It can be argued that you are all three,' I said.

He laughed. 'Good old Watson. There is no need to turn me into a hero. In any case, this technique is used by ordinary people as well.' He smiled. 'I suggest you give it a try.'

'I will keep it in mind, Holmes,' said I, 'the next time I am troubled by lack of work.'

He snorted. 'Work is not your particular addiction. But now,' said he, 'you must tell me all about Brighton. I am sure you enjoyed yourself among your new married friends and the many amusements that seaside resort has to offer. Was it conducive to your own recovery?'

I paused. Holmes stared at me, a small smile curling his lips. This time, I knew I was being mocked. I could not help but smile back. Soon we were both laughing.

'I hated Brighton,' I said. 'It was a bloody bore!'

*Holmes and Watson return
in UNQUIET SPIRITS,
September 2016*

Acknowledgements

For *Art in the Blood*, my parents. For inspiration, Sir Arthur Conan Doyle, truly one of the greats. And for making this book happen, my lovely home team Chuck Hurewitz and Linda Langton. At HarperCollins the wonderful Natasha Hughes.

For inspiration, many actors but especially the elegant, witty Jeremy Brett, the livewire bohemian Robert Downey, Jr and the simultaneously arrogant and vulnerable Sherlock of Benedict Cumberbatch – all of whom personify essential elements of my favourite hero. For Mycroft, the menacing and complex Mark Gatiss, and for Watson, the handsome, dangerous Jude Law and especially Martin Freeman's warm, funny "What the *hell* are you doing?" John. If you hear any of these lovely actors' voices in the book, it's their fault. Oh, all right, it's mine. Though it was my intention and hope that Sir Arthur's prevails.

Special thanks to two renowned Holmes experts:— Les Klinger for his friendship, encouragement, advice and tough notes, and for getting me to "come out" as a Sherlockian. You opened a whole new world to me, Les. And same to my dear friend Catherine Cooke in England. But don't blame Les or Catherine for any errors!

Editorial thanks especially to Lynn Hightower, but also pal Matt Witten, and fellow Oxnardians Patty Smiley, Craig Faustus Buck, Jonathan Beggs, Bob Shayne, Harley Jane Kozak, Jamie Diamond and Nancy Seid. From Scotland Ailsa Campbell, and from France Cynthia Liebow.

Love also to two generous Londoners, Roger Johnson and Steve Emecz, both of whom were instrumental in expanding my Sherlockian horizons, sharing great meals, and introducing me to new friends in my favourite city. Merci au Cercle Holmesien de Paris and particularly Hélène, Thierry, Laurence, Véronique and Cyril.

Medical historian Dr Lindsay Fitz and chemist Christopher A. Zordan advised on transfusions and disappearing inks. Fellow Sherlockian author Dan Andriacco did me a favour which is appreciated beyond words. So many other Sherlockians played a role, among them new friends Luke Benjamen Kuhns, Matthew J. Elliott, Mary Platt, Anne Lewis, Jacquelynn Bost Morris, Tom Ue, Becky Simpson, Martin Moore, Crystal Noll, Charlotte Ann Walters, Jean Upton, Lynn Gale, Marek Ujma, Alex Anstey, Paul Annett, David Stuart Davies, Jerry and Chrys Kegley, Maggie Schpak, Robert Stek, Charlie Mount, as well as Emma Grigg and Jules Coomber of Sherlockology. A very special thank you to Steve Doyle and Mark Gagen. Gratitude to Paul Gilbert for the Sherlock set visit and to the folks at

Hartswood for allowing me to read some *Sherlock* scripts in preparation for a talk. All of these people exemplify the Sherlockian spirit of generosity and great fun. Apologies to anyone I've left out.

Family by blood Chris Simpson and Kirstin Kay, and by choice Jaz Davison, were key in their support and in-the-trenches help. Hugs to Paul Cheslaw, Karen Essex, Ann Cheslaw, Miranda Andrews, and Christine Sofiane for their encouragement, and my writing students from UCLA Extension, particularly fellow author Colette Freedman.

The illustrations were made possible by the massively talented Robert Mammana (source photographer and Vidocq) and my brilliant and handsome actor friends Rob Arbogast and Paul Denniston, who modelled for a perfect Holmes and Watson in the illustrations (and onstage). Thanks Miguel Perez, Samara Bay, Jonathan Le Billon, and Brad Bose who modelled for various characters, Ray Bengston for author photos and video, Joe Blaustein for art encouragement: Various talented design contributers include Stuart Bache, Tanya Johnston, and Patrick Seeholzer's group. Thanks also to Megan Beatie. Jane Acton and Rachael Young at Four Colman Getty, as well as HarperCollins' own Victoria Comella, Jean Marie Kelly and Louise Swanell. Ryan Johnson's evocative original Sherlock Holmes music written for the trailer provided my "soundtrack" while I wrote.

A big shout out goes to Filipe Domingues and the welcoming staff of the Park Plaza Sherlock Holmes hotel on Baker Street in London, where much of this novel was written.

Trish Dickey bravely and coercively maintained some sense of order in the chaos surrounding me while Brad Bose, Liz Poppert, Noel Kingsley, and Anthony Mayatt kept the "transport" working so the mind could continue.

Meditation teacher Shinzen Young not only advised me on Victorian meditation practices, but his direct teaching made the sustained focus of this marathon project possible.

Special thanks goes to David Roth who generously and tirelessly worked some serious magic at the end. Thank you, David.

Penultimately, thanks to the wonderful Otto Penzler proprietor of my favourite bookshop and uber Sherlockian whose enthusiasm meant so much to me.

And finally, my biggest thanks to my generous and supportive husband, Alan Kay. No one understands the creative process better. As the far smarter Sherlock in our pairing, he has at the same time grounded me with his callouts in the best Watson tradition, and fuelled me with the finest omelettes in the world. There would be no book without him.

Thank you, Alan. And thank you all. It didn't take a village; it was a whole shire.

For interested readers, illustrated
annotations to *Art in the Blood*
can be found on
www.macbird.com/aitb/notes